To The Nines

Janet Evanovich

review

Copyright © 2003 Evanovich, Inc

The right of Janet Evanovich to be identified as the Author of
the Work has been asserted by her in accordance with the
Copyright, Designs and Patents Act 1988.

First published in Great Britain in 2003
by HEADLINE BOOK PUBLISHING

First published in paperback in Great Britain in 2004
by HEADLINE BOOK PUBLISHING

First published in Great Britain in this paperback edition in 2005
by REVIEW

An imprint of HEADLINE BOOK PUBLISHING

1

ISBN 0 7472 6763 4 (A format)
ISBN 0 7553 2908 2 (B format)

Typeset in New Caledonia by Avon DataSet Ltd, Bidford on Avon
Printed and bound in Great Britain by
Mackays of Chatham plc, Chatham, Kent

Headline's policy is to use papers that are natural, renewable and
recyclable products and made from wood grown in sustainable forests.
The logging and manufacturing processes are expected to conform to
the environmental regulations of the country of origin.

HEADLINE BOOK PUBLISHING
A division of Hodder Headline
338 Euston Road
London NW1 3BH

www.reviewbooks.co.uk
www.hodderheadline.com

This book was spectacularly edited by SuperJen!

Thanks to Denise Margo Moy for suggesting the
title to this book

One

My name is Stephanie Plum and I was born and raised in the Chambersburg section of Trenton, where the top male activities are scarfing pastries and pork rinds and growing love handles. The pastry and pork rind scarfing I've seen firsthand. The love handles grow over time. Thank God for small favors.

The first guy I saw up close and personal was Joe Morelli. Morelli put an end to my virgin status and showed me a body that was masculine perfection . . . smooth and muscular and sexy. Back then Morelli thought a long-term commitment was twenty minutes. I was one of thousands who got to admire Morelli's best parts as he pulled his pants up and headed for the door.

Morelli's been in and out of my life since then. He's currently *in* and he's improved with age.

So the sight of a naked man isn't exactly new to me, but the one I was presently watching took the cake. Punky Balog had an ass like Winnie the Pooh . . . big and fat and furry. Sad to say, that was where the similarity ended because, unlike Pooh Bear, there was nothing endearing or cuddly about Punky Balog.

I knew about Punky's ass because I was in my new sunshine yellow Ford Escape, sitting across from Punky's dilapidated row house, and Punky had his huge Pooh butt plastered against his second-story window. My sometime partner, Lula, was riding shotgun for me and Lula and I were staring up at the butt in open-mouthed horror.

Punky slid his butt side to side on the pane and Lula and I gave a collective, upper-lip-curled-back *eeyeuuw*!

'Think he knows we're out here,' Lula said. 'Think maybe he's trying to tell us something.'

Lula and I work for my bail bonds agent cousin, Vincent Plum. Vinnie's office is on Hamilton Avenue, his big plate-glass front window looking into the Burg. He's not the world's best bonds agent. And he's not the worst. Truth is, he'd probably be a better bondsman if he wasn't saddled with Lula and me. I do fugitive apprehension for Vinnie and I have a lot more luck than skill. Lula mostly does filing. Lula hasn't got luck or skill. The thing Lula has going for her is the ability to tolerate Vinnie. Lula's a plus-size black woman in a size-seven white world and Lula's had a lot of practice at pulling attitude.

Punky turned and gave us a wave with his johnson.

'That's just so sad,' Lula said. 'What do men think of? If you had a lumpy little wanger like that, would you go waving it in public?'

Punky was dancing now, jumping around, wanger flopping, doodles bouncing.

'Holy crap,' Lula said. 'He's gonna rupture something.'

'It's gotta be uncomfortable.'

'I'm glad we forgot the binoculars. I wouldn't want to see this up close.'

I didn't even want to see it from a distance.

'When I was a 'ho I used to keep myself from getting grossed out by pretending men's privates were Muppets,' Lula said. 'This guy looks like an anteater Muppet. See the little tuft of hair on the anteater head and then there's the thing the anteater snuffs up ants with . . . except ol' Punky here's gotta get real close to the ants on account of his snuffer isn't real big. Punky's got a pinky.'

Lula was a 'ho in a previous life. One night while plying her trade she had a near-death experience and decided to change everything but her wardrobe. Not even a near-death experience could get Lula out of Spandex. She was currently wearing a skintight hot pink miniskirt and a tiger-print top that made her boobs look like big round overinflated balloons. It was early June and midmorning and the Jersey air wasn't cooking yet, so Lula had a yellow angora sweater over the tiger top.

'Hold on,' Lula said. 'I think his snuffer is growing.'

This produced another *eeyeuuw* from us.

'Maybe I should shoot him,' Lula said.

'No shooting!' I felt the need to discourage Lula from hauling out her Glock, but truth was, it seemed like it'd be a public service to take a potshot at Punky.

'How bad do we want this guy?' Lula asked.

'If I don't bring him in, I don't get paid. If I don't get paid, I don't have rent money. If I don't have rent money, I get kicked out of my apartment and have to move in with my parents.'

'So we want him real bad.'

'*Real* bad.'

'And he's wanted for what?'

'Grand theft auto.'

'At least it's not armed robbery. I'm gonna be hoping the only weapon he's got, he's holding in his hand right now . . . on account of it don't look like much of a threat to me.'

'I guess we should go do it.'

'I'm ready to rock 'n' roll,' Lula said. 'I'm ready to kick some Punky butt. I'm ready to do the job.'

I turned the key in the ignition. 'I'm going to drop you at the corner so you can cut through the back and take the back door. Make sure you have your walkie-talkie on so I can let you know when I'm coming in.'

'Roger that.'

'And no shooting, no breaking doors down, no Dirty Harry imitations.'

'You can count on me.'

Three minutes later, Lula reported she was in place. I parked the Escape two houses down, walked to Punky's front door, and rang the bell. No one responded so I rang a second time. I gave the door a solid rap with my fist and shouted, 'Bond enforcement! Open the door!'

I heard shouting carrying over from the backyard, a door crashing open and slamming shut, and then more muffled shouting. I called Lula on the talkie, but got no response. A moment later the front door opened to the house next to me and Lula stomped out.

'Hey, so excuse me,' she yelled at the woman behind her. 'So I got the wrong door. It could happen, you know. We're under a lot of pressure when we're making these dangerous apprehensions.'

The woman glared at Lula and slammed and locked her door shut.

'Must have miscounted houses,' Lula said to me. 'I sort of let myself in through the wrong door.'

'You weren't supposed to open *any* door.'

'Yeah, but I heard someone moving around inside. Guess that's 'cause it was the neighbor lady's house, hunh? So what's going on? How come you're not in yet?'

'He hasn't opened the door.'

Lula took a step back and looked up. 'That's because he's still mooning you.'

I followed Lula's line of sight. She was right. Punky had his ass to the window again.

'Hey,' Lula yelled up. 'Get your fat ass off the window and get down here! We're trying to do some bond enforcement!'

An old man and an old woman came out of the house across the street and settled themselves on their front stoop to watch.

'Are you going to shoot him?' the old man wanted to know.

'I don't hardly ever get allowed to shoot anybody,' Lula told him.

'That's darn disappointing,' the man said. 'How about kicking the door down?'

Lula gave the man one of her hand-on-hip *get real* looks. 'Kick the door down? Do I look like I could kick a door down in these shoes? These are Via Spigas. You don't go around kicking down doors in Via Spigas. These are classy shoes. I paid a shitload of money for these shoes and I'm not sticking them through some cheap-ass door.'

Everyone looked at me. I was wearing jeans, a T-shirt topped by a black jeans jacket, and CAT boots. CAT boots could definitely kick down a door, but they'd have to be on someone else's feet because door kicking was a skill I lacked.

'You girls need to watch more television,' the old man said. 'You need to be more like those Charlie's Angels. Nothing stopped them girls. They could kick doors down in all kinds of shoes.'

'Anyways, you don't need to kick the door in,' the old woman said. 'Punky never locks it.'

I tried the door and, sure enough, it was unlocked.

'Sort of takes the fun out of it,' Lula said, looking past the door into Punky's house.

This is the part where if we were Charlie's Angels we'd get into crouched positions, holding our guns in two hands in front of us, and we'd hunt down Punky. This didn't work for us because I left my gun home, in the cookie jar on my kitchen counter, and Lula'd fall over if she tried to do the crouch thing in her Via Spigas.

'Hey Punky,' I yelled up the stairs. 'Put some clothes on and come down here. I need to talk to you.'

'No way.'

'If you don't get down here, I'm going to send Lula up to get you.'

Lula's eyes got wide and she mouthed, *Me? Why me?*

'Come up here and get me,' Punky said. 'I have a surprise for you.'

Lula pulled a Glock out of her handbag and gave it over to me. 'You should take this on account of *you're* gonna be the one going up the stairs first and you might need it. You know how I hate surprises.'

'I don't want the gun. I don't like guns.'

'Take the gun.'

'I don't want the gun,' I told her.

'*Take* the *gun*!'

Yeesh. 'Okay, okay. Give me the stupid gun.'

I got to the top of the stairs and I peeked around the corner, down the hall.

'Here I come, ready or not,' Punky sang out. And then he jumped from behind a bedroom door and stood spread-eagle in full view. 'Ta-dahhhh.'

He was buck naked and slick as a greased pig. Lula and I swallowed hard and we both took a step backward.

'What have you got all over you?' I asked.

'Vaseline. Head to toe and extra heavy in the cracks and crevices.' He was smiling ear to ear. 'You want to take me in, you have to wrestle with me.'

'How about we just shoot you,' Lula said.

'You can't shoot me. I'm not armed.'

'Here's the plan,' I said to Lula. 'We cuff him and put him

in leg irons and then we wrap him in a blanket so he doesn't get my car greasy.'

'I'm not touching him,' Lula said. 'Not only is he an ugly naked motherfucker, but he's a dry-cleaning bill waiting to happen. I'm not ruining this top. I'll never find another top like this. It's genuine fake tiger. And Lord knows what he'd do to rabbit.'

I reached for him with the cuffs. 'Give me your hand.'

'Make me,' he said, waggling his butt. 'Come get me, sweetie pie.'

Lula looked over at me. 'You *sure* you don't want me to shoot him?'

I took my jacket off and snatched at his wrist, but I couldn't hold tight. After three attempts I had Vaseline up to my elbow, and Punky was skipping around going, '. . . Nah, nah, nah. Kiss my can, you can't catch me, I'm the Vaseline man.'

'This guy's in the red zone on the Breathalyzer,' Lula said. 'Think he might also be missing a few marbles in his greased-up jug head.'

'I'm crazy like a fox,' Punky said. 'If you can't catch hold of me, you can't take me in. If you can't take me in, I don't go to jail.'

'If I don't take you in, I don't pay my rent and I get kicked out of my apartment,' I told Punky, lunging for him, swearing when he slid away from me.

'This here's embarrassing,' Lula said. 'I can't believe you're trying to grab this funky fat man.'

'It's my job. And you could help! Take the damn top off if you don't want it to get ruined.'

'Yeah, take your top off, momma. I've got plenty of extra Vaseline for you,' Punky sang out.

Punky turned away from me, I gave him a good hard kick to the back of his knee, and he crashed to the floor. I threw myself on top of him and yelled to Lula to cuff him. She managed to get both cuffs on and my cell phone chirped.

It was my Grandma Mazur on the phone. When my Grandpa Mazur cashed in his two-dollar chips and moved on to the High Rollers' Suite in the sky, my Grandma Mazur moved in with my parents.

'Your mother's locked herself in the bathroom and she won't come out,' Grandma said. 'She's been in there for an hour and a half. It's the menopause. Your mother was always so sensible until the menopause hit.'

'She's probably taking a bath.'

'That's what I thought at first, but she's never in there this long. I went up and yelled and banged on the door just now and there's no answer. For all I know, she's dead. She could have had a heart attack and drowned in the tub.'

'*Omigod.*'

'Anyways, I thought you could get over here and unlock

the door like you did last time when your sister locked herself in the bathroom.'

At Christmastime my sister Valerie locked herself in the bathroom with a pregnancy test kit. The test kit kept turning up positive, and if I was Valerie I would have wanted to spend the rest of my life locked in the bathroom, too.

'I wasn't the one who unlocked the door,' I told Grandma. 'I was the one who climbed onto the roof over the back stoop and went in through the window.'

'Well, whatever you did, you better get over here and do it again. Your father's off somewhere and your sister's out. I'd shoot the lock off, but last time I tried to do that the bullet ricocheted off the doorknob and took out a table lamp.'

'Are you sure this is an emergency? I'm sort of in the middle of something.'

'Hard to tell what's an emergency in this house any more.'

My parents lived in a small three-bedroom, one-bathroom house that was bursting at the seams with my mom and dad, my grandma, my recently divorced, very pregnant sister, and her two kids. Emergencies tended to blend with the normal.

'Hang tight,' I told Grandma. 'I'm not far away. I'll be there in a couple minutes.'

Lula looked down at Punky. 'What are we gonna do with him?'

'We're going to take him with us.'

'The hell you are,' Punky said. 'I'm not getting up. I'm not going anywhere.'

'I don't have time to mess with this,' I said to Lula. 'You stay here and baby-sit and I'll send Vinnie over to do the pickup.'

'You're in trouble now.' Lula said to Punky. 'I bet Vinnie likes greased-up fat men. People tell me Vinnie used to be romantically involved with a duck. I bet he's gonna think you're just fine.'

I hustled down the stairs and out the front door to the Escape. I called Vinnie on the way to my parents' house and gave him the word on Punky.

'What are you, nuts?' Vinnie yelled at me. 'I'm not gonna go out to pick up some greased-up naked guy. I write bonds. I don't do pickups. Read my lips . . . *you're the pickup person.*'

'Fine. Then *you* go to my parents' house and get my mother out of the bathroom.'

'All right, all right, I'll do your pickup, but it's come to a sad state of affairs when I'm the normal member of this family.'

I couldn't argue with that one.

Grandma Mazur was waiting for me when I pulled up to the curb. 'She's still in there,' Grandma said. 'She won't talk to me or nothing.'

I ran up the stairs and tried the door. Locked. I knocked. No answer. I yelled to my mother. Still no response. Damn. I ran down the stairs, out to the garage and got a step ladder. I put the ladder up to the back stoop and climbed onto the small shingled roof that attached to the back of the house and gave me access to the bathroom window. I looked inside.

My mom was in the tub with earphones on, eyes closed, knees sticking out of the water like two smooth pink islands. I rapped on the window, and my mom opened her eyes and gave a shriek. She grabbed for the towel and continued to scream for a good sixty seconds. Finally she blinked, snapped her mouth shut, pointed straight-armed to the bathroom door, and mouthed the word *go*.

I scuttled off the roof, down the ladder, and slunk back to the house and up the stairs, followed by Grandma Mazur.

My mother was at the bathroom door, wrapped in a towel, waiting. 'What the hell were you doing?' she yelled. 'You scared the crap out of me. Dammit. Can't I even relax in the tub?'

Grandma Mazur and I were speechless, standing rooted to the spot, our mouths open, our eyes wide. My mom never cursed. My mom was the practical, calming influence on the family. My mom went to church. My mom *never* said *crap*.

'It's the change,' Grandma said.

'It is *not* the change,' my mother shouted. 'I am *not* menopausal. I just want a half hour alone. Is that too much to ask? A crappy half hour!'

'You were in there for an hour and a half,' Grandma said. 'I thought you might have had a heart attack. You wouldn't answer me.'

'I was listening to music. I didn't hear you. I had the headset on.'

'I can see that now.' Grandma said. 'Maybe I should try that sometime.'

My mother leaned forward and took a closer look at my shirt. 'What on earth do you have all over you? It's in your hair and on your shirt and you have big grease stains on your jeans. It looks like . . . Vaseline.'

'I was in the middle of a capture when Grandma called.'

My mother did an eye roll. 'I don't want to know the details. Not ever. And you should be sure to pretreat when you get home or you're never going to get that stuff out.'

Ten minutes later I was pushing through the front door to Vinnie's office. Connie Rosolli, Vinnie's office manager and guard dog, was behind her desk, newspaper in hand. Connie was a couple years older than me, an inch or two shorter, and had me by three cup sizes. She was wearing a blood red V-neck sweater that showed a lot of cleavage.

Her nails and her lips matched the sweater.

There were two women occupying the chairs in front of Connie's desk. Both women were dark-skinned and wearing traditional Indian dress. The older woman was a size up from Lula. Lula is packed solid, like a giant bratwurst. The woman sitting across from Connie was loose flab with rolls of fat cascading between the halter top and the long skirt of her sari. Her black hair was tied in a knot low on her neck and shot through with gray. The younger woman was slim and I guessed slightly younger than me. Late twenties, maybe. They both were perched on the edges of their seats, hands tightly clasped in their laps.

'We've got trouble,' Connie said to me. 'There's an article in the paper today about Vinnie.'

'It's not another duck incident, is it?' I asked.

'It's about the visa bond Vinnie wrote for Samuel Singh. Singh is here on a three-month work visa and Vinnie wrote a bond insuring Singh would leave when his visa was up. A visa bond is a new thing, so the paper's making a big deal about it.'

Connie handed me the paper and I looked at the photo accompanying the feature. Two slim, shifty-looking men with slicked-back black hair, smiling. Singh was from India, his complexion darker, his frame smaller than Vinnie's. Both men looked like they regularly conned old ladies out of their life savings. Two Indian women stood in the background, behind Vinnie and Singh. The women in the photo were the women sitting in front of Connie.

'This is Mrs Apusenja and her daughter Nonnie,' Connie said. 'Mrs Apusenja rented a room to Samuel Singh.'

Mrs Apusenja and her daughter were staring at me, not sure what to do or say about the globs of goo in my hair and gunked into my clothes.

'And this is Stephanie Plum,' Connie told the Apusenjas. 'She's one of our bond enforcement agents. She's not usually this . . . greasy.' Connie squinted at me. 'What the hell have you got all over you?'

'Vaseline. Balog was covered with it. I had to wrestle him down.'

'This looks sexual to me,' Mrs Apusenja said. 'I am a moral woman. I do not want to become involved with this.' She clapped her hands to her head. 'Look at me. I have my ears covered. I am not hearing this filth.'

'There's no filth,' I shouted at her. 'There was this guy I had to bring in and he was covered in Vaseline . . .'

'Lalalalalala,' Mrs Apusenja sang.

Connie and I rolled our eyes.

Nonnie pulled her mother's hands away from her head. 'Listen to these people,' she said to her mother. 'We need them to help us.'

Mrs Apusenja stopped singing and crossed her arms over her chest.

'Mrs Apusenja is here because Singh's disappeared,' Connie said.

'This is true,' Mrs Apusenja said. 'We are very worried. He was an exemplary young man.'

I skimmed the article. Samuel Singh's bond was up in a week. If Vinnie couldn't produce Singh in a week's time, he was going to look like an idiot.

'We think something terrible happened to him,' Nonnie said. 'He just disappeared. *Poof.*'

The mother nodded in agreement. 'Samuel has been staying with us while working in this country. My family is very close to Samuel Singh's family in India. It's a very good family. Nonnie and Samuel were to be married, in fact. She was to travel to India with Samuel to meet his mother and father. We have a ticket for the plane.'

'How long has Samuel been gone?' Connie asked.

'Five days,' Nonnie said. 'He left for work and he never returned. We asked his employer and they said Samuel didn't show up that day. We came here because we hoped Mr Plum would be able to help us find Samuel.'

'Have you checked Samuel's room to see if anything is missing?' I asked. 'Clothes? Passport?'

'Everything seems to be there.'

'Have you reported his disappearance to the police?'

'We have not. Do you think we should do that?'

'*No*,' Connie said, voice just a tad too shrill, hitting Vinnie's cell phone number on her speed dial.

'We've got a situation here,' Connie said to Vinnie. 'Mrs Apusenja is in the office. Samuel Singh has gone missing.'

At two in the morning when the weather is ideal and the lights are all perfectly timed, it takes twenty minutes to drive from the police station to the bail bonds office. Today, at two in the afternoon, under an overcast sky, Vinnie made the run in twelve minutes.

Ranger, Vinnie's top gun, had ambled in a couple minutes earlier at Vinnie's request. He was dressed in his usual black. His dark brown hair was pulled back from his face and tied into a short ponytail at the nape of his neck. His jacket looked suspiciously like Kevlar and I knew from experience it hid a gun. Ranger was always armed. And Ranger was always dangerous. His age was somewhere between twenty-five and thirty-five and his skin was the color of a mocha latte. The story goes that Ranger had been Special Forces before signing on with Vinnie to do bond enforcement. He had a lot of muscle and a skill level somewhere between Batman and Rambo.

A while ago Ranger and I spent the night together. We

were in an uneasy alliance now, working as a team when necessary, avoiding contact or conversation that would lead to a repeat sexual encounter. At least *I* was avoiding a repeat encounter. Ranger was his usual silent mysterious self, his thoughts unknown, his attitude provocative.

He'd looked me over before taking a chair. 'Vaseline?' he asked.

'I am thinking it must be something sexual,' Mrs Apusenja said. 'No one has told me otherwise. I am thinking this one must be a slut.'

'I am *not* a slut,' I said. 'I had to capture a guy who was all greased up and some of the gunk rubbed off on me.'

The back door burst open and Vinnie came in like gangbusters, followed by Lula.

'Talk to me,' Vinnie said to Connie.

'Not much to tell. You remember Mrs Apusenja and her daughter Nonnie. Samuel Singh rented a room in the Apusenja house and they were at the photo session last week. They haven't seen him in five days.'

'Christ,' Vinnie said. 'National print coverage on this. A week to go. And this sonovabitch goes missing. Why didn't he just come over to my house and feed me rat poison? It would have been an easier death.'

'We think there might be foul play involved,' Nonnie said.

Vinnie made a halfhearted effort to squash a grimace. 'Yeah, right. Give me a refresher course on Samuel Singh. What was his normal routine?' Vinnie had the file in his hand, flipping pages, mumbling as he read. 'It says here he worked at TriBro Tech. He was in the quality control department.'

'During the week Samuel would be at work from seven-thirty to five. Every night he would stay home and watch television or spend time on his computer. Even on weekends he would spend most of his time on the computer,' Nonnie said.

'There is a word to call him,' Mrs Apusenja said. 'I can never remember.'

'Geek,' Nonnie said, not looking all that happy about it.

'Yes! That's it. He was a computer geek.'

'Did he have friends? Relatives in the area?' Vinnie asked.

'There were people at his workplace that he spoke of but he didn't spend time with them socially.'

'Did he have enemies? Debts?'

Nonnie shook her head no. 'He never spoke of debts or enemies.'

'Drugs?' Vinnie asked.

'No. And he would drink alcohol only on special occasions.'

'How about criminal activity? Was he involved with anyone shady?'

'Certainly not.'

Ranger was impassive in his corner, watching the women. Nonnie was leaning forward in her chair, uncomfortable with the situation. Mama Apusenja had her lips pressed tight together, her head tipped slightly, not favorably impressed with what she was seeing.

'Anything else?' Vinnie asked.

Nonnie fidgeted in her seat. Her eyes dropped to the purse in her lap. 'My little dog,' Nonnie finally said. 'My little dog is missing.' She opened her purse and extracted a photo. 'His name is Boo because he is so white. Like a ghost. He disappeared when Samuel vanished. He was in the backyard, which is fenced, and he disappeared.'

We all looked at the photo of Nonnie and Boo. Boo was a small cocker spaniel and poodle mix with black button eyes in a fluffy white face. Boo was a cockapoo.

I felt something tug inside me for the dog. The black button eyes reminded me of my hamster, Rex. I remembered the times when I'd been worried about Rex, and I felt the same sharp stab of concern for the little dog.

'Do you get along okay with your neighbors?' Vinnie asked. 'Have you asked any of them if they've seen the dog?'

'No one has seen Boo.'

'We must leave now,' Mrs Apusenja said, glancing at her watch. 'Nonnie needs to get back to work.'

Vinnie saw them to the door and watched them cross the street to their car. 'There they go,' Vinnie said. 'Hell's message bearers.' He shook his head. 'I was having such a good day. Everyone was saying how good I looked in the picture. Everyone was congratulating me because I was doing something about visa enforcement. Okay, so I took a few comments when I dragged a naked, greased-up fat guy into the station, but I could handle that.' He gave his head another shake. '*This* I can't handle. This has to get fixed. I can't afford to lose this guy. Either we find this guy, dead or alive, or we're all unemployed. If I can't enforce this visa bond after all the publicity, I'm going to have to change my name, move to Scottsdale, Arizona, and sell used cars.' Vinnie focused on Ranger. 'You can find him, right?'

The corners of Ranger's mouth tipped up a fraction of an inch. This was the Ranger equivalent of a smile.

'I'm gonna take that as a yes,' Vinnie said.

'I'll need help,' Ranger told him. 'And we'll need to work out the fee.'

'Fine. Whatever. You can have Stephanie.'

Ranger cut his eyes to me and the smile widened ever so slightly – the sort of smile you see on a man when he's presented with an unexpected piece of pie.

Two

Connie handed a stack of papers over to Ranger. 'Here's everything we have,' she said. 'A copy of the bond agreement, photo, background information. I'll check the hospitals and the morgue, and I'll run a full investigative report. I should have some of it tomorrow.'

This was the information age. Sign up with a service, tap a few keys on the computer, and within seconds facts start pouring in – all the names on the family tree, employment records, credit history, a chronology of home addresses. If you pay enough and search hard enough it's possible to access medical secrets and marital infidelities.

Ranger read through the Singh file and then looked at me. 'Are you available?'

Connie fanned herself and Lula bit into her lower lip.

I blew out a sigh. This apprehension was going to create problems. My involvement with Trenton cop Joe Morelli was on the fast track again. Joe and I had a long, strange history and we probably loved each other. Neither of us felt marriage was the answer right now. It was one of the few things we agreed on. Morelli hated my job and I wasn't crazy about his grandmother. And Morelli and I had clashing views on Ranger's acceptability as a partner. We both agreed Ranger was dangerous and a shade off normal. Morelli wanted me to stay *far* away from Ranger. I thought six to ten inches was sufficient.

'What's the plan?' I asked Ranger.

'I'll take the neighborhood. You talk to Singh's employer, TriBro Tech. TriBro should be cooperative. They put the money up for the visa bond.'

I snapped him a salute. 'Okeydokey,' I said. 'Don't forget about the dog.'

The almost smile returned to Ranger's mouth. 'No stone unturned,' he said.

'Hey,' I said. 'Dogs are people, too.'

The truth was, I didn't give a hoot about Samuel Singh. I know that's not a great attitude, but I was stuck with it. And I certainly didn't care about Mrs Apusenja. Mrs Apusenja was a bridge troll. Nonnie and the dog seemed like they needed help. And the dog pushed a button on me that triggered a rush of protective feelings. Go figure that. I really wanted to find the dog.

Ranger took off and I headed for home to degrease before

questioning Singh's boss. I live in a three-story brick apartment building that houses the newly wed and the nearly dead . . . and me. The building lacks a lot of amenities, but the price is right and I can get pizza delivered. I parked in the lot, took the stairs to the second floor, and was surprised to find my apartment door unlocked. I stuck my head in and yelled, 'Anybody home?'

'Yeah, it's me,' Morelli yelled back from the bedroom. 'I'm missing a set of keys. I thought maybe I left them here last night.'

'I put them in the cookie jar for safekeeping.'

Morelli walked into the kitchen, lifted the lid on the cookie jar, and removed his keys. Morelli looked like a real badass – lean and hard in a black T-shirt, washed-out jeans that fit him great across the butt, and new running shoes. He wore his gun at his hip, out of sight under a lightweight jacket. His hair was dark and his eyes were dark and he looked like he frequently traveled through places where men's hearts were dark.

'I'm not surprised to find the thirty-eight in here,' he said. 'But what's with the box of condoms?'

'They're for an emergency. Like the gun.'

He pocketed the keys and looked me over. 'You get into a fight with the guy who owns the lube gun at Midas?'

'Punky Balog. He thought if he was greased up and naked I wouldn't take him in.'

'Hah,' Morelli said. 'Greased up and naked is your specialty. Are you done for the day?'

'No. I came home to get cleaned. Did you see the article about Vinnie and the visa bond?'

'Yeah.'

'Samuel Singh, the bondee, is missing.'

Morelli grinned. 'That's fun.'

No one wanted to see Vinnie selling used cars in Scottsdale, but we all enjoyed watching him sweat. Vinnie sat on a rotting branch of my family tree. Only a couple roaches from my Aunt Tootie's kitchen sat lower than Vinnie. He was a pervert, a con man, and a paranoid grouch. And in spite of all that (or maybe because of it) he was liked. He was Jersey. How can you not like Jersey?

'As soon as I change my clothes I'm going out to talk to Singh's boss,' I told Morelli.

'I'm surprised Vinnie didn't give this to Ranger.'

Our eyes locked for a long moment while I searched for a reply, thinking a fib might be the way to go.

'Shit, Stephanie,' Morelli finally said, hands on hips, hard set to his mouth. 'Don't tell me you're working with Ranger again.'

Morelli and I were legitimately separated when I slept with Ranger. When Morelli and I got back together, he never asked and I never told. Still, the suspicion was there and the association rankled. And beyond the suspicion, there was a very real concern that Ranger sometimes operated a tad too far left of the law. 'It's my job,' I told Morelli.

'The guy's nuts. He doesn't have an address. The address on his driver's license is an empty lot. And I think he kills people.'

'I'm pretty sure he only kills bad guys.'

'That makes me feel a lot better.'

I didn't actually know if Ranger killed people. Truth is, no one knows much about Ranger. The only thing I know for sure is that he's a primo bounty hunter. And he's the sort of lover who could make a woman forget she values commitment.

'I have to take a shower,' I told Morelli.

'Need help?'

'No! I want to talk to Singh's employer, TriBro Tech. It's on the other side of Route One and I want to get there before the workday ends.'

'I think I'm getting turned on by the Vaseline,' Morelli said.

Everything turns Morelli on. 'Go to work! Catch a drug dealer or something.'

'I'll hold the thought for tonight,' Morelli said. 'Maybe you should come home and take a nap after TriBro.' And he left.

Twenty minutes later, I was out the door. My clean hair was pulled into a ponytail. I was wearing sandals, a short black skirt, and a white sweater with a low scoop neck. I had pepper spray in my purse, just in case. I couldn't match Connie in the cleavage department, but thanks to Victoria's Secret I was making the most of what I had.

TriBro was located in a light industrial park just east of the city. I cut across town, picked up Route I, and counted off two exits. I took the off-ramp directly into the complex, located B Street, and parked in TriBro's lot. The structure in front of me was a single story, cinderblock construction, brick front, sign to the right of the front door. TriBro Tech.

The reception area was utilitarian. Industrial-grade charcoal carpet, commercial-grade dark wood furniture, overhead fluorescent lighting. Large fake potted plant by the door. Very orderly. Very clean. The woman behind the desk was professionally friendly. I introduced myself and asked to speak to Singh's superior.

A man appeared in an open doorway behind the woman. 'I'm Andrew Cone,' he said. 'Perhaps I can help you.'

He was mid-forties, average height, slim build, seriously thinning brown hair, amiable brown eyes. He wore a blue shirt, one button open at the throat, sleeves neatly rolled. Khaki slacks. He ushered me into his office and directed me to a chair across from his desk. His office was tastefully decorated. He had a *World's Best Dad* coffee mug on his desk and framed photos on his bookcase. The photos were of two little boys and a blonde woman. They were at the beach. They were dressed for a party. They were hugging a small spotted dog.

'I'm looking for Samuel Singh,' I told Andrew Cone, passing him a business card.

He smiled at me with slightly raised eyebrows. 'Bond enforcement? What's a nice girl like you doing in a tough job like that?'

'Paying the rent, mostly.'

'And Singh skipped out on you?'

'Not yet. He has another week left on his visa. This is routine monitoring.'

Cone wagged his finger at me. 'That's a fib. Singh's landlady and her daughter were here earlier. They haven't seen Singh in five days. And neither have we. Singh didn't show up for work last Wednesday and we haven't seen or heard from him since. I read the article in today's paper. Unfortunate timing.'

'Do you have any idea where he might be?'

'No, but I don't think it's any place good. He didn't pick up his paycheck on Friday. Usually, only the dead and the deported don't show up for their paycheck.'

'Did he have a locker here? Any friends I might talk to?'

'No locker. I've asked around, but I didn't come up with much. The general opinion is that Singh's likeable enough, but a loner.'

I looked around the office. No clues as to the nature of TriBro's business. 'So what sort of business is this? And what did Singh do for you?'

'TriBro makes very specific parts for slot machines. My father and his two brothers started the business in fifty-two, and now it's owned by me and my two brothers, Bart and Clyde. My mother had hopes for a large family and thought it would simplify things to name her children alphabetically. I have two sisters. Diane and Evelyn.'

'Your parents stopped at five?'

'They divorced after five. I think it was the stress of living in a house with one bathroom and five kids.'

I felt myself smiling. I liked Andrew Cone. He was a pleasant guy and he had a sense of humor. 'And Singh?'

'Singh was a techie, working in quality control. We hired him to temporarily fill in for a woman who was out on maternity leave.'

'Do you think his disappearance could be work related?'

'Are you asking if the Mob rubbed him out?'

'That would be part of the question.'

'We're actually a pretty boring little cog in the casino wheel,' Cone said. 'I don't think the Mob would be interested in Singh's contribution to gambling.'

'Terrorist connection?'

Cone grinned and tipped back in his chair. 'Not likely. From what I hear, Singh was addicted to American television and junk food and would give his life to protect the country that spawned the Egg McMuffin.'

'Did you know him personally?'

'Only as boss to employee. This is a small company. Bart and Clyde and I know everyone who works here, but we don't necessarily socialize with the people on the line.'

Raised voices carried in to us.

'My brothers,' Andrew said. 'No volume control.'

A slightly younger, balder version of Andrew stuck his head in the doorway. 'We got a problem.' He looked my way. 'And you would be who?'

I gave him my card.

'Bond enforcement?'

A third face appeared in the doorway. This face was round and cherubic with eyes peering out from behind wire-rimmed glasses. The face came with a chubby body dressed in homeboy jeans, a Buzz Lightyear sweatshirt that had been washed almost to oblivion and beyond, and ratty sneakers.

'You're a bounty hunter, right?' the baby-faced guy said. 'Do you have a gun?'

'No gun.'

'They always have guns on television.'

'I left my gun home.'

'I bet you don't need one. I bet you're real sneaky. You just sneak up to someone and *bam*, you've got him in handcuffs, right?'

'Right.'

'Are you going to handcuff someone here?'

'Not today.'

'My brothers,' Andrew said, gesturing to the two men. 'Bart and Clyde Cone.'

Bart was wearing a black shirt, black slacks, and black loafers. Black Bart.

'If you're here about Samuel Singh, we have nothing to say on the matter,' Bart said. 'He was very briefly in our employ.'

'Did you know him personally?'

'I did not. And I'm afraid I have to speak to my brother privately. We have a problem on the line.'

Clyde leaned close to me. Friendly. 'There's always a problem on the line,' he said, smiling, not caring much. 'Shit's always breaking. Gizmos and stuff like that.' His eyes got wide. 'How about a taser? Have you ever used a taser?'

Bart pressed his lips together and threw Clyde a dark look.

The look rolled off Clyde. 'I never met a bounty hunter before,' Clyde said, his breath steaming his glasses.

I'd hoped for more information from TriBro. The name of a friend or enemy would have been helpful. Some knowledge of travel plans would have been nice. What I got was a vague idea of the nature of Singh's job and a dinner invitation from Clyde Cone, who I suspected was only interested in my stun gun.

I declined the dinner invitation and I rolled out of the lot. Ranger was working the Apusenjas' neighborhood. I didn't want to step on Ranger's toes, but I worried that Boo the cockapoo wasn't a priority for him. It was getting to be late afternoon. I could cut across town and do a quick drive around, looking for Boo, and then I'd be in a good position to mooch dinner from my mom.

I called Morelli and told him the plan. 'You can mooch dinner, too,' I said.

'Last time I ate dinner at your parents' house your sister threw up three times and your grandmother fell asleep in her mashed potatoes.'

'And?'

'And I'd like to mooch dinner, but I have to work late. I swear to God, I really do have to work late.'

* * *

Nonnie and Mama Apusenja lived a quarter mile from my parents' house, in a neighborhood that was very similar to the Burg. Houses were narrow, two stories, set on narrow lots. The Apusenja house was a two-toned clapboard, painted a bilious green on the top and chocolate brown on the bottom. A ten-year-old burgundy Ford Escort was parked curbside. The small backyard was fenced. I couldn't see all the yard, but what I *could* see didn't contain a dog. I cruised four blocks without a Boo sighting. Also, no Ranger sighting. I turned a corner and my cell phone chirped.

'Yo,' Ranger said.

'Yo yourself,' I told him. 'Do you have Singh in leg irons?'

'Singh is nowhere to be found.'

'And the dog?'

A couple beats of silence. 'What's with you and the dog?'

'I don't know. I just have these *dog* feelings.'

'Not a good sign, babe. Next thing you'll be adopting cats. And then one day you'll get all choked up when you walk down the baby food aisle in the supermarket. And you know what happens after that . . .'

'What?'

'You'll be punching holes in Morelli's condoms.'

I'd have liked to think the scenario was funny, but I was afraid it might be true. 'I visited with the people at TriBro,' I told Ranger. 'I didn't come away with anything useful.'

I caught a familiar reflection in my rear-view mirror. Ranger in his truck. How he always managed to find me was part of the mystery.

Ranger flashed his lights to make sure I saw him. 'Let's talk to the Apusenjas,' he said.

We drove around the block to Sully Street, parked behind the burgundy Escort, and walked to the door together.

Mama Apusenja answered. She was still in the sari and her fat rolls made me think of the Michelin tire guy.

'Well,' she said to me, with a head wag. 'I see you've cleaned yourself up. You must be a terrible burden to your mother. I am feeling so sorry for her not to have a proper daughter.'

I narrowed my eyes and opened my mouth to speak and Ranger leaned into me and rested a hand on my shoulder. Probably he thought I was going to do something rash, like call Mrs Apusenja a fat cow. And in fact he was right. *Fat cow* was on the tip of my tongue.

'I thought it might be helpful to see Singh's room,' Ranger said to Mrs Apusenja.

'Will you be bringing *this one* in with you?'

Ranger's grip on me tightened. '*This one*'s name is Stephanie,' Ranger said pleasantly. 'And yes, she'll be coming with me.'

'I suppose it will be all right,' Mrs Apusenja said

grudgingly. 'I will expect you to be careful. I keep a very nice house.' She stepped back from the door and motioned us in to the living room. 'This is the formal parlor,' she said proudly. 'And beyond that is the dining room. And then the kitchen.'

Ranger and I stood speechless for a moment, taking it all in. The house was filled to bursting with overstuffed furniture, end tables, lamps, trinkets, dried flowers, faded photos, stacks of magazines and bowls of fake fruit. And elephants. There were ceramic elephants, elaborate elephant couch pillows, elephant clocks, foot stools, and planters. Elephants aside, there was no dominant style or color. It was a garage sale waiting to happen.

I watched Ranger scan the room and I suspected he was doing a mental grimace. It would be easy to miss a note in the mess. For that matter, it would be easy to miss Singh. He could be slouched in a chair somewhere and never be noticed.

Mrs Apusenja led the way upstairs, across the short hallway to a small bedroom. She was wearing pink rubber flip-flops that slapped against her heels and hit the floor at an angle so her heel was always half off the shoe. Her toenails were massive, painted a virulent shimmering purple. I was directly behind her and from my angle her ass looked to be about three feet across.

'This is Samuel's room,' she said, gesturing to the open door. 'It's so sad that it's empty. He was such a nice young man. So polite. Very respectful.' She said this cutting a look back at me, sending the message that she knew I had none of those wonderful qualities.

Ranger and I stepped inside the room and I was hit with a wave of claustrophobia. The double bed was neatly made, covered with a green, yellow, and purple-flowered quilted bedspread that shouted *yikes*. The curtains matched the bedspread and hung over seasick green sheers. The walls were plastered with outdated calendars and thumbtacked posters, with subjects ranging from Winnie the Pooh to Springsteen, the Starship *Enterprise*, and Albert Einstein. There was a nightstand beside the bed and a small desk and rickety chair wedged between the bed and the wall.

'You see, it's such a nice room,' Mrs Apusenja said. 'He was lucky to have this room. We have a room in the basement that we also rent out on occasion, but we gave Samuel this room because I knew he would be a suitor for Nonnie.'

Ranger rifled through the nightstand and desk drawers. 'Was Samuel unhappy about anything?'

'No. He was very happy. Why would he be unhappy? He had everything. We even allowed him kitchen privileges.'

'Have you notified his family of his disappearance?'

'I have. I thought perhaps he was suddenly called

home, but they have heard nothing from him.'

Ranger moved on to the desk. He opened the middle drawer and extracted Singh's passport. 'New York is his only entry.'

'This was his first time away from home,' Mrs Apusenja said. 'He was a good boy. He was not one of those good-for-nothing wanderers. He came here to make money for his family in India.'

Ranger returned the passport to the drawer and continued his search. He abandoned the desk and went to the closet. 'What's missing from the room?' Ranger asked Mrs Apusenja. 'What did Singh take with him?'

'So far as I know, just the clothes he was wearing. And his backpack, of course.'

Ranger turned to look at her. 'Do you know what he carried in his backpack?'

'His computer. He was never without his computer. It was a laptop. It always went to work with him. Samuel was very smart. That's how he got such a good job. He said he got his job over the Internet.'

'Do you know his email address?' I asked.

'No. I don't know anything about that. We don't own a computer. We have no need for such a thing.'

'How did Samuel get to work?' Ranger asked.

'He drove himself.'

'Has his car been found?'

'No. He just drove away in the car and that was the last we saw of him and the car. It was a gray Nissan Sentra . . . an older model.'

Ranger did a quick search of the bathroom and Nonnie's room and we all moved downstairs to search the kitchen.

We were still in the kitchen when Nonnie came home.

'Have you found Boo?' Nonnie asked.

'Not yet,' I said. 'Sorry.'

'It's difficult to concentrate on my work with him missing like this,' Nonnie said.

'Nonnie is a manicurist at Classy Nails in the mall,' Mrs Apusenja said. 'She is one of their most popular girls.'

'I never skimp on the top coat,' Nonnie said. 'That's the secret to a superior manicure.'

It was a few minutes after six when Ranger and I left the Apusenjas. There was still time to make dinner at my parents' house, but I was losing enthusiasm for the experience. I was thinking I'd had enough chaos for one day. I was thinking maybe what I wanted to do was get take-out pizza and go home and watch a bad movie.

Ranger lounged against my car, arms crossed over his chest. 'What do you think?'

'Nonnie never asked about Singh. She only asked about Boo.'

'Not exactly the distraught fiancée,' Ranger said.

'If we believe everything we hear, we've got a nice geeky guy who got himself engaged and disappeared along with the dog.'

'The dog could be a coincidence.'

'I don't think so. My Spidey Sense tells me the disappearances are related.'

Ranger grinned at me. 'Your Spidey Sense tell you anything else?'

'Is that a mocking grin?'

'It's the grin of a man who loves you, babe.'

My heart skipped around a little and I got warm in places only Morelli should be warming. 'Love?'

'There's all kinds of love,' Ranger said. 'This kind doesn't come with a ring attached.'

'Nice, but you avoided answering my question about the mocking grin.'

He gave my ponytail a playful tug.

'I'm going back to TriBro tomorrow,' I said. 'I'll make a pest of myself. Find out about the Internet job search. Talk to coworkers. If it's anything other than a random murder, I should be able to get a lead.'

I decided against the family dinner and instead I stopped at Pino's on the way home. I slid the Pino's pizza box onto my kitchen counter, kicked my shoes off, and got a beer out of the fridge. I punched the message button on my machine and listened to my messages while I ate.

'Stephanie? It's your mother. Hello? Are you there?' Disconnect.

Second message. 'Bad news. I'm gonna punk out on lunch tomorrow. The kids are sick.' It was my best friend, Mary Lou Molnar. Mary Lou and I grew up together. We went to school together and we were married within months of each other. Mary Lou's marriage stuck and she had a pack of kids. My marriage lasted about twenty minutes and ended in a screaming divorce.

The third message was from Vinnie. 'What are you doing at home listening to this dumb machine? Why aren't you out looking for Singh? I'm dying here, for crissake. Do something!'

And my mother again. 'I didn't want anything the first time. You don't have to call me back.'

I erased the messages and dropped a tiny piece of pizza into Rex's cage. Rex is my hamster roommate. He lives in a glass aquarium in my kitchen and sleeps in a Campbell's tomato soup can. Rex rushed out of his soup can, shoved the pizza into his cheek pouch, and scurried back to the can. Quality pet time.

I carted the pizza box, the beer, and my purse into the

living room, flopped onto the couch, powered up the television, and found a *Seinfeld* rerun. A couple months ago I entered the computer age and bought myself an Apple iBook. I keep the iBook on my coffee table so I can check my mail and watch television at the same time. Am I a multitasker, or what?

I opened the iBook and signed on. I deleted the junk mail advertising Viagra, mortgage rates, and porn sites. A single message was left. It was from Andrew Cone. *If I can be of any further help, don't hesitate to call.*

The phone jarred me awake at 7.00 a.m.

'Something just came across my desk that I thought you might want to see,' Morelli said. 'I'm at the station and I have a few things to do and then I'll come over.'

I dragged myself out of bed and into the bathroom. I did the shower thing and the hair thing and a half-assed job at the make-up thing. I got dressed in my usual uniform of T-shirt and jeans and felt ready to face the day. I made coffee and treated myself to a strawberry Pop-Tart, feeling righteous because I'd resisted the S'mores Pop-Tart. Best to have fruit for breakfast, right? I gave a corner of the Pop-Tart to Rex and sipped my coffee.

I was pouring myself a second cup of coffee when Morelli arrived. He backed me against a wall, made certain there were no spaces between us, and he kissed me. His pager buzzed and he did some inventive cussing.

'Trouble?' I asked.

He looked at the display. 'The usual crap.' He stepped back and pulled a folded piece of paper out of his jacket pocket. 'I knew there was some sort of mess associated with TriBro, so I ran a search for you. It turned up this newspaper article from two years ago.'

I took the paper from Morelli and read the headline. 'Bart Cone Charged in Paressi Slaying.' The article went on to say that hikers had stumbled over the body of Lillian Paressi just hours after Paressi had been killed with a single shot to the head at close range. The murder had occurred in a wooded area just north of Washington's Crossing State Park. Cone had been spotted leaving the scene and police claimed to have physical evidence linking Cone to the murder.

'What happened?' I asked Morelli.

'He was released. The witness who reported Cone fleeing from the scene recanted part of his story. And the physical evidence tested out negative. Cone had been carrying a twenty-two when the police picked him up for questioning. Paressi had been shot with a twenty-two, but ballistics ruled out Cone's gun as the murder weapon. And there wasn't a DNA match-up. Paressi had been sexually assaulted after her death and the DNA didn't match to Cone.

'As I remember, the guys assigned to the case still thought Cone killed Paressi. They just couldn't get anything to stick on him. And the case has never been solved.'

'Was there a motive?'

'No motive. They were never able to develop a connection between Paressi and Cone.'

'Bart Cone isn't exactly Mr Nice Guy, but it's hard to see him as a killer.'

'Killers come in all sizes,' Morelli said.

Three

Morelli walked me to my car, gave me a dismissive kiss on the forehead, and told me to be careful. He was driving a Piece Of Shit cop car that was parked next to my Ford. It was a Crown Vic that probably had originally been dark blue, but had now faded to a color that defied description. Paint was scraped off the right rear, and part of the back bumper was ripped away. A Kojak light was rolling around on the floor in the back.

'Nice car,' I said to Morelli.

'Yeah, I had a hard choice to make between this and the Ferrari.' He angled into the Vic, cranked it over, and rolled out of the lot.

It was early morning, but already the day was heating up. I could hear the drone of traffic, not far off on Hamilton. The sky was murky above me and I felt the rasp of ozone in the back of my throat. As the day wore on cars, chemical plants, and backyard barbecues would make their contribution to the stew that cooked over Jersey. Fancy-pants wimps in LA rated their pollution and curtailed activity. In Jersey we just call it *air* and get on with life. If you're born in Jersey, you know how to rise to a challenge. Bring on the Mob. Bring on bad air. Bring on taxes and obesity, diabetes, heart disease, and macaroni at every meal. Nothing defeats us in Jersey.

First thing on my activities list was a drive around the Apusenja neighborhood, keeping my eyes peeled for Boo and Singh. Sometimes missing persons turned up surprisingly close to home. They moved in with neighbors, hid out in garages, and sometimes turned up dead in a Dumpster.

Neither Boo nor Singh showed up after fifteen minutes of searching, so I headed across town to Route I and TriBro.

I still didn't have a clear idea of TriBro's product. Parts for slot machines. What did that mean? Gears? Handles? Bells and whistles? Not that it mattered. What mattered was squeezing a lead out of someone.

Black Bart hadn't been impressed with my charm or cleavage. I didn't think I'd get a lot of help from him. Clyde was eager, but not real bright. Andrew seemed like my best shot. I took the turnoff to TriBro and called Andrew on my cell phone.

'Guess what?' I said. 'I'm in the neighborhood. Can I take a couple more minutes of your time?'

'Absolutely.'

Absolutely was a good answer. Very positive. No sign of annoyance. No lecherous side remark. Professional. Andrew was definitely the brother of choice.

I parked in the lot, entered the lobby, and was immediately directed to Andrew's office. More good luck. No Bart or Clyde to slow me down. I took a chair across from Andrew and thanked him for seeing me.

'TriBro has an interest in finding Singh,' he said. 'We signed for the visa bond. If Singh skips, TriBro pays the bill.'

'Do you have other employees on work visas?'

'Not now, but we have in the past. And I have to tell you, Singh isn't the first to disappear.'

I felt my eyebrows raise.

'It's nothing suspicious,' Andrew said. 'In fact, I find it understandable. If I was in a similar position, I might disappear, too. These men come to work for three months and are seduced by the potential for success. Everything is within their reach . . . rental movies, burgers, designer jeans, a new car, microwave popcorn, and frozen waffles. I have some sympathy for their flight, but at the same time TriBro can't keep absorbing bond losses. If this sort of thing continues we'll have to stop using visa workers. And that would be a shame, because they make very good temporary employees.'

'Singh must have had some friends on the job. I'd like to talk to them.'

Andrew Cone sat through a couple beats of silence, his eyes holding mine, his thoughts private, his expression guarded. 'Why don't we put you undercover,' he finally said. 'I can give you Singh's job for a day. We haven't filled it yet.'

'I'm not even sure what you make here.'

'We make little things. Machine-tooled gears and locks. Singh's job primarily consisted of measuring minutia. Each part we supply must be perfect. The first day onboard you wouldn't be expected to know much.' He reached for his phone and his mouth tipped into a small smile. 'Let's see how good you are at bluffing.'

Ten minutes later I was a genuine bogus TriBro employee, following after Andrew, learning about TriBro Tech. The gears and locks that composed the bulk of TriBro's product were made at workstations housed in a large warehouse-type facility adjoining the reception area and offices. The far end of the warehouse was divided off into a long room where the quality-control work was done. Windows looked into the interior. In the entire facility there were no windows looking out. The quality-control area consisted of a series of cubbies with built-in tables, shelves, and cabinets. The tables held an odd assortment of weights, measures, machine-torture devices, and chemicals. A single worker occupied each of the tables. There were seven people in the quality-control area. And there was one unoccupied table. Singh's table.

Andrew introduced me to the area supervisor, Ann Klimmer, and returned to his office. Ann took me table by table and introduced me to the rest of the team. The women were in their thirties and forties. There were two men. One of the men was Asian. Singh would have gravitated to the Asian, I thought. But the women would warm to me faster.

After the introductions and an overview lecture on the operation, I was partnered with Jane Locarelli. Jane looked like she'd just rolled off an embalming table. She was late forties, rail thin, and drained of color. Even her hair was faded. She spoke in a monotone, never making eye contact, her words slightly slurred as if the effort of speech was too much to manage.

'I've worked here for thirty-one years,' she said. 'I started working for the senior Cones. Right out of high school.'

No wonder she looked like a walking cadaver. Thirty-one years under fluorescent lights, measuring and torturing little metal doohickeys. Jeez.

Jane hitched herself up onto a stool and selected a small gear from a huge barrel of small gears. 'We do two kinds of testing here. We do random testing of new product.' She sent me an apologetic grimace. 'I'm afraid that's a little tedious.' She displayed the gear she held in her hand. 'And we test parts which have failed and been returned. That sort of testing is much more interesting. Unfortunately, today we're testing new product.'

Jane carefully measured each part of the gear and examined it under a microscope for flaws. When she was done, she reached into the barrel and selected another gear. I had to bite back a groan. Two gears down. Three thousand gears to go.

'I heard Singh didn't show up for work one day,' I said, going for casual curious. 'Was he unhappy with the job?'

'Not sure,' Jane said, concentrating on the new gear. 'He wasn't very talkative.' After extensive measuring, she decided the gear was okay and went on to a third.

'Would you like to try one?' she asked.

'Sure.'

She handed the gear over and showed me how to measure.

'Looks good to me,' I said after doing the measuring thing.

'No,' she said, 'it's off on one side. See the little burr on the edge of the one cog?' Jane took the gear from me, filed the side, and measured again. 'Maybe you should just watch a while longer,' she said.

I watched Jane do four more gears and my eyes glazed over and some drool oozed from between my lips. I quietly slid from my stool and moved to the next cubicle.

Dolly Freedman was also testing new gears. Dolly would drink some coffee and measure. Then she'd drink more coffee and perform another test. She was as thin and as pale as Jane, but not as lifeless. She was cranked on coffee. 'This is such a bullshit job,' Dolly said to me. She looked around. 'Anyone watching?' she asked. Then she took a handful of gears and dumped them into the perfect gear bucket. 'They looked good to me,' she said. Then she drank more coffee.

'I'm going to be doing Samuel Singh's job,' I told her. 'Do you know what happened to him? I heard he just didn't show up for work one day.'

'Yeah, that's what I heard, too. No one's said much about him. He was real quiet. Carried his computer around and spent all his breaks on the computer.'

'Playing computer games?'

'No. He was always plugged into a phone line. Surfing. Doing email. Real secretive about it, too. If someone came over to him he'd close up the computer. Probably was on some porno site. He looked like the type.'

'Slimy?'

'Male. I keep protection in my desk for those types.' She opened her top desk drawer to show me her canister of pepper spray.

I continued to move around the room, saving Edgar, the Asian guy, for last. Several of the women thought Singh looked unhappy. Alice Louise thought he might be secretly gay. No one could fault his work habits. He arrived on time and he did his barrel. No one knew he was engaged. No one had any idea where he lived or what he did in his spare time, other than surf the Net. Everyone had seen the newspaper article and thought Vinnie looked like a weasel.

I called Ranger at noon.

'Yo,' Ranger said.

'Just checking in.'

'How are the folks at TriBro?'

'Not giving me a lot, but it's still early.'

'Go get 'em, babe.' And he disconnected.

I drifted over to Edgar's table midafternoon. Edgar was dropping acid on a small metal bar with threads at either end. One drop at a time. Drip, wait, and measure. Drip, wait, and measure. Drip, wait, and measure. There had to be a thousand bars waiting to be tortured. Nothing was happening. This job made watching grass grow look exciting.

'We're testing a new alloy,' Edgar said.

'This seems more interesting than the gear measuring.'

'Only for the first two million bars. After that, it's pretty routine.'

'Why do you keep this job?'

'Benefits.'

'Health insurance?'

'Gambling. If the product fails, one of us goes to Vegas

as a tech rep. And the products fail all the time.'

'What's a tech rep?'

'A technical representative. You know, a repairman.'

'Did Singh ever go to Vegas?'

'Once.'

'And you?'

'On an average, once a month. Failure is usually stress related. And that's my area of expertise.'

'Did Singh like Vegas?'

'Why are you so interested in Singh?' Edgar asked.

'I'm taking over his job.'

'If you were taking over his job you'd be sitting at his desk doing measurements. Instead, you're floating around, talking to everyone. I think you're looking for Singh.'

A point for Edgar. 'Okay, suppose I am looking for Singh. Would you know where to find him?'

'No, but I'd know where to start looking. The day before he disappeared he was in the lunch room calling all the McDonald's places, asking if a guy named Howie worked there. It was pretty strange. He was all excited. And it was the first time I'd ever seen him make a call.'

I looked through the window, into the manufacturing area, and I caught Bart Cone's eye. He was examining a machine, standing with three other men. He glanced up and saw me talking to Edgar.

'That's not a happy face,' Edgar said, his attention shifting to Bart.

'Does he ever have a happy face?'

'Yeah, I saw him smile once when he ran over a toad in the parking lot.'

Bart made a *wait here* gesture to the men at the machine and marched across the work floor to the test area. He wrenched the door open and asked me to follow him out to the offices. I took my purse since it was the end of the day and there wasn't much chance I'd be returning.

Bart was once again dressed in black. His expression was menacing. I followed him into an office that smelled like metal shavings and was a cluttered mess of stacked catalogues and spare parts collected in tattered cardboard boxes. His desk was large, the top heaped with loose papers, disposable coffee cups, more spare parts, a multiline phone, and a workstation computer.

'What the hell were you doing in there?' Bart asked, looking like a guy who might have murdered Lillian Paressi. 'I thought I made it clear that we had nothing to tell you about Singh.'

'Your brother feels otherwise. He suggested I work undercover for a day.'

Bart snatched at his phone and punched a key on speed dial. 'What's the deal with Ms Plum?' he asked. 'I found her in the test area.' His expression darkened at Andrew's answer. He gave a terse reply, returned the handset to the cradle, and glared at me. 'I don't care what my brother told you, I'm going to give you good advice and God help you if you don't follow it. Stay out of my factory.'

'Sure,' I said. 'Okeydokey.' And I left. I might be a little slow sometimes, but I'm not *totally* stupid. I know a genuinely scary dude when I see one. And Bart was a genuinely scary dude.

My cell phone rang as I was pulling out of the lot.

'Stephanie? It's your mother.'

As if I wouldn't recognize her voice.

'We're having a nice chicken for dinner tonight.'

My unmarried sister was nine months pregnant, living with my parents, and had turned into the hormone queen. I'd have to endure Valerie's mood swings to get to the chicken dinner. Valerie's boyfriend, Albert Kloughn, would most likely be there, too. Kloughn was also Valerie's boss and the father of her unborn baby. Kloughn was a struggling lawyer, and he was practically living at the house, trying to get Valerie to marry him. Not to mention Valerie's two little girls by a previous marriage who were nice kids, but added to the bedlam potential.

'Mashed potatoes with gravy,' my mother said, sensing my hesitation, sweetening the offer.

'Gee, I sort of have things to do,' I said.

'Pineapple upside-down cake for dessert,' my mother said, pulling out the big gun. 'Extra whipped cream.' And she knew she had me. I'd never in my life turned down pineapple upside-down cake.

I looked at my watch. 'I'm about twenty minutes away. I'll be a couple minutes late. Start without me.'

Everyone was at the table when I arrived.

My sister, Valerie, was pushed back about a foot and a half to accommodate her beach-ball belly. A couple weeks ago she'd started using the belly like a shelf, balancing her plate on it, tucking her napkin into the neck of her shirt, catching spilled food on her huge swollen breasts. She'd gained seventy pounds with the baby and she was all big boobs and double chins and ham-hock arms. Unheard of for Valerie, who previous to her divorce had been the perfect daughter, resembling the serene and slim Virgin Mary in every way, with the possible exception of virginity and hair style. The hair was Meg Ryan.

Albert Kloughn was at her side, his face round and pink, his scalp gleaming under his thinning sandy hair. He was watching Valerie with unabashed awe and affection. Kloughn wasn't a subtle guy. He hadn't any idea how to hide an emotion. Probably he wasn't great in a courtroom, but he was always fun at the dinner table. And he was surprisingly endearing in an oddball way.

Valerie's two girls from her first and only marriage, Angie and Mary Alice, were on the edges of their seats, hoping for a fun disaster . . . like Grandma Mazur setting the tablecloth on fire or Albert Kloughn spilling hot coffee into his lap.

Grandma Mazur was happily sipping her second glass of wine. My mom was at the head of the table, all business, daring anyone to find fault with the chicken. And my dad shoveled food into his mouth and acknowledged me with a grunt.

'I read in the paper where aliens from a different galaxy are buying up all the good real estate in Albany,' Grandma said.

'They'll get hit hard with taxes,' Kloughn told her. 'They'd be better to buy real estate in Florida or Texas.'

My father never raised his head, but his eyes slid first to Kloughn and then to my grandmother. He muttered something that was too low to carry. I suspected it was in the area of *good grief*.

My father is retired from the post office and now he drives a cab part-time. When my grandmother came to live with my parents, my mother stopped storing the rat poison in the garage. Not that my father would actually take to poisoning my grandmother, but why tempt fate? Better to store the rat poison at Cousin Betty's house.

'If I was an alien I'd rather live in Florida anyway,' Grandma said. 'Florida has Disney World. What's Albany got?'

Valerie looked like she was ready to drop the baby on the dining-room floor. 'Get me a gun,' Valerie said. 'If I don't go into labor soon I'm going to shoot myself. And pass the gravy. Pass it *now*.'

My mother jumped to her feet and handed the gravy boat to Valerie. 'Sometimes the contractions are hardly noticeable in the beginning,' my mother said. 'Do you think you could be having hardly noticeable contractions?'

Valerie's attention was fully focused on the gravy. She poured gravy on everything . . . vegetables, applesauce, chicken, dressing, and a heap of rolls. 'I love gravy,' she said, spooning the overflow into her mouth, eating the gravy like soup. 'I *dream* about gravy.'

'It's a little high in saturated fats,' Kloughn said.

Valerie glanced sideways at Kloughn. 'You're not going to lecture me on my diet, are you?'

Kloughn sat up straight in his seat, his eyes wide and birdlike. 'Me? No, honest, I wouldn't do anything like that. I like fat women. Just the other day I was thinking how fat women were soft. Nothing I like better than big, soft, squishy pillows of fat.'

He was nodding his balding head, trying hard, running down dark roads of panic.

'Look at me. I'm nice and fat, too. I'm like the Doughboy. Go ahead, poke my stomach. I'm just like the Doughboy,' Kloughn said.

'Omigod,' my sister wailed. 'You think I'm fat.' She went into open-mouthed sobbing and the plate slid from her stomach and crashed onto the floor.

Kloughn bent to retrieve the plate and farted. 'That wasn't me,' he said.

'Maybe it was me,' Grandma said. 'Sometimes they sneak out. Did I fart?' she asked everyone.

My eyes inadvertently went to the kitchen door.

'Don't even *think* about it,' my mother said. 'We're all in this together. Anyone sneaks out the back way, they answer to me.'

When the table was cleared and the dishes were done, I made my move to leave.

'I need to talk to you,' my mother said, following me out of the house to stand curbside, where we had privacy.

The bottom of the sun had sunk into the Krienskis' asbestos shingle roof, a sure sign that the day was ending. Kids ran in packs, burning off the last of their energy. Parents and grandparents sat on small front porches. The air was dead still, heavy with the promise of a hot tomorrow.

Inside my parents' house, my father and grandmother sat glued to the television. The muffled rise and fall of a sitcom laugh track escaped the house and joined the mix of street noise.

'I'm worried about your sister,' my mother said. 'What's to become of her? A baby due in two weeks and no husband. She should marry Albert. You have to talk to her.'

'No way! One minute she's all smiley face and crying because she loves me so much and then next thing I know she's grumpy. I want the old Valerie back. The one with no personality. And besides, I'm not exactly an expert at marriage. Look at me . . . I can't even figure out my *own* life.'

'I'm not asking a lot. I just want you to talk to her. Get her to understand that she's having a baby.'

'Mom, she knows she's having a baby. She's as big as a Volkswagen. She's already done it twice before.'

'Yes, but both times she did it in California. It's not the same. And she had a husband then. And a house.'

Okay, now we're getting somewhere. 'This is about the house, right?'

'I feel like the old lady who lived in a shoe. Remember the rhyme? She had so many children she didn't know what to do? One more person in this house and we're going to have to sleep in shifts. Your father's talking about renting a

Porta Potti for the backyard. And it's not just the house. This is the Burg. Women don't go off and have babies without husbands here. Every time I go to the grocery, I meet someone who wants to know when Valerie is getting married.'

I thought this was a good deal. It used to be that people wanted to know when *I* was getting married.

'She's in the kitchen eating the rest of the cake,' my mother said. 'She's probably got it topped with gravy. You could go in and talk to her. Tell her Albert Kloughn is a good man.'

'Valerie doesn't want to hear this from me.'

'What's it going to take?' my mother wanted to know. 'German chocolate torte?'

The German chocolate torte took hours to make. My mother hated to make the German chocolate torte.

'German chocolate torte and a leg of lamb. That's my best offer,' she said.

'Boy, you're really serious.'

My mother grabbed me by the front of my shirt. 'I'm desperate! I'm on the window ledge on the fortieth floor and I'm looking down.'

I did an eye roll and a sigh and I trudged back into the house, into the kitchen. Sure enough, Valerie was at the small kitchen table, snarfing down cake.

'Mom wants me to talk to you,' I said.

'Not now. I'm busy. I'm eating for two, you know.'

Two elephants. 'Mom thinks you should marry Kloughn.'

Valerie forked off a huge piece and shoved it into her mouth. 'Kloughn's boring. Would you marry Kloughn?'

'No, but then I won't even marry Morelli.'

'I want to marry Ranger. Ranger is hot.'

I couldn't deny it. Ranger was hot. 'I don't think Ranger's the marrying type,' I said. 'And there would be a lot of things to consider. For instance, I think once in a while he might kill people.'

'Yeah, but not random, right?'

'Probably not random.'

Valerie was scraping at the leftover smudges of whipped cream. 'So that would be okay. Nobody's perfect.'

'Okay, then,' I said. 'Good talk. I'll pass this on to Mom.'

'It isn't as if I'm antimarriage,' Valerie said, eyeing the grease and drippings left in the roasting pan.

I backed out of the kitchen and ran into my mom.

'Well?' she asked.

'Valerie's thinking about it. And the good news is . . . she's not antimarriage.'

Streetlights were on when I cruised into my parking lot. A dog barked in a nearby neighborhood of single-family homes, and I thought of Boo. Mrs Apusenja had told Ranger and me that she'd tacked lost dog signs up at local businesses and at street corners. The signs had a photo of the dog and offered a small reward, but there'd been no takers.

Tomorrow I'd track down Howie. It was my Spidey Sense again. I had a feeling Howie was important. Singh had been trying to call him. It had to mean something, right?

I let myself into my apartment and said howdy to Rex. I checked my phone messages. Three in all.

The first was from Joe. 'Hey, cupcake.' That was it. That was the whole message.

The second was from Ranger. 'Yo.' Ranger made Joe look like a chatterbox.

The third was a hang-up.

I ambled into the living room, slouched onto the couch, and grabbed for the remote. A splash of color caught my eye from across the room. The color was coming from a vase of red roses and white carnations, sitting on an end table. The flowers hadn't been there this morning. A white envelope was propped against the vase.

My first thought was that someone had broken into my apartment. Ranger and Morelli did this on a regular basis, but they'd never left me flowers, and I was pretty certain they hadn't left them this time, either. I did a quick backtrack to the kitchen with my heart beating way too hard and too fast in my chest. I took my gun out of the brown bear cookie jar and started creeping through my apartment. There were only two rooms left unseen. Bedroom and bath. I looked into the bathroom. No creepy deranged killers lurking behind the shower curtain. None on the toilet. The bedroom was also monster free.

I shoved the gun under the waistband of my jeans and returned to the flowers. There was a message printed on the outside of the white envelope. *Tag. You're it.* I had no idea what this meant. I opened the envelope and removed three photos. It took a moment for the images to register. I clapped a hand to my mouth when I figured it out. They were pictures of a gunshot victim. A woman. Shot between the eyes. The photos were close-ups that were too tight in to reveal the woman's identity. One photo showed part of an eyebrow and an open sightless eye. The other two recorded the destruction to the back of her head, the exit point.

I dropped the photos, ran to the phone, and dialed Joe.

'Someone broke into my apartment,' I said. 'And they left me flowers and some ph-ph-photos. Should I call the police?'

'Honey, I am the police.'

'So I'm covered. Okay, just checking.'

'Do you want me to come over?'

'Yes. Drive fast.'

Four

Morelli stood, hands on hips, staring at the flowers on the table and the photos still spread out on the floor. 'It's like you have a sign on your door welcoming nuts and stalkers to walk in. Everyone breaks into your apartment. I've never seen anything like it. You have three top-of-the-line locks on your door and it doesn't deter anyone.' He glanced over at me. 'Your door was locked, right?'

'Yes. It was locked.' Yeesh. 'Do you think this is serious?'

Morelli looked at me like I was speaking a foreign language. 'Someone broke into your apartment and left you gunshot pictures. Don't *you* think it's serious?'

'I'm completely freaked out, but I was really hoping you'd tell me I was overreacting. I was going for the outside chance that you'd think this was someone's idea of a joke.'

'I hate this,' Morelli said. 'Why can't I have a girlfriend who has normal problems . . . like breaking a fingernail or missing a period or falling in love with a lesbian?'

'Now what?' I asked.

'Now I call this in and get a couple guys out here to collect evidence and maybe look for prints. Do you have any idea what this is about?'

'No idea at all. Not a clue. Nothing.'

The phone rang and I went to the kitchen to answer it.

'I definitely think it might work between Ranger and me,' Valerie said. 'You're pals with him. You could fix me up.'

'Valerie, you're nine months pregnant. This isn't a good time for a fix-up.'

'You think I should wait until after I deliver?'

'I think you should wait until never.'

Valerie did a big sigh and disconnected.

Ranger on a fix-up date. Can you see this?

'You're smiling,' Morelli said.

'Valerie wants to get fixed up with Ranger.'

Now Morelli was smiling. 'I like it. Wear body armor when you tell Ranger.' Morelli opened the refrigerator, took out a piece of leftover pizza, and ate it cold. 'I think it would be smart to get you out of this apartment. I don't know what this is about, but I'm not comfortable ignoring it.'

'And I would go where?'

'You'd go home with me, cupcake. And there'd be benefits.'

'Such as?'

'I'd warm up your pizza.'

Morelli lived in a two-story row house he inherited from his Aunt Rose. It was about a half mile from my parents' house with an almost identical floor plan. Rooms were stacked one behind the other – living room, dining room, kitchen. There were three bedrooms and a bath upstairs. Morelli had added a half bath downstairs. He was slowly claiming the house as his own. The wood floors were all newly sanded and varnished, but Aunt Rose's filmy old-fashioned curtains remained. I liked the mix and in an odd way would be sorry to see the house turn over entirely to Joe. There was something comforting about the curtains enduring beyond Aunt Rose. A tombstone is okay, but curtains are so much more personal.

We stood on the small front porch and Morelli cautioned me as he unlocked his door. 'Brace yourself,' he said. 'Bob hasn't seen you in a couple days. I don't want you knocked on your ass in front of the neighbors.'

Bob was a big scruffy red-haired dog that Morelli and I shared. Technically I suppose he was Morelli's dog. Bob had originally come to live with me, but in the end had chosen Morelli. One of those guy things, I guess.

Morelli opened the door and Bob bounded out, catching

me at chest level. What Bob lacked in manners he made up for in enthusiasm. I hugged him to me and gave him some big loud kisses. Bob endured this for a beat and then turned tail and hurled himself back inside, galloping from one end of the house to the other with ears flapping and tongue flopping.

A half hour later I was all settled in with my car parked at the curb behind Morelli's truck, my clothes in the guest room closet, and Rex's hamster cage sitting on Morelli's kitchen counter.

'I bet you're tired,' Morelli said, flipping the lights off in the kitchen. 'I bet you can't wait to get into bed.'

I gave him a sideways look.

He slung an arm around my shoulders and steered me in the direction of the stairs. 'I bet you're so tired you don't even want to bother getting into pajamas. In fact, you might need some help getting out of all these clothes.'

'And you're volunteering for the job?'

He kissed me at the nape of my neck. 'Am I a good guy, or what?'

I woke up in a tangle of sheets and nothing else. Sunlight was streaming through Morelli's bedroom window and I could hear the shower running in the bathroom. Bob was at the foot of the bed, watching me with big brown Bob eyes, probably trying to decide if I was food. Depending on Bob's mood, food could be most anything . . . a chair, dirt, shoes, a cardboard box, a box of prunes, a table leg, a leg of lamb. Some foods sat better with Bob than others. You didn't want to be too close after he ate a box of prunes.

I pulled on a pair of jeans and a T-shirt and trudged downstairs, hair uncombed, following the smell of coffee brewing. A note on the counter told me Bob had been fed and walked. Morelli was better at this cohabitation stuff than I was. Morelli was invigorated by sex. An orgasm for Morelli was like taking a vitamin pill. The more orgasms he had, the sharper he got. I'm the opposite. For me, an orgasm is like a shot of Valium. A night with Morelli and the next morning I'm a big contented cow.

I was coffee mug in hand, debating the merits of toast versus cereal, when Morelli's doorbell rang. I scuffed to the door with Bob close on my heels and I opened the door to Morelli's mother and grandmother.

The Morelli men are all charming and handsome. And with the exception of Joe, they're all worthless drunks and womanizers. They die in barroom fights, kill themselves in car crashes, and explode their livers. The Morelli women hold the family together, ruling with an iron hand, spotting a fib a mile away. Joe's mother was a revered and respected pillar of the community. Joe's Grandma Bella sent a chill down the spine and into the heart of all who crossed her path.

'Ah-hah!' Grandma Bella said. 'I knew it. I knew they were living together in sin. I had a vision. It came to me last night.'

Two doors down Mrs Friolli stuck her head out her front door so she didn't miss anything. I was guessing Grandma Bella's vision came to her last night after Mrs Friolli called her.

'How nice to see you,' I said to the women. 'What a nice surprise.' I turned and shrieked up the stairs. *Joe! Get down here!*

It was always a shock to stand next to Mrs Morelli and realize she was only five foot, four inches in her chunky two-inch-heeled shoes. She was a dominant and fearful force in a room. Her snapping black eyes could spot a speck of dust at twenty paces. She was a fierce guardian of her family and sat at the head of the table of the large Morelli tribe. She'd been widowed a lot of years and had never shown any interest in trying marriage a second time. Once around with a Morelli man was more than enough for most women.

Grandma Bella was half a head shorter than Joe's mom, but no less fearsome. She kept her white hair pulled into a bun, tied at the nape of her narrow chicken neck. She wore somber black dresses and sensible shoes. And some people believed she had the ability to cast a spell. Grown men scurried for cover when she turned her pale old woman's eye on them or pointed her bony finger in their direction.

'This is a temporary arrangement,' I told Mrs Morelli and Bella. 'I had to leave my apartment for a couple days and Joe was nice enough to let me stay here.'

'Hah!' Bella said. 'I know your type. You take advantage of my grandson's good nature and the next thing you know, you've seduced him and you're pregnant. I know these things. I see them in my visions.'

Jeez. I hoped these visions weren't too graphic. I didn't like the idea of being naked and woman-on-top in Bella's home movies.

'It's not like that,' I said. 'I'm not going to get pregnant.'

I felt Joe move in behind me.

'What's up?' Joe asked his mother and grandmother.

'I had a vision,' Bella said. 'I knew she was here.'

'Lucky me,' Joe said. And he ruffled my hair.

'I see babies,' Bella said. 'Mark my words, this one is pregnant.'

'That would be nice,' Joe said, 'but I don't think so. You're getting your visions confused. Stephanie's sister is pregnant. Right kitchen, wrong pot.'

My breath stuck in my chest. Did he say it would be nice if I was pregnant?

When Joe left for work I ran a computer check on McDonald's franchises in the area. I started dialing the numbers that turned up, asking for Howie, and I got a hit on the third McDonald's. Yes, I was told, a guy named Howie worked there. He would be in at ten.

It was early so I packed off in my happy yellow car and I checked in at the office before cutting across town to look for Howie.

'Anything happening?' I asked Connie.

'Vinnie's at the pokey, writing bail. Lula hasn't come in yet.'

'Yes she has,' Lula said, bustling through the door, big tote bag on her shoulder, take-out coffee in one hand, brown grocery bag in the other. 'I had to stop at the store on account of I need special food. There's a new man in my life and I've decided I'm too much woman for him, so I'm losing some weight. I'm gonna turn myself into a supermodel. I'm gonna lose about a hundred pounds.

'It'll be easy because I joined FatBusters last night. I got everything I need to lose weight now. I got a notebook to write in every time I eat something. And I got a FatBusters book that tells me how to do it all. Every single food's got a number assigned to it. All you gotta do is add up those numbers and make sure you don't go over your limit. Like my limit is twenty-nine.'

Lula set the bag on the floor, plopped herself down on the couch, and took out a small notepad. 'Okay, here I go,' she said. 'This here's my first entry in my notebook. This here's the beginning of a new way of life.'

Connie and I exchanged glances.

'Oh boy,' Connie said.

'I know I've tried diets in the past and they haven't worked out, but this is different,' Lula said. 'This one's realistic. That's what they say in the pamphlet. It's not like that last diet where all I could eat was bananas.' She paged through her FatBusters book. 'Let's see how I'm doing. No points for coffee.'

'Wait a minute,' I said. 'You never get plain coffee. I bet that's a caramel mochaccino you're drinking. I bet that's at least four points.'

Lula narrowed her eyes at me. 'It says here coffee's got no points and that's what I'm writing. I'm not getting involved with all that detail bullshit.'

'You have anything else for breakfast?' Connie asked.

'I had a egg. Let's see what an egg's gonna cost me. Two points.'

I looked over her shoulder at the book. 'Did you cook

that egg yourself? Or did you get it on one of those fast-food breakfast sandwiches with sausage and cheese?'

'It was on a sausage-and-cheese sandwich. But I didn't eat it all.'

'How much didn't you eat?'

Lula flapped her arms. 'Okay, I ate it all.'

'That's got to be at least ten points.'

'Hunh,' Lula said. 'Well, I still got a lot of points left for the rest of the day. I got nineteen points left.'

'What's in the grocery bag?'

'Vegetables. You don't get any points for vegetables, so you can eat as much as you want.'

'I didn't know you were a big vegetable eater,' Connie said.

'I like beans when you put them in a pan with some bacon. And I like broccoli . . . except it's got to have cheese sauce on it.'

'Bacon and cheese sauce might up your points,' Connie said.

'Yeah, I'm gonna have to wean myself off the bacon and cheese sauce if I want to get to supermodel weight.'

'I'm heading out to look for a guy named Howie. Supposedly he and Singh were buddies,' I said to Connie. 'Anything new come in that I should know about?'

'We got a new skip this morning, but Vinnie doesn't want

anyone working on anything other than Singh. Vinnie's in a state over this Singh thing.'

'Maybe I should go look for Howie with you,' Lula said. 'If I stay here I'll file all day and filing makes me hungry. I don't know if I got enough vegetables for a full day of filing.'

'Bad idea. Howie works at a fast-food place. You have no willpower when it comes to that stuff.'

'No problemo. I'm a changed woman. And anyway, I got my fill of fast food for the day. I had a good fast-food breakfast.'

A half hour later, Lula and I parked in the McDonald's lot. Lula had gone through a bunch of celery and was halfway into a bag of carrots.

'This isn't doing much for me,' she said, 'but I guess you gotta sacrifice if you want to be a supermodel.'

'Maybe you should wait in the car.'

'Hell no, I'm not missing out on the questioning. This could be an important lead. This Howie guy and Singh are supposed to be friends, right?'

'I don't know if they're friends. I just know Singh tried to find Howie the day before he disappeared.'

'Let's do it.'

As soon as I was through the door to the restaurant I

spotted Howie. He was working a register and he looked to be in his early twenties. He was dark-skinned and slim. Pakistani, maybe. I knew he was Howie because he was wearing a name tag. Howie P.

'Yes?' he asked, smiling. 'What will it be?'

I slid a card across to him and introduced myself. 'I'm looking for Samuel Singh,' I said. 'I understand you're friends.'

He went immobile for a moment while he held my card. He appeared to be studying it, but I had a suspicion his mind wasn't keeping up with his eyes.

'You are mistaken. I do not know Samuel Singh,' he finally said, 'but what would you like to order?'

'Actually, I'd just like to talk to you. Perhaps on your next break?'

'That would be my lunchtime at one o'clock. But you must order now. It is a rule.'

There was a big guy standing behind me. He was wearing a sleeveless T-shirt, scruffy cutoffs, and mud-clogged grungy boots.

'Cripes, lady,' he said. 'You think we got all day? Give him your order. I gotta get back to work.'

Lula turned and looked at him and he moved to another register. 'Hunh,' Lula said.

'I *must* take your order,' Howie said.

'Fine. Great. I'll have a cheeseburger, a large fries, a Coke, and an apple pie.'

'Maybe some chicken nuggets,' Lula said.

'No nuggets,' I told Howie. 'What about Samuel Singh?'

'First, you must pay me for your food.'

I shoved a twenty at him. 'Do you know where Singh is?'

'I do not. I am telling you I do not know him. Would you like extra ketchup packets with this cheeseburger? I have extra ketchup packets to give at my discretion.'

'Yeah, extra ketchup would be great.'

'If it was me, I would have gotten some chicken nuggets,' Lula said. 'Always good to have nuggets.'

'You're not eating this, remember?'

'Well, maybe I could have had a nugget.'

I took my bag of food. 'You have my card. Call me if you think of anything,' I said to Howie. 'I'll try to stop back at one.'

Howie nodded and smiled. 'Yes. Thank you. Have a good day. Thank you for eating at McDonald's.'

'He was nice and polite,' Lula said when we got back to the car, 'but he didn't give us a lot.' She looked at the bag of food. 'Boy, that smells good. I can smell the fries. Wonder how many points it would cost me to eat a French fry?'

'No one can eat just one French fry.'

'I bet supermodels eat just one French fry.'

I didn't like the way Lula was looking at the bag. Her eyes were too wide and sort of bugged out of her head. 'I'm going to throw this food away,' I said. 'I got it so I could talk to Howie. We don't really need this food.'

'It's a sin to throw food away,' Lula said. 'There's children starving in Africa. They'd be happy to get this food. God's gonna come get you if you throw that food away.'

'First off, we're not in Africa, so I can't give this food to any of those starving kids. Second, neither of us needs this food. So God's just going to have to understand.'

'I think you might be blaspheming God.'

'I'm *not* blaspheming God.' But just in case, I did a mental genuflect and asked for forgiveness. Guilt and fear remain long after blind belief.

'Give me that food bag,' Lula said. 'I'm going to save your immortal soul.'

'No! Remember the supermodel. Have some carrots.'

'I hate those fucking carrots. Give me that bag!'

'Stop it,' I said. 'You're getting scary.'

'I need that burger. I'm outta control.'

No shit. I was afraid if I didn't get rid of the bag Lula would squash me like a bug. I eyed the distance between me and the trash receptacle and I was pretty sure I could outsprint Lula, so I took off at a run.

'Hey!' she yelled. 'You come back here.' And then she pounded after me.

I reached the trash and shoved the bag in. Lula knocked me out of the way, took the top off the trash receptacle, and retrieved the bag of food.

'This here's good as new,' she said, testing a couple French fries. She closed her eyes. 'Oh man, they just made these fresh. And they got a lot of salt. I love it when they got a lot of salt.'

I took a couple fries from the box. She was right. They were great fries. We finished the fries, Lula broke the cheeseburger in half, and we ate the cheeseburger. Then we each ate half of the apple pie.

'Would have been nice to have some nuggets,' Lula said.

'You're a nut.'

'It's not my fault. That was a bogus diet. I can't go around eating plain-ass vegetables all day. I'll get weak and die.'

'Wouldn't want that to happen.'

'Hell no,' Lula said.

We went back to the car and I called Ranger. 'Having any luck?' I asked him.

'I found someone who saw Singh with the dog the day after it disappeared. It looks like Singh ran as opposed to getting himself whacked. And you were right, he took the dog with him.'

'Any idea why he might want to disappear?'

'The future mother-in-law would do it for me.'

'Anything else?'

'No. Have you got something?'

'I have a guy who says he doesn't know Singh, but I don't believe him.' And I have horrific photos of a dead woman. Best to wait until I'm alone with Ranger to tell him about the horrific photos. Lula isn't always great at keeping a secret and Morelli asked me not to share the details.

'Later,' Ranger said.

I called Connie next. 'I need an address for a guy named Howie P. He works at the McDonald's on Lincoln Avenue. See if you can get his address out of the manager.'

Five minutes later Connie got back to me with the address.

'This is the deal,' I said to Lula. 'We're going to check out Howie's apartment. We are *not* going to break in. You accidentally smash a window or bust down a door, and I swear I'll never take you on a case with me again.'

'Hunh,' Lula said. 'When did I ever bust down a door?'

'Two days ago. And it was the *wrong* door.'

'I didn't bust that door. I just tapped it open.'

Howie lived in a hard-times neighborhood a short distance from his job. He rented two rooms in a house that was originally designed to contain one family and now was home to seven. Paint peeled off the clapboard siding, and window ledges rotted in the sun. The small yard was hard-packed dirt, the perimeter marked by chain-link fencing. A fringe of weed clung to life at the base of the fence.

Lula and I stood in the dark, musty foyer and ran through the names on the mailboxes. Howie was 3B. Sonji Kluchari was 3A.

'Hey, I know her,' Lula said. 'Back when I was a 'ho. She worked the corner across from me. If she's living in three A you can bet there's eight other people in there with her. She's a scabby ol' crackhead, doing whatever she has to so she can get her next fix.'

'How old is she?'

'She's my age,' Lula said. 'And I'm not saying how old I am, but it's twenty-something.'

We climbed the stairs to the second-floor landing, which was illuminated by a bare twenty-watt bulb hanging from a ceiling cord, and then we went to the third floor, which clearly had been the attic. The third-floor landing was small and dark and smelled like rot. There were two doors. Someone had scrawled 3A and 3B on the doors with black magic marker.

We knocked on 3B. No answer. I tried the door. Locked.

'Hunh,' Lula said. 'Looks flimsy. Too bad you got all these

rules about breaking things. I bet I could lean on this door and it'd fall down.'

That was a good possibility. Lula wasn't a small woman.

I turned and knocked on 3A. I knocked louder the second time and the door opened and Sonji peered out at us. She was bloodless white with red-rimmed eyes and yellow straw hair. She was rail thin and I would have put her age closer to fifty than twenty. Not easy being a crackhead 'ho.

Sonji stared at Lula, recognition struggling through the dope haze.

'Girl,' Lula said. 'You look like shit.'

'Oh yeah,' Sonji said, flat-voiced, dull-eyed. 'Now I remember. Lula. How you doin', you big ugly 'ho.'

'I'm not a 'ho anymore,' Lula said. 'I'm working for a bail bondsman and we're looking for a scrawny little Indian guy. His name's Samuel Singh and he might know Howie.'

'Howie?'

'The guy across the hall from you.'

I showed Sonji a photo of Singh.

'I don't know,' she said. 'These guys all look the same to me.'

'Anybody living over there besides Howie?' I asked her.

'Not that I know. From what I can tell, Howie's not exactly Mr Social. Maybe Singh came over once . . . or somebody who looked like him. Don't think anybody but Howie's living there. But hell, what do I know?'

I gave Sonji my card and a twenty. 'Give me a call if you see Singh.'

Sonji disappeared behind her closed door and Lula and I trudged down the stairs. We went outside, walked around the building to the backyard, and looked up at Howie's single window.

'Could be me living here,' Lula said. 'I still got some pain from what that maniac Ramirez did to me, but it's turned out it was a favor. He stopped me from being a 'ho. When I got out of the hospital I knew I had to change my life. God works in strange ways.'

Benito Ramirez was an insane boxer who loved inflicting pain. He'd beaten Lula to within an inch of her life and tied her to my fire escape. I found her body, bloody and battered. Ramirez wanted the beating to serve as a lesson for Lula and for me.

I thought getting brutalized like that was a pretty harsh wake-up call.

'So what do you think?' Lula asked. 'You think Singh could be hiding out up there?'

It was possible. But it was a long shot. There were a million reasons why Singh could have been looking for Howie. And for that matter, I wasn't even sure I had the right guy. There were a lot of McDonald's around. Singh could have been calling McDonald's in Hong Kong for all I knew.

I'd been keeping watch for the gray Sentra, but it hadn't surfaced. It could be in a nearby garage. Or it could be in Mexico.

A rusted fire escape clung precariously to the back of the building. The ladder had been dropped and hung just a few inches from the ground. 'I could go up the fire escape,' I said. 'Then I could look in the window.'

'Now *you're* the nut. That thing's falling apart. No way I'm going up that rusted-out piece of junk.'

I grabbed a rail and pulled. The rail held tight. 'It's in better shape than it looks,' I said. 'It'll hold me.'

'Maybe. But it sure as hell won't hold *me*.'

Only one of us needed to go anyway. I'd be up and down in a couple minutes. And I'd be able to see if there was any indication of Singh or the dog. 'You need to stay on the ground and do lookout anyway,' I told Lula.

Five

Nothing ventured, nothing gained. I went hand over hand up the ladder and pulled myself onto the first level. I climbed the second ladder, steadied myself on the third-floor platform, and looked into Howie's window. Howie lived directly under the roof. There were rafters where the ceiling should be and the floor was chipped linoleum. Howie had a sofa that was lumpy and faded, but looked comfy in a dilapidated sort of way. He had a small television and a card table and two metal folding chairs. That was the extent of his furniture. A sink hung on a far wall. A half refrigerator had been placed beside the sink. There were two wood shelves over the refrigerator. Howie had stacked two plates, two bowls, and two mugs on one of the shelves. The other shelf held condiments, a couple boxes of cereal, a jar of peanut butter, and a bag of chips.

When you come right down to it, this is really all anyone needs, isn't it? A television and a bag of chips.

I could see the front door and a doorway leading to another room, but the second room wasn't visible. The bedroom, obviously. I tried the window, but it was either locked or painted shut.

'Coming down,' I said to Lula. 'No dog biscuits on the kitchen shelf.' I put my foot on the ladder and it disintegrated in a shower of rust flakes and chunks of broken metal. The chunks of metal crashed onto the second-floor platform and the whole thing pulled away from the building, and with more of a sigh than a screech the entire bottom half of the fire escape landed on the ground in front of Lula.

'Hunh,' Lula said.

I looked down at Lula. Too far to jump. The only way off the platform was through Howie's apartment.

'Are you coming down soon?' Lula asked. 'I'm getting hungry.'

'I don't want to break his window.'

'You got any other choices?'

I dialed Ranger on my cell phone.

'I'm sort of stuck,' I told Ranger.

Ten minutes later, Ranger opened Howie's apartment door, crossed the room, unlocked and raised the window, and looked out at the mangled mess of metal on the ground. He raised his eyes to mine and the almost smile twitched at the corners of his mouth. 'Good job, Destructo.'

'It wasn't my fault.'

He dragged me through the window, into the apartment. 'It never is.'

'I wanted to see if there were any signs that Singh or the dog had been here. I don't have much to tie Howie to Singh, but once I get past Howie I have *nothing*.'

Ranger closed and locked the window. 'I don't see any boxes of dog biscuits.'

'Poor little Boo.' The instant I said it I knew it was a mistake. I clapped my hand over my mouth and looked at Ranger.

'I could help you with these maternal urges,' Ranger said.

'Get me pregnant?'

'I was going to suggest a visit to the animal shelter.' He grabbed me by the front of my shirt and pulled me close. 'But I could get you pregnant if that's what you really want.'

'Nice of you to want to help,' I said, 'but I think I'll pass on both offers.'

'Good decision.' He released my shirt. 'Let's take a look at the rest of the apartment.'

We moved from the living room to the bedroom and found more clutter, but no evidence of Singh or Boo. Howie had placed a double mattress on the floor and covered it with an inexpensive quilt. There were two cardboard boxes filled with neatly folded pants and shirts and underwear. The poor man's dresser. No closet in the room. A bare bulb hung from the ceiling. It was the only light source. A laptop computer with a cracked screen was on the floor near the only outlet.

I looked around. 'No bathroom.'

'There's a common bathroom on the second floor.'

Yikes. Howie shares a bathroom with the scabby 'ho and her crackhead friends. I tried to remember if he used gloves when he handled my food.

'Spartan,' I said to Ranger.

'Adequate,' Ranger said. He looked down at the mattress. 'I don't think Howie's been sharing his apartment with anyone lately.'

I was feeling a little panicky about being alone in a room with a mattress and Ranger, so I scooted out of the room and out of Howie's apartment. Ranger followed and closed and locked Howie's door. We descended the stairs in silence.

Ranger was smiling when we got to the front foyer. Not the half smile, either. This was a full-on smile.

I narrowed my eyes at the smile. 'What?'

'It's always fun to see you get worried about a mattress.'

Lula hustled over. 'So what's going on?' Lula asked. 'You find anything up there? Any dog hairs in the bedroom?'

'Nothing. It was clean,' I told her.

Lula turned her attention to Ranger. 'I didn't hear you breaking any doors down.'

'It wasn't necessary to break the door down.'

'How'd you do it then? You use a pick? You use some electronic gizmo? I wish I could open doors like you.'

'I'd tell you, but then I'd have to kill you,' Ranger said.

It was an old line, but it was worrisome when Ranger said it.

'Hunh,' Lula said.

'Tell me about Boo and Singh,' I said to Ranger. 'Who saw them? Where were they?'

'A kid working the drive-through window at Cluck in a Bucket saw him. He remembered Singh and the dog because the dog was barking and jumping around. He said Singh got a bucket of chicken and two strawberry shakes and the dog ate two pieces of chicken before Singh got the window rolled up to drive off.'

'Guess he was hungry.'

'Speaking of hungry,' Lula said. 'We haven't had lunch yet.'

'We just had a cheeseburger,' I told her.

'We shared it. That don't count. If you share, it's a snack.'

'I want to go back to talk to Howie at one o'clock. Can you wait until then?'

'I guess. What are we going to do in the meantime?'

'I want to wander around the neighborhood. Maybe snoop in a few garages.'

Lula looked up and down the street. 'You're going to snoop in *this* neighborhood? You got a gun on you?'

Ranger reached behind him, under his shirt, and pulled out a .38. He pulled my T-shirt out of my jeans and he shoved the .38 under my waistband and draped my shirt over the gun. The gun was warm with his body heat and his fingers had been even warmer sliding across my belly.

'Thanks,' I said, trying to keep my voice from cracking.

He curled his hand around my neck and kissed me lightly on the lips. 'Be careful.' And he was gone. Off to make the world a better place in his shiny new black Porsche.

'He had his hand in your pants and he kissed you,' Lula said. 'I'm wetting myself.'

'It wasn't like that. He gave me a gun.'

'Girl, he gave you more than a gun. I tell you, he ever put his hand in *my* pants I'll stop breathing and faint dead away. He is so hot.' Lula did some fanning motions with her hand. 'I'm getting flashes. I think I'm sweating. Look at me. Am I sweating?'

'It's ninety degrees out,' I said. 'Everyone's sweating.'

'It's not ninety,' Lula said. 'I just saw the temperature on the bank building. It's only seventy-eight.'

'Feels like ninety.'

'Ain't that the truth,' Lula said.

An alley ran behind the houses. Cars were parked in the

alley and garages opened to the alley. Lula and I walked to the end of the block and then cut down the alley, peering into filthy garage windows, cracking garage doors to look inside. Most of the garages were used for storage. A few were empty. None contained a gray Nissan. We walked three more blocks and three more alleys. No dog. No car. No Singh.

It was 1.15 when I parked in the McDonald's lot. Lula went inside to order and I walked to the outdoor seating area where Howie was eating lunch.

Howie was hunched over his tray, concentrating on his burger, attempting invisibility.

'Hey,' I said, sitting across from him. 'Nice day.'

He nodded his head without making eye contact. 'Yes.'

'Tell me about Samuel.'

'There is nothing to tell you,' he said.

'He called you at work last week.'

'You are mistaken.' He had his fists balled and his head down. He gestured for emphasis and knocked his empty soda cup over. We both reached for the cup. Howie caught it first and set it straight. 'You must stop bothering me now,' he said. 'Please.'

'Samuel is missing,' I said to Howie. 'I'm trying to find him.'

For the first time, Howie picked his head up and looked at me. 'Missing?'

'He disappeared the day after he called you.'

For a fleeting moment Howie looked relieved. 'I know nothing,' he repeated, dropping his eyes again.

'What's the deal?' I asked Howie. 'Did you owe him money? Did you go out with his girlfriend?'

'No. None of those things. I truly do not know him.' Howie's eyes darted from one side of the lot to the other. 'I must go inside now. I do not like associating with the customers. Americans are a crazy people. Only the games are good. The American games are righteous.'

I looked around. I didn't see any crazy people . . . but then, I'm from Jersey. I'm used to crazy.

'Why do you think Americans are crazy?'

'They are very demanding. Not enough fries in the box. The fries are not hot enough. The sandwich is wrapped wrong. I cannot control these things. I do not wrap the sandwiches. And they are very loud when they tell you about the wrappings. All day people are shouting at me. "Go faster. Go faster. Give me this. Give me that." Wanting an Egg McMuffin at eleven o'clock when it is a rule you cannot have an Egg McMuffin past ten-thirty.'

'I hate that rule.'

Howie gathered his wrappers onto his tray. 'And another

thing. Americans ask too many questions. How many grams of fat are in a cheeseburger? Are the onions real? What do I know? The onions come in a bag. Do I look like the onion man to you?'

He stood at his seat and took his tray in two hands. 'You should leave me alone now. I am done talking to you. If you continue to stalk me, I will report you to the authorities.'

'I'm not stalking you. This isn't stalking. This is asking a couple questions.'

There was a momentary lull in the ambient traffic noise. I heard something go *pop pop*. Howie's eyes got wide, his mouth opened, the tray slid from his hands and crashed to the concrete patio. Howie's knees buckled and he collapsed without uttering a word.

A woman screamed behind me and I was on my feet, thinking, He's been shot, help him, take cover, do something! My mind was racing, but my body wasn't responding. I was paralyzed by the unfathomable horror of the moment, staring down at Howie's unblinking eyes, mesmerized by the small hole in the middle of his forehead, by the pool of blood that widened under him. Just a moment ago I was talking to him and now he was dead. It didn't seem possible.

People were scrambling and shouting around me. I didn't see anyone with a gun. No one in the lot had a gun in his hand. I didn't see anyone armed on the road or in the building. Howie seemed to be the only victim.

Lula ran to me with a big bag of food in one hand and a large chocolate shake in her other hand. 'Holy crap,' she said, eyes bugged out, looking down at Howie. 'Holy moly. Holy Jesus and Joseph. Holy cow.'

I eased away from the body, not wanting to crowd Howie, needing some distance from the shooting. I wanted to make time stand still, to back up ten minutes and change the course of events. I wanted to blink and have Howie still be alive.

Sirens screamed on the highway behind us and Lula furiously sucked on the shake. 'I can't get anything up this freakin' straw,' she shrieked. 'Why do they give you a straw if you can't suck anything up it? Why don't they give you a goddamn spoon? Why do they make these things so freakin' thick anyways? Shakes aren't supposed to be solid. This here's like trying to suck up a fish sandwich.

'And don't think I'm hysterical, either,' Lula said. 'I don't get hysterical. You ever see me hysterical before? This here's *transference*. I read about it in a magazine. It's when you get upset about one thing only you're really upset about something else. And it's different from hysterical. And even if I was hysterical, which I'm not, I'd have a perfect right. This guy got shot dead in front of you. If you'd have moved an inch to the left you probably would have lost an ear. And he's dead. Look at him. He's dead! I *hate* dead.'

I grimaced at Lula. 'Good thing you're not hysterical.'

'You bet your sweet ass,' Lula said.

A Trenton PD blue and white angled to a stop, lights flashing. Seconds later, another blue and white pulled in. Carl Costanza was riding shotgun in the second car. He rolled his eyes when he saw me and reached for the radio. Calling Joe, I thought. His partner, Big Dog, ambled over.

'Holy crap,' Big Dog said when he saw Howie. 'Holy moly.' He looked over at me and winced. 'Did you shoot him?'

'No!'

'I got to get out of here,' Lula said. 'Cops and dead people give me diarrhea. Anybody wants to talk to me, they can send me a letter. I didn't see anything anyway. I was getting extra sauce for my chicken nuggets. I don't suppose you'd want to give me your car keys?' she asked me. 'I'm starting to feel transference coming on again. I need a doughnut. Calm me down.'

Costanza was pushing people around, laying out crime scene tape. An EMS truck arrived, followed by a plainclothes cop car and Morelli's POS.

Morelli jogged over to me. 'Are you okay?'

'Pretty much. I'm a little rattled.'

'No bullet holes?'

'Not in me. Howie wasn't so lucky.'

Morelli looked down at Howie. 'You didn't shoot him, did you? Tell me you didn't shoot him.'

'I didn't shoot him. I never even carry a gun!'

Morelli dropped his eyes to my waist. 'Looks to me like you're carrying one now.'

Shit. I'd forgotten about the gun.

'Well, I *almost never* carry a gun,' I said, doing my best to smooth out the bulge in my T-shirt. I looked around to see if anyone else noticed. 'Maybe I should lose the gun,' I said to Morelli. 'There might be a problem.'

'Besides carrying concealed without a permit?'

'It might not be registered.'

'Let me guess. Ranger gave you the gun.' Morelli stared down at his feet and shook his head. He muttered something indiscernible, possibly in Italian. I opened my mouth to speak and he held a hand up. 'Don't say anything,' he said. 'I'm working hard here. Notice I'm not ranting over the fact that not only are you partners with Ranger, but you were stupid enough to take a gun from him.'

I waited patiently. When Morelli mutters in Italian it's a good idea to give him some room.

'Okay,' he said, 'this is what we're going to do. We're going to walk over to my car. You're going to get in, take the gun out of your goddamn pants, and slide the gun under the front seat. Then you're going to tell me what happened.'

An hour later, I was still sitting in the car, waiting for Morelli to leave the scene, when my cell phone rang.

It was my mother. 'I heard you shot someone,' she said. 'You've got to stop shooting people. Elaine Minardi's daughter never shoots anyone. Lucille Rice's daughter never shoots anyone. Why do I have to be the one to have a daughter who shoots people?'

'I didn't shoot anyone.'

'Then you can come to dinner.'

'Sure.'

'That was too easy,' my mother said. 'Something's wrong. Omigod, you really did shoot someone, didn't you?'

'*I didn't shoot anyone,*' I yelled at her. And I disconnected.

Morelli opened the driver's side door and angled himself behind the wheel. 'Your mother?'

I sagged in the seat. 'This is turning into a really long day. I told my mother I'd show up for dinner.'

'Let's go over this one more time,' Morelli said.

'One of Singh's coworkers told me Singh tried to make a phone call to Howie the day before he disappeared. I questioned Howie just now and he denied knowing Singh. I'm pretty sure he was lying. And when I told him Singh was missing I could swear he looked relieved. He ended the interview by telling me Americans are crazy. He stood to go inside and *pop pop* . . . he was dead.'

'Only two shots.'

'That's all I heard.'

'Anything else?'

'Off the record?'

'Oh boy,' Joe said. 'I hate when a conversation with you starts like that.'

'I happened to accidentally wander into Howie's apartment this morning.'

'I don't want to hear this,' Morelli said. 'They're going to go to Howie's apartment and dust for prints and you're going to be all over the place.'

I chewed on my lower lip. Unfortunate timing. Who knew Howie would get killed?

Morelli raised eyebrows in question. 'So?'

'The apartment is clean,' I told him. 'No sign that Singh's been there. No diary detailing secret activities. No hastily scribbled notes that someone wanted him dead. No evidence of drugs. No weapons.'

'It could have been a random shooting,' Morelli said. 'This isn't a great neighborhood.'

'He was in the wrong place at the wrong time.'

'Yeah.'

Not for a single second did either of us believe that to be

true. Deep inside I knew Howie's death was tied to Singh and to me. That he was killed in my presence wasn't a good thing.

Morelli's eyes softened and he ran a fingertip along my jaw line. 'Are you sure you're okay?'

'Yeah. I'm okay.' And I was . . . sort of. My hands had stopped shaking and the pain in my chest was subsiding. But I knew that somewhere hiding in my head were sad thoughts of Howie. The sadness would creep forward and I would cram it back into crevices thick with brain gunk. I'm a firm believer in the value of denial. Anger, passion, and fear spill out of me in real time. Sadness I save until the edge dulls. Someday three months from now I'll stroll down the cereal aisle of a supermarket and burst into tears for Howie, a man I didn't even know, for crissake. I'll stand in front of the cereal boxes and blow my nose and blink the tears out of my eyes so no one realizes I'm an emotional idiot. I mean, what about Howie's life? What was it like? Then I'll think about Howie's death and I'll go hollow inside. And then I'll go to the freezer section and get a tub of coffee-flavored Häagen-Dazs ice cream and eat it all.

Morelli turned the engine over and chugged out of the lot. 'I'll take you back to the office so you can get your car. I have paperwork to do at the station. If I'm not home by five-thirty, go to dinner without me. I'll catch up with you as soon as I can.'

Lula and Connie weren't looking happy when I got to the office.

'We only have a couple days left before everyone finds out Singh's skipped,' Connie said. 'Vinnie's freaking. He's locked in his office with a bottle of gin and the real estate section from the Scottsdale paper.'

'I don't need this cranky shit he's pulling, either,' Lula said. 'I had a bad day. I didn't lose any weight and the guy we wanted to talk to got dead. And every time I think about poor ol' Howie I get hungry on account of I'm a comfort eater. I relieve my stress with comfort food.'

'You've eaten everything but the desk,' Connie said. 'It'd be cheaper to get you addicted to drugs.'

Vinnie stuck his head out his office door. 'You get one crappy lead and he gets himself killed,' Vinnie yelled at me. 'What's with that?' And he pulled his head back into his office and slammed the door shut.

'See, that's what I mean,' Lula said. 'Makes me want some macaroni and cheese.'

Vinnie stuck his head out of his office again. 'Sorry,' he said. 'I didn't mean to say that. I meant to say . . . uh, I'm glad you're not hurt.'

We all went silent, thinking about how awful it actually had been. And how it could have been worse.

'The world's a crazy place,' Lula finally said.

I needed to get out and do something to take my mind off Howie. My car keys were lying on Connie's desk. I pocketed the keys and gave my shoulder bag a hitch up. 'I'm heading out to talk to the Apusenjas. Nonnie should be getting home from work soon.'

'I'll go with you,' Lula said. 'I'm not letting you go out alone.'

Nonnie was home when I arrived. She answered the door on my second knock and peered out at me, first surprised, then cautiously happy. 'Did you find him?' she asked. 'Did you find Boo?'

'I haven't found him, but I have something I'd like to run by you. Did Samuel ever mention a man named Howie?'

'No. I've never heard him speak of Howie.'

'Samuel was on the computer all the time. Did you ever get a chance to see what he was doing? Did he get mail? Do you think he might have gotten email from Howie?'

'I saw a mail from work one time. Samuel was at the kitchen table. He sometimes preferred to sit there because his room was small. I came to the kitchen for a glass of tea and I passed behind him. He was typing a letter to someone named Susan. The letter was nothing, really. It only said *thank you for the help*. Samuel said it was work related. That is the only time I have seen any of his computer mails.'

'Did he ever get mail from the post office?'

'He received a few letters from his parents in India. My mother would know more of that. She collects the mail. Would you like to talk to my mother?'

'No!'

'Who is that?' Mrs Apusenja called from the hall.

Lula and I put our heads down and took a deep breath.

'It is two women from the bonds agency,' Nonnie said.

Mrs Apusenja rumbled to the door and elbowed Nonnie aside. 'What do you want? Have you found Samuel?'

'I had a couple questions to ask Nonnie,' I said.

'Where is the man named Ranger?' Mrs Apusenja said. 'I can tell you are just his worthless assistant. And who is this fat woman with you?'

'Hunh,' Lula said. 'There was a time when I would have kicked your nasty ass for calling me fat, but I'm on a diet to be a supermodel and I'm above all that now.'

'Such language,' Mrs Apusenja said. 'Just as I would expect from sluts.'

'Hey, watch who you're calling a slut,' Lula said. 'You're starting to get on my nerves.'

'Get off my porch,' Mrs Apusenja said. And she shoved Lula.

'Hunh,' Lula said. And she gave Mrs Apusenja a shot to the shoulder that rocked her back on her heels.

'Disrespectful whore,' Mrs Apusenja said to Lula. And she slapped her.

This was where I took two steps back.

Lula grabbed Mrs Apusenja by the hair and the two of them stumbled off the porch to the small front yard. There was a lot of bitch slapping and name calling and hair pulling. Nonnie was shouting for them to stop and I had my stun gun in my hand just in case it looked like Lula was going to lose.

An old lady tottered out of the house next door and turned her garden hose on Lula and Mrs Apusenja. Lula and Mrs Apusenja broke apart, sputtering. Mrs Apusenja turned tail and scuttled into her house, her soaked sari leaving a trail of water behind her that looked like slug slime.

The old lady shut the water off at the spigot on her front porch. 'That was fun,' she said. And she disappeared into her house.

Lula squished to the car and climbed in. 'I could have taken her if I'd had more time,' Lula said.

I dropped Lula off at the office and drove on autopilot to Hamilton and eased into the stream of traffic. Hamilton is full of lights and small businesses. It's a road that leads to everything and everywhere and at this time of the day it was clogged with cars going nowhere. I turned from Hamilton, cut through a couple side streets, and swung into my apartment building lot. I parked and looked up at my building and realized I'd driven myself to the wrong place. I wasn't living here these days. I was living with Morelli. I thunked my head on the steering wheel. 'Stupid, stupid, stupid.'

I was on the third thunk when the passenger side door swung open and Ranger took the seat next to me. 'You should be careful,' Ranger said. 'You'll shake something loose in there.'

'I didn't see you in the lot when I pulled in,' I said. 'Were you waiting for me to come home?'

'I followed you, babe. I picked you up a block from the office. You should check your mirrors once in a while. Could have been a bad guy on your tail.'

'And you're a good guy?'

Ranger smiled. 'Are you parked here for any special reason? I thought you moved in with Morelli.'

'Navigation error. My mind wasn't on my driving.'

'Do you want to tell me about it?'

'The shooting?'

'Yeah,' Ranger said. 'And anything else I should know about.'

I told him about the shooting and then I told him about the flowers and the photos.

'I could keep you safer than Morelli,' Ranger said.

I believed him. But I would also be more restricted. Ranger would lock me up in a safe house and keep a guard with me 24–7. Ranger had a small army of guys working for him who made Marine commandos look like a bunch of sissies.

'I'm okay for now. Is there any word on the street about Bart Cone? Like does he rape and murder women?'

'The street doesn't talk about Bart Cone. The street doesn't even *know* Bart Cone. The Cone brothers run a tight factory and pay their bills on time. I had Tank ask around. The only interesting thing he turned up was the murder inquiry. Two months after the police dropped Bart as a suspect, Bart's wife left him. He's the nuts-and-bolts guy at the factory. Has an engineering degree from MIT. Smart. Serious. Private. The direct opposite of Clyde, who spends most of his day reading comic books and gets together several times a week with his friends to play Magic.'

'Magic?'

'It's one of those role-playing card games.'

'Like Dungeons and Dragons?'

'Similar. Andrew is the people person. Manages the human resources side of the business. He's been married for ten years. Has two kids, ages seven and nine.' Ranger's pager went off and he checked the readout. 'Do you have any candidates for the flowers and photos?'

'I've made my share of enemies since I've had this job. No one stands out. Bart Cone crossed my mind. The business with the murder is hard to ignore even though the charge didn't stick. And the break-in occurred right after I was at the factory. Sort of a strange set of coincidences. If he's the nuts-and-bolts guy maybe he knows how to open locks.'

'Don't go walking in the woods with him,' Ranger said. And he was gone.

Six

I opened the front door to Morelli's house and Bob exploded out at me. He knocked me to one side, took the concrete and brick stairs in a single bound, and ran up the street. He stopped and turned and ran back full speed. He got to Morelli's property line, applied the brakes, hunched, and pooped.

Lesson number one when cohabitating with a man and a dog: Never be the first to arrive home.

I went to the backyard, got the snow shovel from the shed, and used the shovel to flip the poop into the street. Then I sat on the stoop and waited for a car to run over the poop. Two cars drove by, but both of them avoided the poop. I gave a sigh of resignation, went into the kitchen, got a plastic baggie, scooped the poop up off the street, and threw it into the garbage. Sometimes you just can't catch a break.

Bob looked like he still had lots of energy, so I snapped

the leash on him and we took off. The sun was warm on my back and Joe's neighborhood felt comfortable. I knew a lot of the people who lived here. It was an older population consisting of parents and grandparents of kids who went to school with me. From time to time a house would turn over to the new generation and a stroller or baby swing would appear on the porch. Sometimes I'd look at the strollers and my biological clock would tick so loud in my head and my heart it would blur my vision, but more often than not there were days like today when I came home to a load of fresh poop and babies didn't seem all that alluring.

Bob and I went for a nice long walk and we were on our way home. Two people, Mrs Herrel and Mrs Gudge, popped out of their houses to ask if it was true that I shot someone today. Word travels fast in the Burg and its surrounding neighborhoods. Story accuracy isn't always a top priority.

I crossed the street and saw a car pull to the curb in front of Joe's house half a block away. There were two women in the car. Joe's mother and grandmother. Damn. I'd rather face Howie's killer. I had a moment of indecision, wondering if I'd been spotted, if it was too late to sneak off. Joe's mother got out of the car, our eyes caught, and my fate was sealed.

By the time Bob and I got to Joe's house, Grandma Bella

was out of the car and on the sidewalk beside Joe's mother.

'I had a vision,' Grandma Bella said.

'I didn't shoot anyone,' I told her.

'You were dead in my vision,' Grandma Bella said. 'Cold as stone. The blood drained from your lifeless body. I saw you go into the ground.'

My jaw went slack and the world lost focus for a moment.

'Don't pay attention to her,' Joe's mother said. 'She has these visions all the time.' Mrs Morelli gave me a loaf of bread in its white paper bakery bag. 'I came over to give Joe this bread. It's fresh baked from Italian People's. Joe likes it in the morning with his coffee.'

'I saw you in the box,' Grandma Bella said. 'I saw them close the lid and put you in the ground.'

Bella was doing a bang-up job of creeping me out. This wasn't a good time to tell me I was going to die. I was working hard not to get overwhelmed by the shooting, the photos, and the flowers.

'Stop that,' Joe's mother said to Bella. 'You're scaring her.'

'Mark my words,' Bella said, shaking her finger at me.

The two women got back into the car and drove off. I took Bob and the bread into the house. I gave Bob fresh water and a bowl filled with dog crunchies. I sliced the end off the bread and ate it with strawberry jam.

A tear slid out of my eye and rolled down my cheek. I

didn't want to give in to the tear, so I wiped it away and looked in at Rex. Rex was sleeping, of course. 'Hey!' I said real loud into the cage. Still no movement. I dropped a chunk of the bread and jam a couple inches away from the soup can. The soup can vibrated a little and Rex backed out. He stood blinking in the light for a moment, whiskers whirring, nose twitching. He scurried over to the bread, ate all the jam, shoved the remaining bread into his cheek pouch, and scuttled back into his soup can.

I checked the phone machine. No messages. I opened my iBook, went online, and my screen filled with more of the penis enlargement, hot chicks with horses, get out of debt ads.

'We can send a man to the moon, but we can't find a way to stop junk mail!' I yelled at the computer.

I calmed myself and deleted the garbage. I was left with one piece of mail. No subject in the subject line. The body of the letter was short: *Did you like my flowers? Were you impressed with my marksmanship this afternoon?*

My stomach went hot and sick and my vision got cobwebby. I put my head between my legs until the ringing stopped in my ears and I was able to breathe again.

This was from Howie's killer. He knew my email address. Not that my email address was a secret. It was printed on my business cards. Still, the message was chilling and eerily invasive. It tied the flowers and the photos to the shooting. It was a message from a madman.

I typed back to him. *Who are you?*

Seconds later, my message was returned as undeliverable.

I saved the email to show to Morelli and I shut down.

'My day is in the toilet,' I told Bob. 'I'm taking a shower. Don't let any maniacs in the house.' I stood up as tall as I could and I made sure my voice was steady. The bravado was partly for Bob and partly for me. Sometimes if I acted brave, I almost became a little brave. And just in case Bob fell asleep on the job, I went to the closet in Morelli's room, helped myself to his spare gun, and took it into the bathroom with me.

Grandma Mazur was waiting at the door when I pulled up. 'What do you think of my new hair?' she asked.

It was punk-rock-star red and stuck out in little spikes. 'I think it's fun,' I told Grandma.

'It brings out the color of my eyes.'

'And it's flattering to your skin tone.' Definitely drags attention away from the liver spots.

'It's a wig,' she said. 'I got it at the mall today. Me and Mabel Burlew went shopping. I just got home. I missed all the excitement when everybody thought you shot someone again.'

Albert Kloughn came in behind me. 'What about shooting someone? Do you need a lawyer? I'd give you a real good rate. Business has been a little slow. I don't know why. It's not like I'm not a good lawyer. I went to school and everything.'

'I don't need a lawyer,' I told him.

'Too bad. I could use a high-profile case. That's what really helps your practice to take off. You gotta win something big.'

'What do you think of my hair?' Grandma asked Kloughn.

'It's nice,' he said. 'I like it. It's real natural looking.'

'It's a wig,' Grandma said. 'I got it at the mall.'

'Maybe that's what I should get,' Kloughn said. 'Maybe I'd get more cases if I had more hair. A lot of people don't like bald men. Not that I'm bald, but it's starting to get thin.' He smoothed his hand over his few remaining strands of hair. 'You probably didn't notice that it was thin, but I can tell when the light hits it just right.'

'You should try that chemical stuff you pour on your head,' Grandma said. 'My friend Lois Grizen uses it and she grew some hair. Only problem was she used it at night and it rubbed off on her pillow and got on her face and now she has to shave twice a day.'

My father looked up from his paper. 'I always wondered what was wrong with her. I saw her in the deli last week and she looked like Wolfman. I thought she had a sex change.'

'I have everything on the table,' my mother said. 'Come now before it gets cold. The bread will go stale.'

Valerie was already at the table with her plate filled. My mother had put out an antipasto platter, fresh bread from People's, and a pan of sausage-and-cheese lasagna. Nine-year-old Angie, the perfect child and an exact replica of Valerie at that age, sat hands folded, patiently waiting for food to be passed. Her seven-year-old sister, Mary Alice, thundered down the stairs and galloped into the room. Mary Alice has for some time now been convinced she's a horse. Outwardly she has all the characteristics of a little girl, but I'm beginning to wonder if there's more to the horse thing than meets the eye.

'Blackie tinkled in my bedroom,' Mary Alice said. 'And I had to clean it up. That's why I'm late. Blackie couldn't help it. He's just a baby horse and he doesn't know any better.'

'Blackie's a new horse, isn't he?' Grandma asked.

'Yep. He came to play with me just today,' Mary Alice said.

'It was nice of you to clean it up,' Grandma said.

'Next time you should put his nose in it,' Kloughn said. 'I heard that works sometimes.'

Valerie impatiently looked around the table. She folded her hands and bowed her head. 'Thank God for this food,' Valerie said. And she dug in.

We all crossed ourselves, mumbled *thank God*, and started passing dishes.

There was a rap on the front door, the door opened, and Joe strolled in. 'Is there room for me?' he asked.

My mother beamed. 'Of course,' she said. 'There's always room for you. I set an extra plate just in case you could make it.'

There was a time when my mother warned me about Joe. *Stay away from the Morelli boys*, my mother would say. *They can't be trusted. They're all sex fiends. And no Morelli man will ever amount to anything*. A while back my mother had decided Joe was the exception to the rule and that somehow, in spite of genetic disadvantage, he'd actually managed to grow up. He was financially and professionally stable. And he could be trusted. Okay, so he was still a sex fiend, but at least he was a monogamous sex fiend. And most important, my mother had come to think that Joe was her best, and possibly *only*, shot at getting me off the streets and respectably married.

Grandma shoveled a wedge of lasagna onto her plate. 'I've got to get the facts straight on the shooting,' she said. 'Mitchell Farber just got laid out and Mabel and me are going to his viewing at Stiva's funeral parlor right after dinner, and people are gonna be on me like a rash.'

'There's not much to tell,' I said. 'Lula and I stopped for lunch and the man eating across from me was shot. No one knows why, but it's not a great neighborhood. It was probably just one of those things.'

'One of those things!' my mother said. 'Accidentally dinging your car door with a shopping cart is one of those things. Having someone shot right in front of you is *not* one of those things. Why were you in such a bad neighborhood? Can't you find a decent place to have lunch? What were you thinking?'

'I bet there's more to it than that,' Grandma said. 'I bet you were after a bad guy. Were you packin' heat?'

'No. I wasn't armed. I was just having lunch.'

'You aren't giving me a lot to work with here,' Grandma said.

Kloughn turned to Morelli. 'Were you there?'

'Yep.'

'Boy, it must be something to be a cop. You get to do all kinds of cool stuff. And you're always in the middle of everything. Right there where the action is.'

Joe forked off a piece of lasagna.

'So what do you think about Stephanie being there? I mean, she was sitting right across from this guy, right? How far away? Two feet? Three feet?'

Morelli sent me a sideways glance and then looked back at Kloughn. 'Three feet.'

'And you're not freaked? If it was me, I'd be freaked. But

hey, I guess that's the way it is with cops and bounty hunters. Always in the middle of the shooting.'

'I'm never in the middle of the shooting,' Joe said. 'I'm plainclothes. I investigate. The only time my life is in danger is when I'm with Stephanie.'

'How about last week?' Grandma asked. 'I heard from Loretta Beeber that you were almost killed in some big shoot-out. Loretta said you had to jump out of Terry Gilman's second-story bedroom window.'

I swiveled in my seat and faced Joe and he froze with his fork halfway to his mouth. There'd been rumors about Joe and Terry Gilman all through high school. Not that a rumor linking Morelli to a woman was unusual. But Gilman was different. She was a cool blonde with ties to the Mob and an ongoing relationship with Morelli. Morelli swore the relationship was professional and I believed him. That isn't to say that I liked it. It bore a disturbing parallel to my relationship with Ranger. And I knew that as hard as I tried to ignore the chemistry between Ranger and me, it still simmered below the surface.

I narrowed my eyes just a tiny bit and leaned forward, invading Morelli's space. 'You jumped out of Terry Gilman's window?'

'I told you.'

'You didn't tell me. I would have remembered.'

'It was the day you wanted to go out for pizza and I said I had to work.'

'And?'

'And that was it. I told you I had to work. Can we discuss this later?'

'I wouldn't put up with that,' Valerie said, working the lasagna around in her mouth, grabbing a meat-and-cheese roll-up from the antipasto tray. 'I ever get married again, I want full disclosure. I don't want any of this "I have to work, honey" baloney. I want all the answers up front, in detail. You don't keep your eyes open and next thing your husband's in the coat closet with the baby-sitter.'

Unfortunately, Valerie was speaking from firsthand experience.

'I've never jumped out of a window,' Kloughn said. 'I thought people just did that in the movies. You're the first person I've ever met who jumped out of a window,' he said to Morelli. 'And a bedroom window, too. Did you have your clothes on?'

'Yeah,' Morelli said. 'I had my clothes on.'

'How about your shoes? Did you have your shoes on?'

'*Yes*. I had my shoes on.'

I almost felt sorry for Morelli. He was making a major effort not to lose his temper. A younger Morelli would have broken a chair over Kloughn's head.

'I heard Terry didn't hardly have anything on,' Grandma said. 'Loretta's sister lives right across from Terry Gilman and she said she saw the whole thing and Terry was wearing a flimsy little nightie. Loretta's sister said even from across the street you could see right through the nightie and she thinks Terry got a boob job because Terry's boobs were perfect. Loretta's sister said there was a big to-do with the police showing up on account of all the shooting.'

I tried to control my eyebrows from jumping halfway up my forehead. 'Nightie? Shooting?'

'Loretta's sister was the one who *called* the police,' Joe said. 'And there wasn't a lot of shooting. A gun accidentally discharged.'

'And the nightie?'

The anger disappeared and Morelli tried unsuccessfully to stifle a smile. 'It wasn't exactly a nightie. She was wearing one of those camisole tops and a thong.'

'No kidding!' Kloughn said. 'And you could see through it, right? I bet you could see through it.'

'That does it,' I said, standing at my seat, throwing my napkin onto the table. 'I'm out of here.' I stomped out of the dining room into the foyer and stopped with my hand on the door. 'What did you make for dessert?' I yelled to my mother.

'Chocolate cake.'

I wheeled around and flounced off to the kitchen. I cut a good-size wedge from the cake, wrapped it in aluminum foil, and swept out of the house. Okay, so I was acting like an idiot. At least I was an idiot with cake.

I took to the road and drove off, spewing indignation and self-righteous fury. I was still fuming when I reached Joe's house. I sat there for a couple beats, considering my predicament. My clothes and my hamster were in the house. Not to mention my safety and great sex. Problem was, there was all this . . . emotion. I know emotion covers a lot of ground, but I couldn't hang a better name on my feelings. *Wounded* might be in the ballpark. I was stung that Morelli couldn't keep from smiling when he thought back to Gilman in her thong and camisole. Gilman and her perfect boobs. *Unh.* Mental head slap.

I opened the aluminum foil and ate the chocolate cake with my fingers. When in doubt, eat some cake. Halfway through the cake I started to feel better. Okay, I said to myself, now that we have some calm, let's take a look at what happened here.

To begin with, I was a big fat hypocrite. I was all bent out of shape over Morelli and Gilman when I had the exact same situation going on between Ranger and me. These are working relationships, I told myself. Get over it. Grow up. Have some trust here.

Okay, so now I've yelled at myself. Anything else going on? Jealousy? Jealousy didn't feel like a fit. Insecurity? Bingo. Insecurity was a match. I didn't have a *lot* of insecurity. Just enough insecurity to surface at times of mental health breakdown. And I was definitely having a mental health breakdown. The denial thing wasn't working for me.

I put the car in gear and drove to my apartment building. I wouldn't stay long, I decided. I'd just go in and retrieve a few things – like my dignity, maybe.

I parked in the lot, shoved the door open, and swung from behind the wheel. I beeped the car locked with the remote and headed for the back door to my building. I was halfway across the lot when I heard a sound behind me. *Phunf.* I felt something sting my right shoulder blade and heat swept through my upper body. The world went gray, then black. I put my hand out to steady myself and felt myself slide away.

I was swimming in suffocating blackness, unable to surface. Voices only partially penetrated. Words were garbled. I ordered myself to open my eyes. Open them. *Open them!*

Suddenly there was daylight. The images were blurred, but the voices snapped into focus. The voices were calling my name.

'Stephanie?'

I blinked a couple times, clearing my vision, recognizing Morelli. My first words were, 'What the fuck?'

'How do you feel?' Morelli asked.

'Like I've been hit by a truck.'

A guy I didn't know was bending over me, opposite Joe. A paramedic. I had a blood pressure cuff on and the paramedic was listening.

'She's looking better,' he said.

I was on the ground in the parking lot and Joe and the paramedic brought me up to sitting. An EMS truck idled not far off. There was a lot of equipment beside me. Oxygen, stretcher, medical emergency kit. A couple Trenton cops stood hands on hips. A small crowd was gathered behind the cops.

'We should take her to St Francis to have her checked by a doctor,' the medic said. 'They might want to keep her overnight.'

'What happened?' I asked Morelli.

'Someone shot you in the back with a tranquilizer dart. The impact was partially absorbed by your jacket, but you got enough tranq to knock you out.'

'Am I okay?'

'Yeah,' Morelli said. 'I think you're okay. More than I can say for me. I just had three heart attacks.'

'I don't want to go to St Francis. I want to go home . . . wherever that is.'

The medic looked over at Morelli. 'Your call.'

'I'll take responsibility,' Morelli said. 'Help me get her to her feet.'

I walked around for a couple minutes on shaky legs. I was feeling really crappy, but I didn't want to broadcast it. I didn't want to overnight in the hospital. They take your clothes away and hide them and make you sleep in one of those cotton gowns that your ass hangs out of. 'Jeez,' I said. 'What was I shot with, an elephant gun?'

Morelli had the dart in a plastic evidence bag in his pocket. He held the bag out for me to see. 'Looks to me to be more large dog size.'

'Oh great. I was shot with a dog dart. That doesn't even make good bar conversation.'

Morelli eased me into his truck. 'We'll leave your car here. I don't think we want to put you behind the wheel yet.'

I wasn't going to argue. I was developing a monster headache.

There was a single red rose on the dash. A square white card in a plastic evidence bag had been placed beside the rose.

Morelli gestured at the rose. 'That was left on your windshield.' He reached across and took the card and turned it so I could read the message. *You should be more careful. If you make it too easy, the fun will be gone.*

'This is creepy,' I said. 'This is definitely psycho.'

'It started right after you became involved with Singh,' Morelli said.

'Do you think it's Bart Cone?'

'He'd be on the list, but I'm not convinced he's the one. I can't see him leaving roses. Bart Cone doesn't strike me as a man who has a flare for the dramatic.'

I wanted it to be Bart Cone. He was an easy mark. I had a fantasy scenario going in my head. Stephanie and Lula break into Bart's home, find the tranquilizer gun stashed beside the gun that killed Howie, and call the police. The police immediately arrest Bart. And Stephanie lives happily ever after. Needless to say, the fantasy scenario didn't include Stephanie doing time for illegal entry. 'This has moved way beyond my comfort zone,' I said to Morelli. 'If I wasn't shot full of tranquilizer you'd be seeing some first-rate hysteria.'

Morelli left-turned out of the lot. 'What were you doing here, anyway?'

'I was returning to my apartment because you liked looking at Gilman in her thong.'

'Shit,' Morelli said. 'You're such a *girl*.'

I closed my eyes and rested my head on the seat back. 'You're lucky I'm drugged.'

'Did you notice anything unusual when you parked? A strange car? A paranoid schizophrenic lurking in the shadows?'

'Nothing. I wasn't looking. I was making the most of my indignation.'

By the time we reached Morelli's house the sun was low in the sky and the night insects were singing. I looked down the street, more for comfort than from fear. Hard to believe anything bad could happen on Morelli's street. Mrs Brodsky was sitting on her porch and Aunt Rose's second-story curtains, filmy behind the glass, floated like a protective charm. Morelli's neighborhood felt benign. Of course, none of that stopped Morelli from doing his cop thing. He'd been checking his tail all the way over, making sure we weren't followed. He parked and helped me out of the truck, hustling me into the house, partially shielding me with his body.

'I appreciate the effort,' I said, sinking onto his couch. 'But I hate when you put yourself in danger to protect me.'

Bob climbed up next to me, leaving no room for Morelli. Bob had a piece of dog biscuit stuck to his head.

'How does he always get food stuck to him?' I asked Morelli.

'I don't know,' Morelli said. 'It's a Bob mystery. I think stuff falls out of his mouth and he rolls in it, but I'm not sure.'

'About Gilman . . .' I said.

'I can't talk about Gilman. It's police business.'

'This isn't one of those James Bond things where you sleep with Gilman to get information out of her, is it?'

Morelli slouched into a chair and clicked the television on. 'No. This is one of those Trenton cop things where we threaten and bribe Gilman to get information out of her.' He found a ball game, adjusted the sound, and turned to me. 'So are you sleeping with me tonight?'

'Yes. But I have a headache.' I closed my eyes and tried to relax. 'Omigosh!' I said, my eyes popping open. 'I forgot to tell you. I have an email from Howie's killer and it links the killing and the flowers.'

Morelli was long gone by the time I dragged myself out of bed. I shuffled into the bathroom, took a shower, dressed in jeans and T-shirt, and found my way to the kitchen. I got coffee brewing and put a couple slices of bread in the toaster while I drank my orange juice and checked my email. I suspected there would be a message from the killer. I wasn't disappointed. *Now the hunter is the hunted*, the email read. *How does it feel? Does it excite you? Are you prepared to die?*

Bob was sitting beside me, waiting for bread crumbs to fall out of my mouth.

'I'm not excited,' I told Bob. 'I'm scared.' The words echoed in the kitchen and made my breath catch in my chest. I didn't like the way the words sounded and decided not to say them out loud again. I decided to give denial another chance. Some thoughts are best kept silent. That's not to say I was going to ignore being scared. I was going to try very, very hard to be very, very careful.

I signed off and called Morelli and told him about the latest email. Then I called Lula and asked her to pick me up. I wanted to go back to TriBro and my car was still parked in my apartment building lot. I needed a ride. And I needed a partner. I wasn't going to stay inside, hiding in a closet, but in all honesty I didn't want to go out alone.

Ten minutes later, Lula rolled to a stop in front of Morelli's house. Lula drove a big ol' red Firebird that had a sound system that could shake the fillings loose in your teeth. The front door to Joe's house was closed and locked and I was in the kitchen in the back of the house . . . and I knew Lula had arrived because Shady's bass was giving me heart arrhythmia.

'You don't look so good,' Lula said when I got into the car. 'You got big bags under your eyes. And your eyes are all bloodshot. You must have really had a good time last night to look this bad this morning.'

'I was shot with a tranquilizer dart last night and I had a

killer hangover from it until about four this morning.'

'Get out! What were you doing getting shot with a tranquilizer dart?'

'I wasn't doing anything. I was walking from my car to my apartment building and someone shot me in the back.'

'Get out! Did you find out who did it?'

'No. The police are investigating.'

'I bet it was Joyce Barnhardt. Joyce would do something like that, trying to even the score for all the times we zapped her with the stun gun and you let Bob poop on her front lawn.'

Joyce Barnhardt. I'd forgotten about Joyce Barnhardt. She'd be a prime contender, too, except for the Howie shooting. Joyce wasn't a killer.

I went to school with Joyce and she'd made my life a misery. Joyce publicized secrets. When she didn't have a secret she fabricated stories and started rumors. I wasn't the only one singled out, but I was a favorite target. A while back, Vinnie hired Joyce to do some apprehension work and once again Joyce and I crossed paths.

'I don't think it's Joyce,' I told Lula. 'I think the tranq incident is related to the Howie shooting.'

'Get out!'

If Lula said *get out* one more time I was going to choke her until her tongue turned blue and fell out of her head.

'And you're probably in danger when you hang with me,' I told Lula. 'I'd understand if you wanted to bail.'

'Are you shitting me? Danger's my middle name.'

Seven

We were out of Joe's neighborhood and moving across town. Lula had Eminem cranked up. He was rapping about trailer-park girls and how they go round the outside, and I was wondering what the heck that meant. I'm a white girl from Trenton. I don't know these things. I need a rap cheat sheet.

I was checking the rear-view mirror now. I didn't want a second dart between the shoulder blades. It was time to be vigilant. I had no indication that the creep who was stalking me knew I was living with Joe. And I was riding in Lula's car. So maybe today would be uneventful.

We hit Route 1 and I noticed there was a cooler on the back seat. 'Are you still on the diet?' I asked. 'Is the cooler filled with vegetables?'

'Hell no. That was a bogus diet. You could waste away and die on that diet. I'm on a new diet. This here's the all-protein diet that I'm on. I'm going to be a supermodel in no time on this diet. All I have to do is stay away from the carbs. Carbohydrates are the enemy. I can eat all the meat and eggs and cheese I want, but I can't eat any bread or starch or any of that shit. Like, I can have a burger but I can't eat the roll. And I can only eat the cheese and grease on the pizza. Can't eat the crust.'

'How about doughnuts?'

'Doughnuts are gonna be a problem. Don't think there's anything I can eat on a doughnut.'

'So what's in the cooler?'

'Meat. I got ribs and rotisserie chicken and a pound of crispy bacon. I can eat meat until I grow a tail and moo. This is the *best* diet. I can eat things on this diet that I haven't been able to eat in years.'

'Like what?'

'Like bacon.'

'You always eat bacon.'

'Yeah, but I feel guilty. It's the guilt that puts the weight on.'

Lula turned into the industrial park and wound around some until she came to TriBro.

'Now what?' she asked. 'You want me to go on in with you? Or you want me to stay here and guard the chicken?'

'*Guard* the chicken?'

'Okay, so I'm gonna *eat* the chicken. That's the good part

of this diet. You eat all the time. You could shove pork roast and leg of lamb down your throat all day long and it's okay. Long as you don't have biscuits with it. I had a steak for breakfast. A whole steak. And then I had a couple eggs. Is that a diet, or what?'

'Sounds a little screwy.'

'That's what I thought at first, but I bought a book that explains it all and now I can see where it makes sense.'

'Keep your eyes open while you're *guarding* the chicken. I shouldn't be more than a half hour. Call me on my cell if you see anyone suspicious in the lot.'

'You mean like someone setting up a dart gun?'

'Yeah. That would be worth a phone call.'

I'd gotten in touch with Andrew first thing this morning, before leaving the house. I told him I needed some information and he said he'd be happy to help. Andrew, the people person. Hopefully I could get to him without crossing paths with Bart. I hated to admit it, but I was afraid of Bart.

I did a brisk walk across the lot to the building entrance and hurried through the large glass door. The woman at the desk smiled and waved me through to Andrew's office. I thanked her on a *whoosh* of expelled air. I'd just had two bad parking lot experiences and many of my body functions, like breathing, now stopped when I set foot on parking-lot pavement.

Andrew stood and smiled when I entered his office. 'You didn't say much on the phone. How's the Singh search going?'

'We're making progress. I'm looking for a woman named Susan. I was hoping you could check through your employee list and pull out the Susans.'

'Susan is a pretty common name. What's the connection to Singh?'

'It's vague. She's just a name that turned up and I thought I should check it through.'

Andrew turned to his computer, typed in a series of commands, and the screen filled with the employee database. Then it executed a search for all Susans.

'We employ eight Susans,' he finally said. 'When I set the age at forty or below, I'm left with five Susans. I'll give you a printout and you can talk to them if you want. All are married. None work in Singh's department, but he would have had a chance to mingle with the general population during breaks and at lunch. We're a relatively small company. Everyone knows everyone else.'

Clyde appeared in the open doorway. He was wearing a faded Star Trek T-shirt and new black jeans that were pooled around his ankles. Scruffy sneakers peaked out from under the jeans. He had a can of Dr Pepper in one hand and a bag of Cheez Doodles in the other. He had a Betty Boop tattoo on his chunky left arm.

'Hey, Stephanie Plum,' Clyde said. 'I was taking a break and I heard you were here. What's up? Anything exciting going on? Did you find Samuel Singh?'

'I haven't found Singh, but I'm working on it.' My eyes strayed to Betty Boop.

Clyde grinned and looked down at Betty. 'It's a fake. I got it last night. I'm too chicken to get a real one.'

'Stephanie has a list of people she'd like to talk to,' Andrew said. 'Do you have time to take her around?'

'You bet. Sure I do. Is this part of the investigation? How do you want me to act? Should I be casual?'

'Yeah,' I said. 'You should be casual.'

Clyde reminded me a lot of Bob with the unruly hair and goofy enthusiasm.

'These are all Susans,' Clyde said, looking at the list. 'That's a lead, right? Some woman named Susan knows where Singh is hiding. Or maybe some woman named Susan bumped Singh off! Am I close? Am I getting warm?'

'It's nothing that dramatic,' I told Clyde. 'It was just a name that popped up as a possible friend.'

'I know all these women,' Clyde said, leading me out of Andrew's office. 'I can tell you all about them. The first Susan is real nice. She has two kids and a beagle. And the beagle's always at the vet. I think her whole paycheck goes to the vet. The dog eats everything. One time he was real sick and they X-rayed him and found out he had a stomach full of loose change. Her husband works here, too. He's in shipping. They live in Ewing. They just bought a house there. I haven't seen the house, but I think it's one of those little tract houses.'

Clyde was right about the first Susan. She was very nice. But she only knew Singh from a distance. And the same was true for the other four Susans. And I believed them all. None of the Susans seemed like girlfriend material. None of them looked like sharpshooters or killers. They all looked like they might send roses and carnations.

'Those are all the Susans,' Clyde said. 'None of them worked out, huh? Do you have any other leads? Any clues we could work on next?'

'Nope. That's it for now.'

'How about lunch?'

'Gee, sorry. I have a friend waiting for me in the parking lot.' Thank God.

'I'm a pretty interesting guy, you know,' he said. 'I have a lot going on.' His eyes got round. 'You haven't seen my office yet. You *have* to see my office.'

I glanced at my watch. 'It's getting late . . .'

'My office is right here.' He galloped down the hall and opened the door to his office. 'Look at this.'

I followed him and stepped into his office. One wall was

floor-to-ceiling shelves and the shelves were filled with action figures. Star Trek, professional wrestlers, GI Joe characters, Star Wars, Spawn, about two hundred Simpsons figures.

'Is this an awesome collection, or what?' he asked.

'It's fun.'

'And I collect comic books, too. Mostly action comics. I have a whole stack of original Spider-Man McFarlanes. Man, I wish I could draw like him.'

I looked around the room. Large old wooden partner's desk with desk chair, computer with oversize LCD monitor, trash basket filled with squashed Dr Pepper cans, framed poster of Barbarella behind the desk, single chair in front of the desk, dog-eared comics piled high on the chair seat. None of the catalogues and product samples I saw in Bart's office.

'So,' I said, 'what's your part in the business?'

Clyde giggled. 'I don't have one. Nobody trusts me to do anything. Now, on the surface that might seem a little insulting, but if you examine it more closely you see that I have a good deal. I collect a paycheck for staying out of the way! How good is that?'

'Does it get boring? Do you have to sit here all day?'

'Yeah, I guess sometimes it's a little boring. But everyone's nice to me and I get to do all the things I like. I can play with my action figures and read comics and play games on the computer. It isn't like I'm mentally retarded . . . it's just that I screw up a lot. The truth is, I'm not real interested in making thingamabobs.'

'What would you like to do?'

He shrugged. 'I don't know. I guess I'd like to be Spider-Man.'

Too bad Clyde wasn't older. He'd be perfect for Grandma Mazur.

Lula was sound asleep with the driver's seat tipped back when I returned to the car. I jumped in and locked my door and nudged Lula.

'Hey,' I said. 'You're supposed to be on lookout.'

Lula sat up and stretched. 'There wasn't anything to see. And I got sleepy after eating all that chicken. I ate the whole thing. I even ate the skin. I love skin. And you know how all other diets tell you not to eat the skin? Well, guess what? I'm doing the skin diet now, girlfriend.'

'That's great. Let's get out of here.'

'Something happen in there to make you in such a rush to take off?'

'Just feeling antsy.'

'Fine by me. Where we going next?'

I didn't know. I was out of leads. Out of ideas. Out of courage. 'Let's go back to the office.'

* * *

Lula and I saw the black truck simultaneously. It was parked in front of Vinnie's office. It was a new Dodge Ram. It didn't have a speck of dust on it. It had bug lights on the cab, oversize tires, and a license plate that was probably made in someone's basement. Ranger drove a variety of cars. All of them were black. All were new. All were expensive. And all were of dubious origin. The Ram was his favorite.

'Be still my beating heart,' Lula said. 'Does my hair look okay? Am I starting to drool?'

I wasn't nearly so excited. I suspected he was waiting for me. And I worried that it wasn't going to be a good conversation.

I followed Lula into the office. Connie was at her desk, head down, furiously shuffling papers. Vinnie's door was closed. Ranger was slouched in a chair, elbows on the arms, fingers steepled in front of him, his eyes dark and intense, watching us.

I smiled at Ranger. 'Yo,' I said.

He smiled back but he didn't yo.

'We're just checking in,' I said to Connie, leaning on the front of her desk. 'Do you have anything for me?'

'I have skips piling up on my desk,' Connie said, 'but Vinnie doesn't want anyone even *looking* at them until Singh is found.'

'No calls? No messages?'

Ranger unfolded himself and crossed the room, standing close behind me, sucking me into his force field. 'We need to talk.'

A flash of heat rippled through my stomach. Ranger always evoked a mixture of emotion. Usually that mixture was attraction followed by a mental eye roll.

'Sure,' I said.

'Now. Outside.'

Lula scurried behind the file cabinets and Connie bent into the nonsense paper shuffling. No one wanted to get caught in the line of fire when Ranger was in a mood. I followed Ranger out the door to the sidewalk and stood blinking in the sun.

'Get into the truck,' Ranger said. 'I feel like driving.'

'I don't think so.'

The line of his mouth tightened.

'Where are we going?' I asked.

'Do you want a full itinerary?'

'I don't want to get locked up in a safe house.'

'I'd love to lock you up in a safe house, babe, but that wasn't my plan for the day.'

'Promise? Cross your heart and hope to die?'

There was a slight narrowing of his eyes. Ranger wasn't feeling playful. 'I guess you have to decide if it's more dangerous to be in the truck with me or to stand out here as a potential target for the sniper.'

I stared at Ranger for a beat.

'Well?' he asked.

'I'm thinking.'

'Christ,' Ranger said. 'Get in the damn truck.'

I climbed into the truck and Ranger drove two blocks down Hamilton and turned into the Burg. He wound through the Burg and parked on Roebling in front of Marsilio's restaurant.

'I thought you wanted to drive,' I said.

'That was the original plan, but you smell like rotisserie chicken and it's making me hungry.'

'It's from Lula. She's on this diet where she eats meat all day.'

Bobby V met us at the door and gave us a table in the back room. The Burg is famous for its restaurants. They're stuck all over the place in the neighborhood, between houses, next to Betty's bridal shop and Rosalie's beauty parlor. Most are small. All are family affairs. And the food is always great. I'm not sure where Bobby V fits in the scheme of things at Marsilio's, but he's always on hand to direct traffic and shmooze. He's a snappy dresser, he's got a handful of rings and a full head of wavy silver hair, and he looks like he wouldn't have much trouble breaking someone's nose. If you're in bad with Bobby V don't even bother showing up, because you won't get a table.

Ranger sat back in his chair, took a moment to scan the menu, and ordered. I didn't need the menu. I always got the fettuccini Alfredo with sausage. And then because I didn't want to die, I got some red wine to help unclog my arteries.

'Okay,' Ranger said when we were alone. 'Talk to me.'

I filled him in on the shooting, the dart, the email. 'And what really has me freaked is that Joe's grandma saw me dead in one of her visions,' I said, an involuntary shiver ripping through me.

Ranger was motionless. Face impassive.

'Every lead I get ends up in the toilet,' I told him.

'Well, you must be doing something right. Someone wants to kill you. That's always a good sign.'

I guessed that was one way of looking at it. 'Problem is, I'm not ready to die.'

Ranger looked at the food in front of me. Noodles and sausage in cheese and cream sauce. 'Babe,' he said.

Ranger's plate held a chicken breast and grilled vegetables. He was hot, but he didn't know much about eating.

'Where are you now?' Ranger wanted to know. 'Do you have any more leads to follow?'

'No leads. I'm out of ideas.'

'Any gut instincts?'

'I don't think Singh's dead. I think he's hiding. And I think the freak who's stalking me is directly or indirectly associated with TriBro.'

'If you had to take a guess, could you pull a name out of a hat?'

'Bart Cone is the obvious.'

Ranger made a phone call and asked for the file on Bart Cone. In my mind I imagined the call going into the nerve center of the Bat Cave. No one knows the source of Ranger's cars, clients, or cash. He operates a number of businesses which are security related. And he employs a bunch of men who have skills not normally found outside a prison population. His right-hand man is named Tank and the name says it all.

Tank walked into the restaurant twenty minutes later with a manila envelope. He smiled and nodded a hello to me. He helped himself to a slice of Italian bread. And he left.

Ranger and I read through the material, finding few surprises. Bart was divorced and living alone in a townhouse north of the city. He had no recorded debts. He paid his credit cards and his mortgage on time. He drove a two-year-old black BMW sedan. The packet included several newspaper clippings on the murder trial and a profile on the murdered woman.

Lillian Paressi was twenty-six years old at the time of her death. She had brown hair and blue eyes and from the photo in the paper she looked to be of average build. She was pretty in a girl-next-door way, with curly shoulder-length hair and a nice smile. She was unmarried, living alone in an apartment on Market just two blocks from the Blue Bird luncheonette, where she'd worked as a waitress.

In a very general sort of way I suppose she resembled me. Not a good thought to have when investigating an unsolved murder that had serial killer potential. But then half the women in the Burg fit that same description, so probably there was no reason for me to be alarmed.

Ranger reached over and tucked a brown curl behind my ear. 'She looks a little like you, babe,' Ranger said. 'You want to be careful.'

Super.

Ranger looked at my pasta dish. I'd eaten everything but one noodle. A smile twitched at the corner of his mouth.

'I don't want to get fat,' I told him.

'And that noodle would do it?'

I narrowed my eyes. 'What's your point?'

'Do you have room for dessert?'

I sighed. I always had room for dessert.

'You're going to have dessert at the Blue Bird luncheonette,' Ranger said. 'I bet they have good pie. And while you're eating the pie you can talk to the waitress. Maybe she knew Paressi.'

Halfway across town I rechecked the reflection in my side mirror for the fourth time. 'I'm pretty sure we're being followed by a black SUV,' I said.

'Tank.'

'Tank's following us?'

'Tank's following you.'

Ordinarily I'd be annoyed at the invasion of privacy, but right now I was thinking privacy was overrated and it wasn't a bad idea to have a bodyguard.

The Blue Bird sat cheek to jowl with several small businesses on Second Avenue. This wasn't the most prosperous part of town, but it wasn't the worst, either. Most of the businesses were family owned and operated. The yellow brick storefronts were free of graffiti and bullet holes. Rents were reasonable and encouraged low-profit businesses: a shoe repair shop, a small hardware store, a vintage clothing store, a used book store. And the Blue Bird luncheonette.

The Blue Bird was approximately the size of a double-wide railroad car. There was a short counter with eight stools, a pastry display case and cash register. Booths stretched along the far wall. The linoleum was black-and-white checkerboard and the walls were bluebird blue.

We took a booth and looked at the menu. There was the usual fare of burgers and tuna melts and pie. I ordered lemon meringue and Ranger ordered coffee, black.

'Excuse me?' I said, palms down on the Formica tabletop. 'Coffee? I thought we came here for pie.'

'I don't eat the kind of pie they serve here.'

I felt a flash of heat go through my stomach. I knew firsthand the kind of pie Ranger liked.

The waitress stood with pencil poised over her pad. She was late fifties with bleached blond hair piled high on her head, heavily mascaraed eyes, perfectly arched crayoned-on eyebrows, and iridescent white lipstick. She had big boobs barely contained in a white T-shirt, her hips were slim in a black Spandex miniskirt, and she was wearing black orthopedic shoes.

'Honey, we got *all* kinds of pie,' she said to Ranger.

Ranger cut his eyes to her and she took a step backward. 'But then maybe not,' she said.

'I'm not usually in this neighborhood,' I told the waitress, 'but my little sister knew a girl who used to work here. And she always said the food was real good. Maybe you knew my sister's friend. Lillian Paressi.'

'Oh honey, I sure did. She was a sweetheart. Didn't have an enemy. Everyone loved Lillian. That was a terrible thing that happened to her. She was killed on her day off. I couldn't believe it when I heard. And they never caught the guy who did it. They had a suspect for a while, but it didn't turn out. I tell you, if I knew who killed Lillian he'd never come to trial.'

'Actually, I lied about my sister,' I said. 'We're investigating Lillian's murder. There've been some new developments.'

'I figured,' the waitress said. 'You get to be a good judge of people with a job like this and Rambo's got "fed" written all over him. A local cop would have ordered pie.'

Ranger looked at me and winked and I almost fell off my seat. It was the first time he'd ever winked at me. Somehow Ranger and winking didn't go together.

'Did Lillian have a boyfriend?' I asked.

'Nothing serious. She was going out with this one guy, but they broke up. She hadn't seen him for a couple months. His name was Bailey Scrugs. You don't forget a name like Bailey Scrugs. The cops talked to him early on. So far as I know she wasn't dating anyone when she was killed. She was real depressed after breaking up with Scrugs and she spent a lot of time on her computer. Chat rooms and stuff.

'Do you want to know what I think? I think it was one of them random killings. Some nut saw her out walking in the woods. The world's full of nuts.'

'I know this all happened a while ago,' I said, 'but try to think back. Was Lillian ever worried? Scared? Upset? Anything unusual happen to her?' Like was she ever shot with a tranquilizer dart?

'The police asked me all those same questions. At the time I couldn't think of anything to tell them. But there was something that popped into my head months later. I couldn't decide if I should go tell someone. It was sort of an odd thing and all that time had passed, so I ended up keeping it to myself.'

'What was it?' I asked.

'This is probably stupid, but a couple days before she was killed someone left a red rose and a white carnation on her car. Stuck them under her windshield wiper with a card. And the card said *Have a nice day*. Lillian was kind of upset about it. She brought them in here and threw them away. I guess that's why it bothered me when I remembered. She didn't say anything more about them, like who they were from or anything. Do you think the flowers might have been important?'

'Hard to say,' Ranger told her.

'You should talk to her neighbor,' the waitress said to us. 'Carl. I don't remember his last name. They were real good friends. Nothing romantic. Just good friends.'

I ate my pie and Ranger drank his coffee. Neither of us

said anything until we were out of the cafe and into his truck.

'Shit,' I said. 'Shit, shit, shit, shit, shit.'

'I have a house in Maine,' Ranger said. 'It's nice there at this time of year.'

It was a tempting offer. 'Is there an outlet mall nearby? Is it close to a Cheesecake Factory? A Chili's?'

'Babe, it's a safe house. It's on a lake in the woods.'

Oh boy. Bears, black flies, rabid raccoons, and spiders. 'Thanks for the offer, but I think I'll pass. Just tell Tank to stick close to me.'

Ranger put the truck in gear, turned at the corner, drove two blocks down Market, and parked in front of an old Victorian clapboard house. The front door was unlocked and led to a small foyer. There were six mailboxes lined up on the wall. Beyond the mailboxes, a hand-carved mahogany railing followed a broad staircase to the second and third floors. The carpet was threadbare and the wall covering was faded and had begun to peel at the corners, but the foyer and staircase were clean. An air freshener had been plugged into a baseboard outlet and spewed lemony freshness that mingled with the natural mustiness of the house.

We ran through the names on the mailboxes and found Carl Rosen. Apartment 2B. We both knew chances weren't good that he'd be in, but we took the stairs and knocked on his door. No answer. We knocked on the door across the hall. No answer there, either.

We could get Carl Rosen's work address easy enough, but most people were reluctant to talk in their work environment. Better to wait a couple hours and catch him at home.

'Now what?' I asked Ranger.

'I want to go through Bart Cone's house. It'll be easier to do alone, so I'm taking you back to the office. You should be safe there. I'll pick you up at five and we'll try Rosen again.'

Eight

Mrs Apusenja was sitting in the office when Ranger dropped me off. She was on the couch, arms crossed over her chest, lips pressed tightly together.

She jumped up when I walked in and pointed her finger at me. 'You!' Mrs Apusenja said. 'What do you do all day? Do you look for Samuel Singh? Do you look for poor little Boo? Where are they? Why haven't you found them?'

Connie rolled her eyes.

'Hunh,' Lula said from behind a file cabinet.

'I've only been looking for a couple days . . .' I said.

'This is the fourth day. Do you know what I think? I think you don't know what you're doing. I want someone new on the case. I *demand* someone new.'

We all looked at the door to Vinnie's inner office. It was closed and locked. There was silence behind the door.

Connie got up and rapped on the door. No response.

'*Hey*,' Connie yelled. 'Mrs Apusenja wants to talk to you. Open the door!'

The door still didn't open.

Connie returned to her desk, got a key from the middle drawer, and went back and opened Vinnie's door. 'Guess you didn't hear me,' Connie said, standing hand on hip, looking in at Vinnie. 'Mrs Apusenja wants to talk to you.'

Vinnie came to the door and smiled an oily smile out at Mrs Apusenja. 'Nice to see you again,' he said. 'Do you have some new information for us?'

'I have this for you. The new information is that I will go to the papers if you do not find Samuel Singh. I will ruin you. How does it look for my Nonnie? People will talk. And he owes me two weeks' rent. Who will pay that?'

'Of course we'll find him,' Vinnie said. 'I've got my best man looking for Singh. And Stephanie's helping him.'

'You are a boil on the backside of your profession,' Mrs Apusenja said. And she left.

'How many years have I been in this business? A lot of years, right?' Vinnie asked. 'And I'm good at it. I'm good at writing bond. I do a service for the community. Does the honest law-abiding taxpayer have to pay my salary? No. Does the city of Trenton have to hire cops to go find their scofflaws? No. All because of me. I go get the scumbags at no cost to the general population. I risk my neck!'

Connie and Lula and I raised our eyebrows.

'Well, okay, I risk *Stephanie's* neck,' Vinnie said. 'But it's all in the family, right?'

'Yeesh,' Lula said.

'I should have let Sebring write the damn visa bond,' Vinnie said. 'What was I thinking?'

Les Sebring was Vinnie's competitor. There were several bail bonds offices in the Trenton area, but Sebring's agency was the largest.

'So what are you doing standing here?' Vinnie asked, flapping his arms. 'Go find him, for crissake.' Vinnie looked around and sniffed the air. 'What's that smell? It smells like roast leg of lamb.'

'It was my afternoon snack,' Lula said. 'I got it delivered from the Greek deli. I'm on the all-you-can-eat meat diet. I didn't eat the whole leg, though. I don't want to go overboard.'

'Yeah,' Connie said. 'She only ate half a leg.'

Vinnie stepped back into his office and closed and locked the door.

'Sounds like we should go find this guy,' Lula said.

I'd have liked nothing better than to find Samuel Singh, but I didn't know how. And worse, I was having a hard time focusing on the hunt. I couldn't get Lillian Paressi out of my head. I kept seeing her marching into the Blue Bird, angrily clutching the flowers. Red rose, white carnation. The note was innocuous. Nothing to get angry over. So the flowers had to be part of a continuing harassment. And surely she talked to someone about it. I was hoping Carl Rosen was that someone.

'Earth to Stephanie,' Lula said. 'You got any ideas?'

'No.'

'Me, either,' Lula said. 'I think this diet's clogging things up inside me. This isn't a creative thinker's diet. You need Cheez Doodles to do that shit. And birthday cake. The kind with the lard icing and the big pink and yellow icing roses.'

Connie and I looked at Lula.

'Not that I'm gonna eat anything like that ever again,' Lula said. 'I was just saying that's why I haven't got any good ideas.'

Since we were all out of how-to-find-Singh ideas, I asked Lula if she'd give me a ride so I could move my car to Joe's house.

'Hell yeah,' Lula said. 'I could use some air. It's too nice to be inside on a day like today. And besides, it smells like leg of lamb in here. This office needs some ventilation.'

We were half a block down Hamilton when Lula looked in her rear-view mirror. 'I think we're being followed. That black SUV pulled out right after us and now he's sitting on our bumper.'

'It's Tank. Ranger thinks I need a baby-sitter.'

Lula took another look. 'He's fine. He's not as hot as Ranger. But he's fine all the same. I wouldn't mind having my way with him.'

'I thought you had a new boyfriend?'

'Don't mean I can't think someone else is fine. I'm just going steady, girl. I'm not *dead*.'

In a couple minutes we were at my apartment building and Lula parked in the lot, beside the Escape.

'I think you should go up to your apartment just to check it out and shit,' Lula said. 'I could go with you and I bet King Kong over there'll go, too. And I'd get a chance to see him up close.'

'Sure,' I said. 'I should probably see if everything's okay, anyway.'

We all got out of our cars and walked to the back door. Tank is about six foot six and is built like . . . a tank. He hasn't an ounce of fat on him. He wears his hair in a Marine buzz cut. He was dressed in desert cammies.

We climbed the stairs and walked down the hall. Tank took the key from me and opened the door. He was the first to step through. He looked around and he motioned us in.

It was cool and quiet inside. No flowers. No photos. No killers. I gathered together some clean shirts and underwear and we left.

'I'd forgotten about Tank following me,' I said to Lula. 'He can chauffeur me around if you want to get back to the office.'

'What are you, crazy? If I go back there I'll have to file. And Vinnie's there. Vinnie creeps me out these days. All he does is mope around, worrying about Samuel Singh. It's unnatural. Vinnie's usually out having a nooner with a goat. I hate having him just hang around the office.'

Tank smiled at the part about the nooner, but he didn't say anything. He got into his shiny black SUV. Lula got into her red Firebird. And I got into my yellow Escape. And we all motored off to Joe's house.

Lula parked behind me and immediately got out of her car. 'Are you going in?' she asked. 'I hope you're going in because I've never been in Morelli's house. I'm dying to see the inside. What's the decor? Modern? Traditional? Colonial?'

'Mostly Pizza Hut with a splash of Aunt Rose.'

I opened the door and Bob rushed out at us, nose twitching, eyes wild. He looked from Tank to Lula to me and then his head swung back to Lula and he gave a loud woof.

'What the . . .' Lula said.

Bob gave another woof, chomped down on Lula's purse, ripped it out of her hand, and took off out the door down the street.

'Hey,' Lula yelled. 'Come back with that! That's my purse.' She looked to Tank. 'Do something. I paid good money for that purse.'

Tank whistled, but Bob paid no attention. Bob was at the end of the block, tearing the purse to shreds. We jogged down to Bob and found him gnawing on a pork chop.

'That was my snack,' Lula said. 'It was barbecue. I was looking forward to that pork chop.'

I took Bob by the collar and dragged him back to Morelli's house.

'I'm on a diet,' Lula explained to Tank. 'The fat just melts away on this diet, but you've gotta eat lots of pork chops.'

I locked Bob in the house and Lula and I drove back to the office with Tank following.

'That was sort of embarrassing,' Lula said. 'It's hard to explain a pork chop in your purse.'

'Sorry it all got destroyed.'

'Yeah, I really wanted that pork chop. I don't care so much about the bag. I bought the bag from Ray Smiley, out of the back of his Pontiac. It was one of those things that accidentally fell off a truck.' Lula's eyes got bigger. 'Hey, we should make a stopover at the mall. I could get a new purse and then just for the hell of it we could go into Victoria's Secret and see if Tank follows us in. That's how you tell what a man's really made of. It's one thing for a man to be big and brave and kill a spider. Any man could do that. Trailin' after a woman when she's shopping for thongs and push-up bras is a whole other category of man. And then if you want to see how far you can go with it, you ask him to carry one of those little pink bags they give you.'

I've never been shopping with Ranger so I can't say how he'd do with the Victoria's Secret test. Morelli flunked hands down. Morelli takes off for soft-serve ice cream when I head for Victoria's Secret.

'No time,' I told Lula. 'Ranger's picking me up at five o'clock.' And Ranger doesn't like to be kept waiting.

At precisely five, I saw Ranger's truck ease to a stop in front of the bonds office. I grabbed my bag and my jacket and I went out to meet him. The instant I got in beside Ranger I saw Tank peel away and take off.

'I thought he was supposed to be guarding my body,' I said to Ranger.

Ranger looked at me with dark eyes. 'It's my turn to guard your body, babe.'

Oh boy.

Ever since I could remember I've loved adventure stories and heroes. I guess that's true for all kids. And maybe all adults, too. My best friend Mary Lou Molnar and I would choose up roles when we were kids. I'd be Snake Eyes from

GI Joe or Inspector Gadget or Han Solo. I'd run through the neighbors' yards, shouting, *Thundercats, ho!* And Mary Lou would follow after me, living her own fantasy as Smurfette or Wendy Darling or Marcia Brady. Mary Lou always had a good sense of gender and of her own abilities. Mary Lou's fantasies were close to the reality of her life. I, on the other hand, have never been able to merge the reality with the fantasy. In my mind, I'm still Snake Eyes. In truth, I'm closer to Lucy Ricardo. I don't have a lot of the skills I should have as a crime fighter. I'm not good with guns and I've never found the time to take self-defense. The only black belt in my closet is a narrow snakeskin with a gold buckle.

'Tell me about Bart Cone,' I said to Ranger. 'Was his house filled with florist bills? Photos of murdered women? Body parts in the freezer?'

'None of the above. He has the minimum furniture. A bed, a chair, a table, a desk. No computer on the desk. No television. He had two books at bedside. *Into Thin Air*. And a nuts and bolts catalogue. It didn't look to me like he'd cracked the spine on *Into Thin Air*.'

'Sounds like his wife had a good divorce lawyer.'

'Cone had minimum food in the refrigerator. His medicine chest was filled with antidepressants and sleeping pills.'

'Do you think he's crazy?'

'I think he has no life. I think he's the job.'

'Like us.'

Ranger looked over at me. 'You have a life. You shop for shoes. You eat Butterscotch Krimpets. You have a hamster, half ownership of a dog, thirty percent of a cop. And you have a scary family.'

'You think I only have thirty percent of Morelli?'

'I think you have as much as he can give anyone right now.'

'How about you?' I asked. 'How much can you give?'

Ranger kept his eyes on the road. 'You ask a lot of questions.'

'So I've been told.'

It was close to 5.30 when we reached the apartment house on Market. Ranger pulled into the driveway and parked in a small lot to the rear of the house. We took the back entrance and went directly to the second floor. We knocked on Carl Rosen's door. No one answered. Ranger crossed the hall and knocked on 2A. A woman in her fifties opened the door and peered out.

'We're looking for Carl Rosen,' Ranger said. 'I don't suppose you've seen him.'

'No,' the woman said. 'I haven't seen him, but he's usually home by now. Sorry.'

The woman slipped back into her apartment. Her door closed and three locks tumbled into place. Ranger paced away from the door, called Tank, and asked him to run a basic information check on Rosen. Three minutes later the information came back. Carl Rosen worked at the hospital. He drove a '94 blue Honda Civic. He was unmarried. Tank also had previous addresses and jobs and a list of relatives. Ranger disconnected and knocked one more time on Rosen's door. When no one answered, Ranger slid a slim tool into the lock and opened the door. He left me outside to do lookout and he disappeared into the apartment.

Ten minutes later, Ranger walked out of the apartment and locked the door behind him. 'I can't remember the last time I broke into so many places and found so little,' Ranger said. 'Not even a computer. Just the power cord plugged into the wall. Either Rosen takes his laptop with him to work or else someone's gone through his apartment in front of us.'

'Now what?'

'Now we wait.'

I called Morelli and told him I'd be late. I was thinking an hour maybe, but we were still waiting at nine o'clock. We were sitting on the floor outside Rosen's apartment, backs to the wall, legs outstretched.

'My ass is asleep,' I said to Ranger.

'And you'd like me to do something about it?' Ranger asked.

'Just making conversation.'

'There are a lot of reasons why Rosen might not be home yet, but I have a bad feeling in my gut that this isn't going to turn out good,' Ranger said.

'How much longer do you want to sit here?'

'Let's give him until ten.'

'Okay,' Morelli said, 'tell me again. You were doing *what* with Ranger?'

'We wanted to talk to Carl Rosen, but he never came home.' I told Morelli about the waitress at the Blue Bird and how she remembered about the flowers.

'Christ,' Morelli said. 'That never came out in any of the investigation. I've read through the file. Carl Rosen was questioned, along with everyone else in that apartment building, but no one ever said anything about flowers.'

'I guess they didn't think it related.'

'Tomorrow morning I'll talk to Ollie. He was the principal on the case.'

Oh great. Blubber-butt Ollie. The bane of my existence. The guy who once tried to arrest me for impersonating a bounty hunter.

It was late. And I was tired. I'd done nothing for hours

and it had sapped my energy. Spending time with Ranger was an odd experience. I was always aware of the sexual pull, magnified by the silence that surrounded him. The attraction had changed since we'd had the one night together. We knew the power of it now. We set boundaries after that night. His were different from mine. My boundaries were physical and Ranger's were emotional. I still knew almost nothing about him. And I suspected it would always be that way.

I had one task left before going to bed. I needed to check my email. Not a pleasant experience any more. I knew there'd be a message from the killer. I had a terrible feeling of dread that it would be about Carl Rosen.

I tapped my code into AOL and waited for my mail to appear. A chill slid along my spine when I saw the subject line: *Tally ho.*

Dear prey, the email began, *so sorry you couldn't get to talk to Carl, but that might have ruined the hunt. Alas, it's necessary to eliminate participants. After all, this is a survival game, isn't it?*

Morelli was reading over my shoulder. 'Doesn't sound good for Carl.'

'This guy thinks he's playing a game.'

'Have you run across any paranoid schizophrenics lately? Any completely wacko nut cases?'

'My path is littered with them. Have you guys had any luck tracking the emails?'

'No. Hiding the origin of an email requires some sophistication, but it's possible. The Mercer County Prosecutor's Office is working with us. We'll see what we can do with this new one. I'm going to confiscate your computer for a while.'

'Were you able to locate the flower source?'

'They didn't come from any of the local florists. This guy probably picked them up at a supermarket. We have notices up in all the supermarket lunchrooms for checkers to watch for red roses and white carnations going out. We've dusted your apartment for prints, but nothing worthwhile came up.'

'This is very creepy.'

'Yeah,' Morelli said. 'Let's go to bed and I'll take your mind off your problems.'

I woke up the next morning thinking maybe I only had thirty percent of Morelli, but it was a damn good thirty percent.

My schedule for fighting crime began considerably later in the day than Morelli's, so by the time I wandered into the kitchen Morelli was already at work. I got coffee brewing and dropped a frozen waffle into the toaster. The morning paper was on the table. I did a fast scan, but saw nothing about a body found floating in the Delaware.

I took a mug of coffee and padded out to the living room, opened the door, and looked up and down the street for Tank. No Tank in sight. That didn't mean he wasn't there.

I called Ranger and told him about the latest email. 'I don't suppose you've seen Carl Rosen this morning?' I asked.

'No. His car hasn't surfaced. And he didn't show up for work.'

'Is Tank out there? I didn't see him.'

'He saw *you*. He said you were frightening.'

'I haven't taken a shower yet. My hair might be a little unruly.'

'Takes a lot to scare Tank,' Ranger said. And he was gone.

I took a shower and I did the full-on hair thing. Hot rollers, gel, the works. I tweezed my eyebrows, painted my toenails, and spent an hour applying make-up. I shrugged into a swirly flowered skirt and finished it all off with a stretchy little white knit top. I was Jersey Girl right down to the strappy sandals with the four-inch heels. Not only did I have to do some image correction for Tank, but I'd be damned if I was going to die needing a pedicure.

I clacked out of the house carrying my big leather shoulder bag and took off for the office in the Escape. I looked great, but I couldn't run for a damn in the shoes so I had sneakers in my shoulder bag . . . just in case I had to chase down a bad guy.

I turned onto Hamilton and Andrew Cone called.

'I have something for you,' he said. 'This is really good. Can you stop around?'

Andrew sounded excited. Maybe this was my lucky day. Hot dog.

Connie was at her desk when I swung in. 'Uh-oh,' she said, 'big hair and full face paint, high heels, and a Barbie shirt. What's going on?'

'It's too complicated to explain.' And I wasn't sure I understood, anyway. 'Where's Lula?'

'She's up the street. She's still on the diet. Went through all her meat in a half hour and had to walk up to the coffee shop for some bacon.'

'Lula *walked* to the coffee shop? That's two blocks away. Lula never walks anywhere.'

'She parked in back and got blocked in by someone. I guess she figured it was faster to walk.'

'She must have really needed the bacon.'

'She was on a mission.'

I moseyed over to the door, looked up the street, and spotted Lula at the end of the block. She was walking fast in her Via Spiga heels, holding a white food bag against her chest. Two dogs, a beagle and a golden retriever, trotted close behind Lula. A third dog crossed the street and joined the pack. Every couple steps Lula would turn and yell something at the dogs. When the beagle jumped for the bag when Lula was half a block away, Lula let out a shriek and started running.

'Stop running,' I yelled at her. 'You're making it worse. They think it's a game.'

They were snapping at her heels now and barking.

'Do something,' Lula yelled. 'Shoot them!'

'Drop the bag! They want the bacon.'

'No way I'm giving up my bacon.'

Lula was running knees high, arms pumping. She was wearing the Via Spigas and a short black Spandex skirt that was hiked up to her waist, showing Hamilton Avenue what a big woman looks like in a red satin thong.

'Open the door!' Lula shouted. 'I can make it. I'm almost there. Just hold the damn door open!'

Lula tossed the dogs a slice of bacon from the bag, the dogs dove after the bacon, and Lula rushed past me into the office. I slammed the door shut and we all stood looking at the dogs milling around outside.

Lula tugged her skirt down. 'Tank's out there, isn't he?'

'Yep.'

'I explained pretty good about the pork chop, but I'm at a loss here.'

'It speaks for itself,' I said to Lula.

Grease stains were starting to show through the bag. 'I

love this diet,' Lula said. 'I love pork chops. And I love ribs. And I love bacon. I love bacon most of all.'

Lula was eating bacon like it was popcorn, chomping on it out of the bag, rolling her eyes in gastronomic ecstasy.

'How much bacon do you have there?' Connie wanted to know.

'Three pounds minus the one strip I gave up to the dogs.'

'Sounds like a lot of bacon,' Connie said.

'I'm pushing the boundaries of science here,' Lula said. 'I'm gonna be a supermodel with a smile on my face on account of I'm gonna be full of bacon.'

'I need to go to TriBro,' I said. 'I'm looking for someone to ride shotgun.'

'That would be me,' Lula said.

Lula and Tank waited in the lot while I went in to talk to Andrew Cone.

'This is really good,' Cone said. 'I had to tell you this in person. First thing this morning I found an email from one of the people I do business with in Vegas. Bill Weber. He said Samuel Singh filled out a job application and Weber was emailing to check references. I got so excited, I called the guy. Got him out of bed. Forgot about the time change.'

'Singh's in Vegas? And he was dumb enough to list you as a reference?'

Cone bobbed his head up and down, smiling wide. 'Yes.'

'I bet he even gave a street address.'

'He did.' Cone slid a piece of paper my way with all the information neatly printed out. 'I told Weber about the visa bond and he's going to string Singh along until you get there. You're going to go get him, right?'

'Right.'

Lula was looking kind of sick when I got back to the car.

'How much of that bacon did you eat?' I asked her.

'I ate it all. It didn't seem like so much while I was eating it, but it doesn't feel like it fits in my stomach now.'

I called Ranger and told him about Singh. 'He's in Vegas, waiting for you to go get him,' I said.

'I'm having a small legal problem with Nevada on a weapons violation,' Ranger said. 'You're going to have to make the capture. Take Tank. I don't want you to go alone.'

Good grief.

Nine

Lula was up straight in her seat. 'What's this about Vegas?'

'Samuel Singh is in Vegas and Ranger can't make the capture. So either I go or Vinnie farms the capture out to a Vegas agency.'

'Don't even suggest farming it out. All my life I've wanted to go to Vegas. I hear there's a shopping center that's just like being in Venice with canals and boats and everything. And there's all those casinos and fancy hotels. There's the Strip. *The Strip!* I could get to see the Strip.' Lula stopped and blinked. 'You were gonna take me, right?'

'Ranger wants me to go with Tank.'

'Tank? Are you shittin' me?' Lula pulled back, eyes bugged out with the injustice of it all. 'Hunh. I get to go along on all the chicken-shit stuff. Sit in the car while you go into TriBro. And I'm the one goes to the back door when you go to the front door on a bust. I *always* get the back door. Do

I complain? Hell no. I guess I know where I stand here.'

I narrowed my eyes at her. 'Are you done?'

'No way. I'm not done. And I'm feeling anxious now. I need a burger or something.'

'You just ate three pounds of bacon!'

'Yeah, but the dogs ate one of those strips.'

I drove out of the lot and headed for the office. 'Okay, fine. I'll take you to Vegas if you can clear it with Connie.'

'I knew it,' Lula said. 'I knew you wouldn't go without me. We're a team, right? We're like those two cops in the *Lethal Weapon* movies. We're like Mel Gibson and Danny Glover.'

More like Thelma and Louise, driving off a cliff.

The office was quiet when we walked in. No Mrs Apusenja. No Vinnie. Only Connie, sitting at her desk, reading the latest Nora Roberts.

'I found Singh,' I told her. 'He's in Vegas.'

'Vegas! I *love* Vegas,' Connie said.

'You see? Everybody's been to Vegas but me,' Lula said. 'It's not fair. I lead a deprived life. Bad enough I grew up underprivileged and all and now I'm the only one not been to Vegas.'

'Let me go get my violin,' Connie said.

'What do you want to do about this now that I've found him?' I asked Connie. 'Can we forcibly bring him back? Has he violated his bond agreement?'

'The bond agreement states that he can't leave the tristate area without permission. So the answer is yes, you can forcibly bring him back. I'll page Vinnie to double-check, but I'm sure he'll want Singh brought back here.'

'Ranger can't go to Vegas to make the capture,' I told Connie.

Connie nodded. 'He's got an outstanding weapons violation. Stepped on a few toes last time he was in Nevada. His lawyer's working on it.'

'So that leaves me, I guess,' I said. 'And Lula.'

'I get the picture,' Connie said.

'And Tank,' I added. 'Ranger said I should take Tank.'

'Anyone else?' Connie asked, turning to the computer. 'You want a permit for a parade?'

'Boy, this here's going to be fun,' Lula said. 'And what with this new diet, I'll probably be real thin by the time I get there.'

'It's only a five-hour flight,' I told her.

'Yeah, but this diet works fast.'

'Okay, here we go,' Connie said. 'I've got us on a flight out of Newark at four o'clock. We have a plane change in Chicago and we arrive in Vegas at nine. It's not a direct flight, but it's the best I can do.'

'Us?'

'You don't think I'm going to send you and Lula to Vegas

without me, do you? I'm feeling lucky. I'm going straight to the craps table. I'm not going to page Vinnie, either. I'm going to leave him a note.'

We didn't have a lot of time if we were going to catch a four o'clock flight. 'Here's the plan,' I said. 'It doesn't make sense to take more than one car. I'll tell Tank he's driving and he can pick all of us up. Everyone go home and pack and be ready to go in an hour. And remember, there's tight security now. No guns, no knives, no pepper spray, no nail files.'

'What? How am I supposed to travel without a nail file?' Lula wanted to know.

'You have to put it in your suitcase and check your suitcase.'

'What if I break a nail getting onto the plane and I got to file it down?'

'You'll have to gnaw it down with your teeth. I'll get you in an hour.'

Tank was parked in front of the bonds office and he was being surveillant. I went out to him and gave him the game plan. He said his assignment was to stick to me and he didn't need to pack.

'Not even a toothbrush?' I asked. 'Not even an extra pair of tighty whiteys?'

Tank almost smiled.

Okay then. I ran to my car and took off for my apartment. I hit the ground running when I got to my building. I took the stairs two at a time, barefoot with my shoes in my hands. Tank was ahead of me in the hall. He opened my apartment door and stepped inside. Four eight-by-ten glossies were spread across the floor. We bent to look at them without touching anything. They were photos of a man with half his head blown away. Like the first set of photos, they were enlarged to hide the victim's identity. My first thought, of course, was of Carl Rosen.

'Do you recognize him?' Tank asked.

'No.'

Tank closed the front door and gave me a gun. 'Stay here while I check the rest of the apartment.' Moments later he was back. 'No one here. No more photos that I can see. I didn't go through your drawers.'

'Okay,' I said, 'here's what we do. We leave these photos exactly where they are. We try not to disturb any prints that might have been left. I pack as fast as possible and we get the hell out. When we're ready to board I'll call Morelli. If I call him now I'll have to stay for questioning and we'll never make the plane.'

'Works for me,' Tank said.

Ten minutes later I was out of the apartment, a change of clothes and essential make-up in a tote bag slung over my shoulder. We left my car in the lot and took Tank's SUV.

Connie lived in the Burg, so she was next on the pickup list. We beeped once when we pulled to the curb and Connie hustled out to us. Connie's house was a narrow single family, similar to my parents' duplex, but half of Connie's house had been chopped away. Vito Grecci used to live in the adjoining half house. Vito was a Mob bagman who came in with a light bag one time too many. Next day Vito's house mysteriously caught fire and Vito turned up in the Camden landfill. Fortunately for Connie, the fire didn't go beyond the brick firewall between the two adjoining houses. Connie bought Vito's fire-gutted half at a bank auction, tore the trashed house down, and never rebuilt. Connie liked having the empty lot. She put a big free-standing pool with a wraparound cedar deck in the newly created side yard. And she set up a shrine to the Virgin for sparing her house.

Lula lived on the other side of Hamilton, down by the train station. There wasn't a lot of money in the neighborhood, but year after year it held its own. Lula rented a tiny two-room apartment on the second floor of a small house. The house was gray clapboard with touches of Victorian trim. Last year the owner painted the trim pink. In a weird way it seemed just right for Lula.

Lula was on the curb waiting when we drove down her street. She had two huge suitcases with her, a big leather purse hung on her shoulder, and she was holding a large canvas tote.

Tank smiled. 'I bet they're all filled with pork chops.'

'We're only staying overnight,' I told Lula when she climbed into the backseat next to Connie.

'I know that, but I like to be prepared. And I couldn't decide what to wear. I got a whole suitcase filled with shoes. You can't go to Vegas without a change of shoes. How many shoes did you bring?' Lula asked me.

'The shoes I'm wearing and sneakers.'

'How about you?' she asked Connie.

'Four pairs of shoes,' Connie said.

'Dog,' Lula said to Tank. 'How many shoes you got?'

Tank looked at Lula in the rear-view mirror and didn't say anything.

Lula turned and checked out the luggage in the back of the SUV. 'I don't even see any Tank suitcases,' Lula said. 'Where's your suitcases?'

'Tank hasn't got any suitcases,' I said. 'Tank's traveling light.'

'Where's he keep his extra tighty whiteys?' Lula wanted to know.

Tank cut another look at Lula. 'I don't wear tighty whiteys,' he said.

'You *devil*!' Lula yelled. 'I bet you go commando.'

Lula and Connie fanned themselves in the backseat. Tank kept his eyes on the road, but I could see him smiling.

An hour later, we were in the terminal, standing in line. Seventy-three people in front of us. An airline employee was going person to person, suggesting electronic ticket holders use the automatic ticketing machines. We looked over at the machines with flocks of people gathered around them.

'I don't know,' Lula said. 'Those people trying to use those machines look pissed off. Don't look to me like they're having a whole lot of luck getting tickets out of those machines. Looks to me like after they waste some time they give up and get back in line over here.'

We sent Connie over to investigate and we stayed in line. After a couple minutes Connie came back. 'I think they're just decoys,' Connie said. 'I never saw anybody have any luck getting a ticket out of them.'

'I bet I know,' Lula said. 'You go over there and try to get a ticket and you give them your name and address. And then you don't get a ticket, but you get put on some list for junk mail and telephone solicitors. I bet the airlines make money selling those lists. I bet they get extra on account of they're lists of gullible people who'll buy anything. You didn't give them your name and address, did you, Connie?'

'That's ridiculous,' Connie said. And because she was

snippy when she said it, we all knew she gave the machine her name and address.

Forty-five minutes later, we got to the counter and got ticketed. Lula checked two of her bags. Tank didn't have any bags. I carried my single tote bag with me. Connie had one small suitcase on rollers, which she checked.

'We're on our way now,' Lula said. 'Boy, this is gonna be fun. Hold on. What are we doing in another line?'

'This is the line to go through the security check,' I told her.

'Say what?'

We inched our way along again. I had a low-grade headache from the terminal noise and the tedium and I had a backache from an hour of carrying the tote on my shoulder. Twenty minutes ago I'd dropped the tote onto the floor and now I kicked it along ahead of me. I suspected I was growing pale and in another twenty minutes I'd look like I'd spent fifteen years at TriBro testing nuts and bolts.

I was first in line. Lula stood behind me. Then Connie. Tank was in line behind Connie. We showed our tickets. We flashed our photo IDs. I approached the conveyor belt leading to the scanner. I placed my tote and my purse on the belt.

A security attendant asked me to place my shoes on the belt as well. I looked down at the strappy sandals I'd put on first thing this morning. Brown leather and not a single part of the shoe thicker than an eighth of an inch with the exception of the slim wood stacked stiletto heel, which was a quarter of an inch. Guess security thought I had a bomb in the shoe. Bombs must frequently be hidden in women's strappy sandals.

I took the shoes off and shuffled barefoot along the filthy floor, through the metal detector. I didn't set the detector off but the security attendant told me I was a random female, so I was pulled aside and asked to stand spread eagle. I supposed they thought I had box cutters hidden under my skintight, slightly see-through white stretchy shirt. I was wanded and released. My shoes were returned to me after careful scrutiny.

An attendant in rubber gloves extracted all the items from my tote. Two pairs of bikini panties, a pair of jeans, two little white T-shirts, white socks, sneakers, a travel box of tampons (just in case), hair spray, roller brush, assorted cosmetics. Forty or fifty people passing by admired the panties and a couple women suggested a different brand of tampon.

The items were returned to my bag and I was told I could continue on my way. Lula was causing a scene behind me. She had to go through the same routine and they found fried chicken in her purse.

'You're not allowed to take unpackaged food past security,' the attendant said to Lula.

'What am I supposed to eat?' Lula wanted to know. 'I'm on a diet to be a supermodel. I need this fried chicken. Suppose they don't feed me on the plane?'

'There are kiosks by the gate that sell food,' Lula was told.

I looked at the fried chicken displayed on the examining table. A leg and a breast. I guess security was on the lookout for chicken leg bombs.

'I don't like this,' Lula said, shouldering her bags. 'Had to take my shoes off, my jacket off, got felt up under my bra clip. Had to take my belt off. And look at this, I can't button the top snap on my stretch pants and now everybody knows. This here's been a humiliating experience. And on top of it all they took my chicken.'

Connie had breezed through without a hitch. 'That's the way it is now,' Connie said. 'You want to be safe, right? This is just a small thing to keep us safe.'

'Shut up,' Lula said. 'I hate people who don't get searched.' Her eyes were wild and her lower lip was jutting out. 'I'm feeling a lot of anxiety,' Lula said. 'If this was supposed to make me feel safe it isn't working. All I can think of now is terrorists. I wasn't thinking of terrorists before. I need some ham. Where's the place they sell ham?'

It was announced that our plane was boarding and Tank

still hadn't cleared security. I knew he didn't have weapons on him. He'd locked everything in the truck when we parked. They brought a dog in and two armed guards moved closer. Apparently they were picking up traces of explosives on his shoes and clothes. Wow, big surprise there. He had his identification displayed, including a license to carry, but security was having none of it.

He cut his eyes to me and I sent him a blank-faced look back. No way was I going to come to his rescue. I wasn't taking any chances on guilt by association. I was afraid the airport gestapo would haul my ass off to a back room and give me a body-cavity search.

I grabbed Lula and pulled her along. Connie followed. We only had a couple minutes until boarding.

'What about Tank?' Lula asked.

'He'll catch up with us.' Maybe.

We got to the gate and Lula was wide-eyed, looking everywhere. 'I don't see no kiosk with fried chicken,' she said. 'I just see doughnuts and ice cream and bagels and big pretzels. I can't eat none of that food. Where's the friggin' meat?'

'Maybe we'll get something on the plane,' I said. 'We'll be in the air over dinnertime, so maybe we'll get some dinner.' Yeah, right. If we were flying first class we might get a bag of peanuts.

We were seated three across, six rows back in coach. Lula was on the aisle. I sat next to her. Tank's seat was empty. Connie sat on the other side of the aisle.

I called Morelli and told him about the photos.

'And here's the thing,' I said to Morelli. 'I'm sort of on a plane. Singh is in Vegas and I'm going out to apprehend him. So I was thinking maybe you could just let yourself in and, uh, take charge.'

Silence.

'Joe?'

'This is the sort of thing Ranger usually takes.'

'He has a problem with the state of Nevada.'

'Okay, let me rerun this,' Morelli said. 'You went home to pack and you found more snuff photos. Then you drove to the airport and waited until you were boarded before calling me so it was impossible for me to bring you back to Trenton.'

'Yup. That's about it.'

The conversation deteriorated pretty quickly after that, so I said goodbye and shut my phone off.

The plane filled and the usual announcements were made. No Tank. I was feeling a little worried without my bodyguard. I had Connie and Lula with me. I liked Connie and Lula, but I suspected they were more liability than asset.

The flight attendants closed the doors and the plane began taxiing. Lula was singing with her headset on and her eyes shut. Connie was talking to the woman next to her.

All right, calm down, I told myself. Probably flying to Vegas was safer than staying in Trenton. Tank would get the next plane and everything would be fine. If I'd stayed with Tank I wouldn't be on the plane. I would have had to call Morelli and he would have insisted I return to Trenton.

Minutes after taking off it was announced that no food or beverages would be served. 'What about peanuts?' Lula yelled out. 'Don't we even get any freakin' peanuts?' Lula turned to me. 'I want to get off this plane. I'm hungry and I'm uncomfortable. And look at the seat in front of me. It's all ripped. How am I supposed to have confidence when they can't even keep their seats sewed up? I bet some terrorist was practicing on that seat.'

I put my finger to my eye.

'You getting that nervous eye twitch back?' Lula asked. 'It's from this plane, isn't it? I feel nervous, too. I'm just a bundle of nerves.'

'It's from *you*,' I said. 'Put your headset back on and listen to your music.'

An hour into the flight Lula was fidgeting again. 'I smell coffee,' she said. 'I bet they're gonna give us coffee. Probably they feel bad about treating us like a bunch of cows and they're gonna hand out coffee.' She sniffed the air. 'Hey, I smell *real food*. I smell something cooking.' She hung over the armrest and looked up the aisle at the front of the plane. 'It's not first class,' she said. 'I can see into first class and they're not getting any food, either.'

Now I was smelling it. Definitely coffee. And maybe a tomato sauce and pasta dish. And cookies baking!

'It's like there's ghosts up there,' Lula said. 'I haven't seen a flight attendant walk down the aisle since we took off. It's like they vanished and their ghosts are cooking. I'm dying here. I'm starving. I'm getting weak.'

Connie looked over. 'What's going on?'

'I smell coffee,' Lula said. 'I must be hallucinating from hunger.'

'Maybe the flight attendants are making coffee for the pilots,' Connie said.

'I don't like the sound of that,' Lula said. 'That sounds like an emergency. Like the pilots are tired. Just my luck I get on a plane with a pilot who was up all night. I'm going to be really pissed off if he falls asleep and we crash and we all die and it's before I get to Vegas.'

Connie went back to her magazine, but Lula was still leaning over the armrest into the aisle. 'I can see them!' Lula said. 'It's the flight attendants. Someone pulled the curtain aside and I can see the flight attendants eating. They're having coffee and fresh-baked cookies. Can you freaking believe it? They're not even going to offer any to us.'

I was starting to think crashing and dying might be the way to go. Compared to another two hours in the air, crashing and dying held some appeal.

Lula's eyes were slitty and her forehead was scrunched up. She reminded me of a bull pawing the ground, nostrils flaring, shaggy head steaming. 'I'm not calling them flight attendants anymore,' Lula said. 'I'm calling them stewardesses. See how they like that.'

'Keep it down,' Connie said. 'Maybe they've been working all day and they didn't get a chance to eat.'

'*I've* been working all day,' Lula said. '*I* didn't get a chance to eat. You see anybody feeding me? I guess not. Look at me. I'm beside myself. I feel like the Hulk. Like I'm getting all swollen up with frustration.'

'Well, take it easy,' I said. 'You'll burst something.'

'You know what this is?' Lula said. 'This here's plane rage.'

'Plane rage isn't allowed. It got taken off the allowed activities list along with eating. If you make a scene they'll haul you off in leg irons.'

'I'm tired of being strapped in here, too,' Lula said. 'This seat belt's too tight and it's giving me gas.'

'Anything else?'

'There's no movie.'

* * *

When we landed at Chicago I positioned myself between Lula and the flight attendants.

'Keep your head down and walk,' I told Lula. 'Don't look at them. Don't talk to them. Don't grab any of them by the throat. We need to get on the next plane. Just keep thinking about Vegas.'

Our connecting flight was ten gates down. We started walking and almost immediately we hit fast food. Lula hurried over and ordered seven double cheeseburgers. She threw the buns away and ate the rest.

'I'm impressed,' I said to Lula. 'You're really sticking to this diet.' Hard to believe she was going to lose weight on it, but at least she was trying.

An hour later our row was called to board and Lula, Connie, and I got in line. We reached the gate and I was pulled aside to be searched. Random female.

'Step over here,' the security attendant said. 'And take your shoes off.'

I looked down at the sandals. 'What could you possibly be looking for in these sandals?' I asked.

'It's standard procedure.'

'I've already gone through this at Newark!'

'Sorry. You're going to have to take your shoes off if you want to get on the plane.'

'Uh-oh,' Lula said to me. 'Your face is getting red. Remember about getting to Vegas. Just take the freakin' shoes off.'

'It's not like it's personal,' Connie said. 'You should be happy security precautions are in place.'

'Easy for you to say,' I told her. 'You're not the one getting picked on. You're not the one getting singled out *for a second time*. Your tampons and panties aren't getting pawed through.' I stared down at the shoes. There wasn't any way to hide a weapon in them, but I thought I could do some pretty good damage if I hit the security idiot in the head with one. Spike heel directly into the eyeball, I thought. I visualized the bleeding eyeball falling out of the woman's head and felt much more calm. I stepped out of my sandals and waited peacefully for them to be scrutinized.

When we were seated on the plane Lula turned to me. 'You know, sometimes you can be real scary. I don't know what you were thinking back there when you took those shoes off, but all the hair stood up on the back of my neck.'

'I had airport rage.'

'Fuckin' A,' Lula said.

Lula had airport rage when we landed and her luggage wasn't there.

* * *

Connie had us booked into the Luxor. It was on the Strip, and because the bail bonds conferences were held there every year we got good rates.

'Look at this,' Lula said, head tipped back, taking it all in. 'It's a freaking pyramid. It's like being in some big-ass Egyptian tomb. I *love* this. I'm ready to gamble. Outta my way. I'm looking for the slots. Where's the blackjack tables?'

I didn't know where Lula's energy came from. I'd exhausted myself trying to stay calm while mentally maiming airport employees, screaming kids, and security personnel.

'I'm going to bed,' I told Lula. 'We need to get an early start tomorrow, so don't stay out too late.'

'I can't believe I'm hearing this. You're in Vegas and you're going to bed? Unh uh, girlfriend. I don't think so.'

'I don't gamble. I'm not good at it.'

'You can play slots. There's nothing to slots. You put your money in and you push the button.'

'I'm feeling hot for the craps,' Connie said. 'I'm going to drop my suitcase off in the room and then I'm going to hit the craps tables.'

'You see?' Lula said to me. 'You don't come with, I'm gonna be all alone on account of Connie's gonna play craps.'

Lula had a point. Maybe it wasn't a good idea to have Lula all alone in Vegas. 'Okay,' I said. 'I'll tag along, but I'm not playing. I don't know what I'm doing and I always lose.'

'You gotta play once,' Lula said. 'It wouldn't be right if you came to Vegas and didn't even play one slot. I bet there's even a law that says you gotta play a slot.'

Fifteen minutes later, we were checked into our room. We all applied fresh lipstick, and we were ready to roll.

'Look out, Vegas, here I come,' Lula said, closing the door behind us.

'I'm wearing my lucky shoes,' Connie said, leading the way down the hall. 'I can't lose in my lucky shoes.'

It was the first time I'd ever walked any distance behind Connie and I was knocked over by the sight in front of me. Connie was a small Italian version of Mae West. Her hips were big and round and her boobs were big and round. And when Connie walked everything was in motion. Connie swung her ass down the hall. Connie was a *broad*. Connie belonged in a gangster movie set in Chicago during Prohibition.

We got to the elevator and the three of us stood waiting for the doors to open, cackling and preening in front of the hall mirror. We stepped into the elevator, went down one floor, and two guys got on. One was about five foot ten, had a big beer belly, and looked to be in his sixties. The other was average build, early forties, and was short enough that his eyes were level with my breasts. They were both dressed in tight white jumpsuits with bell-bottoms and big stand-up collars. The jumpsuits were decorated with sequins and glittered under the elevator lights. They had huge rings on their fingers and shoe-polish-black pompadour hairdos with long sideburns. They were wearing name tags. The big guy was named Gus and the little guy was named Wayne.

'We're Elvis impersonators,' the little guy said.

'No shit, Sherlock,' Lula said.

'We're part of a convention. There are fourteen hundred Elvis impersonators here at the hotel.'

'We just got here,' Lula said. 'We're going down to play some slots.'

'We're going to the show,' Gus said. 'We hear Tom Jones is singing in the lounge.'

Lula's eyes got the size of duck eggs and popped out of her eye sockets. 'Tom Jones! Are you shitting me? I *love* Tom Jones.'

'You should come with us,' Wayne said. 'We wouldn't mind having a couple chicks tagging along, right, Gus?'

Lula looked down at little Wayne. 'Listen up, Shorty,' she said. 'I don't do that patronizing, sexist chick shit.'

'We gotta say things like that,' Wayne told her. 'We're Elvis impersonators. We're Vegas, baby.'

'Oh yeah, I guess I could see that. Sorry,' Lula said.

The elevator hit the casino floor and we all got out and

hustled across the casino to the lounge. Me, Connie, Lula, and two over-the-hill Elvis impersonators. We reached the lounge and were stopped by a crush of people waiting to get in.

'Oh man,' Lula said. 'Look at this crowd. We're not gonna get in.'

'They always let Elvis in,' the big guy said, and he started bumping people out of the way with his belly. 'Uh, s'cuze me. The King's comin' through,' he'd say. And then he'd sort of snarl and curl his lip the way Elvis used to.

We were packed up behind him, moving in his wake. All of us getting excited about seeing Tom Jones, willing to step on a few toes to do it. Gus got us a position close to the stage, off to the side. The room lights were dim and the stage was washed in red light. A band was playing. We ordered drinks and Tom Jones was introduced.

The minute Jones came onstage Lula went ape-shit. Lula didn't care about anything but Tom Jones. 'Hey, Tom, honey, look over here,' she yelled out. 'Look at Lula!'

All around us women were throwing room keys and panties onto the stage. And then from the corner of my eye I caught sight of Lula pitching a giant hot-pink satin thong at Tom Jones. It was the biggest thong I'd ever seen. It was a King Kong thong. It hit Tom Jones square in the face. *Wap!*

'Holy crap,' Connie said.

Tom Jones staggered back a step, snagged the thong from off his face, looked at it, and forgot the words to the song he was singing. The band was playing, but Tom Jones was just standing there staring at the thong.

'Maybe I should throw my bra, too,' Lula said.

'*No!*' Connie and I said, worried Tom Jones would go into cardiac arrest at the sight. 'Not a good idea. Overkill.'

Tom Jones snapped out of his coma, stuffed the thong into his tux pocket, and went back to singing.

'I don't think Tom Jones looks all that good,' Connie said to me. 'He looks different somehow. Like he's had a face-lift that went wrong.'

'And he's sort of fat,' I said. 'And he can't sing anymore.'

'That's blasphemous to say about Tom Jones,' Lula said. 'You can't go dissin' Tom Jones.'

Wayne leaned across Lula. 'It's not Tom Jones. I thought you knew that. It's a Tom Jones impersonator. They're having a convention here, too.'

'What?' Lula yelled. 'I gave my underpants to an impostor?'

'He's pretty good, though,' Gus said. 'He's got a lot of the moves down pretty good.'

'I want my underpants back,' Lula shouted to the stage. 'I don't go giving away perfectly good underpants to impostors. You got my underpants under false pretenses. And you can't even sing! I bet these two Elvis impersonators could sing better than you.'

The guy on the stage stopped singing, shaded his eyes against the lights with his hand, and squinted over at us. 'Elvis impersonators? I've got some goddamn Elvis impersonators at my show?'

'Uh oh,' Wayne said. 'Elvis impersonators and Tom Jones impersonators don't get along.'

A low rumble went through the crowd. *Elvis impersonators*, they were grumbling. *The nerve!*

'Get them,' someone shouted. 'Get the dirty lousy Elvis impersonators.'

Someone reached for little Wayne, and Lula stepped in. 'Hold on here,' she said. 'We came with these guys. They're good guys. They got us in here.'

'Get the Elvis impersonators and their *bitches*,' someone yelled. 'The Elvis impersonators have *bitches*!'

The room was packed, and we were getting jostled and shoved. A Cher impersonator with a beard and mustache reached for Connie. Connie cold-cocked him and he went to the floor like a sack of sand. After that it was bedlam.

Lula took to the stage to wrestle Tom Jones for her underpants, and Connie and I scrambled after Lula to help with the thong retrieval. We were getting pelted with beer nuts and wasabi peas, and I could see casino security at the door, trying to make its way through the crowd. Lula ripped the thong out of Tom Jones's hands and we all ran backstage.

'Which way out?' I asked a greasy-haired guy in the wings.

The greasy-haired guy pointed to a door and we all crashed through it, ran down a hall, through another door, and found ourselves back on the casino floor.

Connie smoothed out her skirt and felt to see if she had any beer nuts stuck in her hair. 'That was fun,' she said. 'I'm going to go play craps now.'

'Yeah,' Lula said, stuffing her thong into her purse. 'I'm hitting the slots. I'm gonna start there.'

'Wait a minute,' I said to Lula. 'Where'd you get the thong?'

'I had it in my purse,' Lula said. 'I read somewhere that you should carry emergency undies when you travel.' Lula squinted at my hair. 'You got something green slimed in your hair,' she said. 'It looks like someone got you with one of those fancy drinks.'

Great. 'I'm going back to the room,' I said. 'I'm going to wash my hair and go to bed. I've had enough excitement for one day.'

'What about the slots?' Lula wanted to know.

'Tomorrow.' Maybe.

* * *

At seven in the morning Lula and Connie still hadn't returned to the room. I pulled on jeans and a Lakewood Blue Claws T-shirt that had the message *Got Crabs?* printed on the front. I covered my hair with a baseball cap and went downstairs to look for Lula. I found her in the café eating breakfast with Connie. Lula had about two dozen scrambled eggs and five pounds of sausage links on her plate. Connie had coffee.

Lula looked wired and not much different from everyday Lula. Connie looked like she'd died and come back from the dead. Connie's black hair was completely frazzled, sticking out at odd places. Her mascara had smudged, making the bags under her eyes more pronounced. Most shocking of all . . . she was without lipstick. I'd never seen Connie without lipstick.

I took a seat and I snitched a sausage link from Lula.

'What time is it?' Connie asked.

'Seven-thirty,' I told her.

'Day or night?'

'Day.'

The cafe was located on the perimeter of the casino floor. That's the way it always is in a casino. Everything opens to the floor. The casino was business as usual, but the attendance was light. The tables were populated mostly by bedraggled men in shirtsleeves. Leftovers from the night. The slots had a more alert crowd. Early risers, getting a jump on the day. I wasn't much of a gambler. But I liked the flash and color of the casino. I liked the neon lights, the bells and whistles, and the *ka-ching* of money being won and lost.

'Las Vegas never closes,' Lula said. 'Can you believe it? And I haven't been out of the hotel yet, but there's supposed to be an Eiffel Tower out there and the Brooklyn Bridge and all kinds of shit.'

'What did you do all night?'

'I started with the slots,' Lula said, 'but I wasn't having any luck there, so I went over to the blackjack tables. I did pretty good and then I did really bad. And here I am . . . broke. Good thing Vinnie's buying me breakfast.'

Connie had her head down on the table. 'I lost all my money. I drank too much. And I lost my shoes.'

We all looked under the table. Sure enough, Connie didn't have any shoes.

'I left them someplace,' Connie said. 'I don't know where.'

'That's not even the best part,' Lula said to me. 'Ask Connie about the photograph.'

Connie pulled a cardboard framed photo out of her big leather shoulder bag. It was a picture of Connie and a short guy in a powder blue tuxedo. The short guy had sideburns and an Elvis hairdo. Connie was holding a bouquet of flowers. 'I think I might have gotten married to an Elvis impersonator,' Connie said, dragging herself to her feet. 'I'm going to bed. Wake me up when you get Singh and I'll do the paperwork for the locals.'

Lula watched Connie stagger away. 'I wouldn't hardly recognize her without lipstick,' Lula said. 'She sat down and I didn't know who she was at first.'

'We have to snatch Singh today,' I said to Lula. 'Are you going to be up for it?'

'Damn straight I'm up for it. I'm just getting started. I'm like that Energizer Rabbit dude. How we gonna get this guy?'

'Singh applied for a job at a small casino downtown. My contact's name is Louis Califonte. He's the casino manager. Cone said I should call Califonte at nine o'clock. I'm hoping we can get Singh to come into the casino. It'll be easier to apprehend him there.'

'Get Singh to come in tonight so I can have the day to go shopping. I gotta see the talking statues at Caesars. And we gotta stay to see the fountains at the Bellagio. It wouldn't be right if we left before we saw the fountains.'

Shopping would be fun, but there were other things on my mind. Photos of dead people. Carl Rosen missing. Red roses and white carnations. Plus I've never made an out-of-state apprehension and I was counting on Tank's help.

I ate a second sausage and I punched Ranger's number into my phone.

'Have you heard from Tank?' I asked Ranger.

'Tank's here. By the time he got security straight he couldn't get a flight out. The earliest flight we could get him on is today's four o'clock.'

'Probably we don't need him. Connie has me on a seven-thirty out of Vegas. I don't expect problems. Connie will get me the paperwork necessary to bring Singh back restrained and she'll make the arrangements with the local police.' Now if I just felt half as confident as I sounded, I'd be in good shape. 'Unfortunately the hardware's packed in Lula's suitcase. And the airlines lost both her bags.'

'I'll have everything you need delivered to your room by noon.'

'Did Tank tell you about the photos?'

'Yeah. And I heard from Morelli, too. He's not happy.'

'Did Carl Rosen ever show up?'

'You don't want to know about Rosen, babe.'

I blew out a sigh and disconnected. Even at seven in the morning, smoke hung in the air on the casino floor. I squinted into the haze and wondered if they were matching the new photos to Rosen. I called Morelli at home. When he didn't pick up I realized it was ten on the East Coast and I tried his cell.

'Yeah,' Morelli answered. Halfway through the morning and sounding pissed off.

'Guess who?'

Silence.

I grimaced at Lula.

'He should chill,' Lula said, shoveling eggs. 'We're working hard here. We got a job to do.'

'I heard that,' Morelli said. 'Tell Lula I've got an outstanding arrest from when she was on the street.'

'Tell me about the photos and Carl Rosen.'

'They're working on the photos now, but at first glance they look like a match. We found Rosen late last night. Someone dumped him at the corner of Laurel Drive and River Road. He had a white carnation stuffed down his pants and you've seen the photos, so I don't have to describe his head.'

'Any suspects?'

'A few. No arrests, if that's what you're asking.'

I wasn't looking forward to returning to Trenton. It felt safer in Vegas. Far away from Carl Rosen and the carnation freak. I could easily stay here and sit by the pool and do a little shopping and tell Vinnie the apprehension was more complicated than expected.

'Connie tells me you have a flight out at seven-thirty tonight,' Morelli said. 'Do you already have Singh in custody?'

'No. If I have problems today, Connie will change the flight.'

There was a moment's pause. 'Are you expecting problems?'

'I'm *hoping* for problems. If there are problems I might get to stay another day. Maybe another week. It feels safer here than it does in Trenton.'

I disconnected and waited while Lula ate the last sausage.

'From the conversation I just heard between you and Ranger, I'm guessing they didn't deliver my bags yet,' Lula said. 'So I'm going shopping. I gotta get some clothes. All that dumb-ass airline gave me was a toothbrush.'

'I thought you gambled all your money away.'

'Yeah, but if I shop here in the hotel it goes on our room bill and Vinnie pays. It's only right he pays anyway, on account of this is a business disaster.'

I returned to the room and took a shower while Lula went shopping. We were all packed together to save some money. The room had an Egyptian motif and two queen-size beds. Connie was sound asleep with a pillow over her face. She didn't seem to be bothered by my presence, so I ordered room service coffee and a bakery basket and put a call in to Lou Califonte.

Lou suggested he call Singh and ask him to come in to

discuss a job. I was expecting a handcuff delivery sometime this morning, so I asked that Singh be given an early afternoon appointment. Califonte said he'd call back as soon as everything was in place.

I could see the mountains from my room. They were shimmering in the morning heat, smokey blue, lost behind haze. The valley floor leading to the mountains was flat desert broken by roads and strip malls and the backside of the Strip. I could see the billboard and neon sign for the Rio Hotel and Casino.

There was no place else on earth like Vegas. Even Disney couldn't compete with this. I'd been to Vegas twice before. Several years ago and then last year for the PBUS conference. I was always shocked at how fast Vegas grew. Trailer parks, McMansions, artificial lakes and fountains, bigger and more spectacular hotels and malls. They erupted overnight. It was magic. Good old-fashioned American capitalist magic.

It was close to nine when Lula came bustling in. 'Just give me a minute to jump in the shower and get dressed and I'm ready to roll,' Lula said. 'This here's a shopping paradise. They got stuff here that I didn't even know existed. Everything's Spandex and sequins. It's a retired 'ho's dream come true.'

By ten we were in a rental Taurus, heading out of town.

Lula was reading the map, directing me to the address Singh had given Califonte on his job application. I wasn't making the bust at Singh's house, but I wanted to see it anyway. I wanted to make sure nothing weird was going on.

Much of the sprawl in Vegas is given up to high-end gated golf course communities. We were deep into the sprawl, but we were on the wrong side of the tracks. We were driving past block after block of small dusty Southwest houses, not a ghetto situation of graffiti and uncollected trash, more an area of neglect by necessity. Screen doors were askew, yards were hardscrabble weed and desert dirt, cars had seen a lot of hot, dry miles.

Connie had checked on Singh's address before we left and found he was living with a woman named Susan Lu, a cocktail waitress at Caesars. So here was the Susan in Singh's life. I was guessing Singh met Lu on his business trip, communicated with her by email, and decided to move in.

The house was typical of the neighborhood. It was a modest single-story stucco bungalow. A Joshua tree grew in the front yard. The small backyard was fenced. I didn't see Boo, but then most of the yard wasn't visible from the street.

'Sure would be tempting to knock on his door and drag his bony ass out here,' Lula said. 'Then we could lock him in the trunk and go shopping.'

'We aren't that good,' I said to Lula. 'We don't even have

handcuffs. I'm not taking a chance on screwing this up.'

My cell phone rang. It was Lou Califonte. He was calling to tell me that he hadn't been able to get in touch with Singh. He'd spoken to Susan Lu and Lu told him Singh went out early this morning and hadn't yet returned. Lu expected Singh back by lunchtime. Califonte set up a tentative meeting for two o'clock.

'Don't you hate that?' Lula said. 'Right in the middle of our time here. How are we supposed to have any fun like that? I hear Siegfried and Roy got their tigers on display. How many chances you think we're gonna get to see Siegfried's tiger?'

'Just help me get Singh back to the hotel room and you can go off for a couple hours. We don't have to leave for the airport until six-thirty.'

'Yeah, it's not like I gotta check luggage.'

We returned to the room a little after twelve. Connie was still asleep with the pillow over her face. There was a small sealed cardboard box on the coffee table. The delivery from Ranger. And there was a small floral arrangement next to it. Red roses and white carnations. The card with the flowers read: *You're one step behind me again. Singh's been eliminated. The game continues.*

I was totally dumbstruck.

'Hey,' Lula said. 'Are you okay?'

I took a step back, bumped into a chair, and sat down hard. I went lightheaded for a moment. I hadn't been expecting this. I'd been caught totally off guard. The killer knew I was in Vegas. Even worse, he had to be here, too. I was pretty sure he was telling me he'd killed Singh and, according to Susan Lu, Singh was alive this morning.

'I think he's dead,' I said.

'Who's dead?'

'Singh.'

I'd dropped the card on the floor. Lula picked it up and read it. 'I don't get it,' she said.

'Just give me a second and I'll explain it to you.' I found my way to the bathroom and I stood there until I was sure I wasn't going to throw up. Lula was at the bathroom door, watching. I put a hand up. 'I'm getting there,' I said. 'I was just caught by surprise and it knocked the air out of me.' I left the bathroom, walked to the desk, and reread the card. The card was standard hotel stock. The flowers had been sent through the hotel.

I called the concierge and waited on hold while he traced the flowers down. He returned to tell me the order had been phoned in and placed on Carl Rosen's credit card. The hotel wasn't able to access the call origination number.

Ten

Lula was standing over Connie. 'Do you think she's dead? She's not moving under the pillow.'

'Take the pillow off her.'

'Not me. I *hate* dead. If she's dead, I don't want to see.'

I walked over and took the pillow off Connie's face.

Connie opened an eye and looked up at me. 'Did you bring Singh in?'

'No. I think Singh might be dead.'

'Dead or alive,' Connie said. 'It's all the same to me.' She sat up in the bed. 'I can't get any sleep in this hotel. People keep coming in and out delivering stuff. Did you see you got flowers?'

'About the flowers,' I said. And I told them about the carnation killer.

'Holy crap,' Lula said. 'Why didn't you tell me sooner?'

'I didn't know what to say. The whole thing is so bizarre. And the police wanted the details kept from the public while they tried to match the photos to a victim.'

'Hey, I can keep a secret. Look at me. My mouth is zipped,' Lula said.

'You can't keep a secret, ever,' I said. 'You have no sense of secret.'

'That's so not true. I didn't tell you about Joe and Terry Gilman, did I?'

For a couple beats no one in the room said anything. We just stared at each other with our mouths open.

'I didn't say that,' Lula said.

I felt my eyebrows pull together. 'What about Joe and Terry Gilman?'

'You keep doing that and you're going to need Botox,' Lula said.

'Are you talking about the jumping out the window incident?'

'No. I'm talking about the coming out of the motel looking chummy incident.'

'When?'

'I guess it must have been about two weeks ago. It was a Saturday afternoon and I was going shopping at Quaker Bridge and you know how there are a couple motels on Route One that are mostly by the hour? Well, I saw them coming out of one of those skanky motels. It was the one with the blue trim and the wishing well in the front. I almost ran off the road.'

'You're sure it was Joe and Terry?'

'I bet they were doing police business,' Lula said. 'That's why I didn't tell you. I knew you'd get that look that you got now. And you'd get all huffy and make a big thing for nothing.'

I used my fingertips to smooth away the frown line in my forehead. 'I don't get huffy. Do I look huffy?'

'Fuckin' A,' Lula said.

At least she took my mind off the flower freak. It's always nice to have a choice of things to worry about.

'Open the box from Ranger,' I said to Lula. 'I have to call Morelli and tell him about the flowers.'

Morelli answered on a sigh. 'Yeah?'

I meant to start out with the facts about the flowers, but the wiring between my brain and my mouth got crossed and I started with Terry Gilman. 'So,' I said to Morelli as my opening line, 'have you seen Terry Gilman lately?'

'I saw her yesterday. Why?'

'You are such a jerk.'

There was a beat of silence where I figured Morelli was staring down at his shoe and counting his lucky stars he never married me. 'That's what you called to tell me? I'm a jerk?'

'I called to tell you I just got a floral arrangement. Red roses and white carnations.' I read the card to him. 'The flowers were ordered through the hotel and placed on Carl

Rosen's credit card. You might want to remind the Rosen family to cancel Carl's cards. It looks like the killer lifted Rosen's MasterCard.'

'He's loving this,' Morelli said. 'This is like a chess game. And he's winning. He's taking your pieces one by one.'

'This particular piece was with Susan Lu first thing this morning and hasn't been heard from since. I don't suppose you have Bart Cone in custody?'

'Not in custody, but he's being watched. He's not in Vegas. I'm almost sure of it.'

'What about the other Cones?'

'All three were in for questioning late yesterday afternoon. It's Saturday so they're not at work, but I'll make sure they're tracked down and accounted for.'

'I'm going back out to talk to Susan Lu,' I said to Morelli. 'I'll call you if anything turns up.'

'I'd feel better if you just stayed in your hotel room until your plane. Let the Vegas police talk to Susan Lu.'

'I'll be fine. Ranger had a care package dropped off for me. And I've got Lula and Connie to watch my back.'

'Oh *shit*,' Morelli said.

'This is like Christmas,' Lula said, opening the box from Ranger. 'I love getting presents. Look at this. Pepper spray. One for each of us. And handcuffs. Not the cheap-ass kind, either. These are good-quality cuffs. And leg shackles. And a thirty-eight Smith and Wesson snubby revolver. Guess that would be yours since I shoot a Glock. And here's a box of rounds for your thirty-eight.' Lula pawed through the packing. 'Hey, there's no Glock. Where's *my* gun?' She dumped the box upside down and a note and a stun gun fell out.

I took the note and left the stun gun for Lula.

Call if you need help. I'll come to your room at six to take you to the airport. Erik. His phone number was printed at the bottom of the note.

Lula was reading over my shoulder. 'Who's Erik?'

'Ranger said he was sending hardware to replace what we lost in luggage. It looks like Erik comes with the hardware.'

I loaded the .38 and slipped it into my purse. I stuffed the personal-size pepper spray canister into my jeans pocket, I stuck the cuffs half in and half out of the back of my pants, and then I shrugged into a lightweight zipper-front sweatshirt that was going to make me sweat, but it covered the cuffs. I called to ask that the car be brought around from valet parking.

'I'm going, too,' Connie said. 'Give me five minutes to jump in the shower.'

A half hour later the three of us left the room for the lobby, Lula on one side of me, Connie on the other. Connie had made a phone call to a local bondsman and had arranged for a second arms delivery. As a result, Connie and Lula now wore two guns apiece. They each had a gun at the small of their back and they each had one in their purse. My fear of getting shot by the carnation killer was considerably less than my fear that I'd get shot by Connie or Lula.

'You know what I think?' Lula said in the elevator. 'I think we're an accident waiting to happen.'

I could ask Erik to ride along with us, but I'd had some past experience with Ranger's men and there was no guarantee that Erik would be any less scary than the carnation killer. 'Just keep your eyes open. We'll be fine.'

Connie didn't say anything. Connie had some Mafia skeletons in her closet and Connie took soldiering seriously.

It was after one when we pulled into Susan Lu's driveway. Lula, Connie, and I got out and went to Lu's front door.

Susan Lu was about five feet, four inches with a flat dish face and glossy straight black hair. She looked older than Singh. I placed her somewhere between forty and forty-five. She was surprised to find us on her porch and immediately bristled. Probably we looked like door-to-door missionaries, so I understood the bristle. I looked over her shoulder at a small curly white dog scratching at a baby gate that confined him to the kitchen. Boo.

I identified myself, introduced Lula and Connie, and I

asked if we could come in. Lu said no and we went in anyway. Lu was a lightweight.

I already knew Singh wasn't in the house. The car still wasn't in the driveway. And besides, I was pretty sure he was dead. Still, I asked anyway.

'Is Samuel Singh here?' I asked Susan Lu.

'He isn't,' Lu said. 'He went out first thing this morning for a pack of cigarettes for me and he hasn't returned. He should have been back hours ago. And he isn't answering his cell phone. Men are such shits. Listen, I'd like to chat, but I have to get ready for work and I'm not feeling all that social without my goddamn cigarettes.'

The dog was barking now. *Yap yap yap*. And every time it yapped its little front paws would come off the ground.

'Is that Samuel's dog?'

'Yeah, I don't know what's wrong with it. Usually the little turd just mopes in the corner. I've never seen it trying to get out like this.'

Lula took a step back and nervously shifted foot to foot. God only knows what she had in her purse. Suckling pig, two dozen hamburgers, a twenty-pound turkey.

'Sammy brought the dog with him just to piss off some awful old woman and her daughter. He was boarding with them and he said the old woman was something out of a horror movie. He wanted to take a picture of himself with the dog and send it back to them, but he hasn't gotten around to it. After he gets his picture the dog's going to the pound. Nasty beast.'

I gave Susan Lu my card. 'Tell Samuel to call me when he comes in.'

'Sure.'

Lula, Connie, and I left Lu, got into the car, and I backed out of the driveway. I drove around the block and parked three doors down from Lu, behind a van so we could watch the house.

'You think Singh's gonna show up?' Lula wanted to know.

'Nope.'

'Me, neither.'

'You parking here so you can keep an eye on Lu?'

'Yep.'

'You're waiting for her to leave and then you're gonna snatch the dog, aren't you?'

'Yep.'

Connie was in the backseat, probably reviewing in her mind which of the local bondsmen she'd use to bail us out after we were arrested for breaking and entering.

After fifteen minutes of no air-conditioning, the car started to bake under the desert sun. Lula immediately fell asleep in the heat. She was head back, mouth open. And she was snoring. Loud.

'Holy mother,' Connie said. 'I've never heard anyone snore like this. It's like being locked in a car with a jet engine.'

I gave Lula a shove. 'Wake up. You're snoring.'

'The hell I am,' Lula said. 'I don't snore.' And she went back to snoring.

'I can't take it,' Connie said. 'I've got to get out of the car.'

I joined her and we walked down the street. We were wearing baseball hats and dark glasses but no sunblock and I could feel the sun scorching the exposed skin on my arm.

'Let me run through this,' Connie said. 'Lillian Paressi, Howie at McDonald's, Carl Rosen, and possibly Samuel Singh are all tied to the same serial killer. And now he's targeted you.'

'I don't know about Howie, Carl or Samuel, but Lillian Paressi received red roses and white carnations and a note just before she was killed.'

'Like the flowers and notes you've been getting.'

'Yeah. So I'm guessing he likes to taunt his victims. Likes to get them afraid before he strikes. Some kind of game for him.'

'Are you sure it's a *him*?'

'I'm not sure of anything. In the beginning I suspected Bart Cone, but the police are keeping a close watch on him.

If Cone's still in Trenton and Singh turns up dead, that eliminates Cone from the suspect list.'

When we got back to the car, Lula was still snoring and there were two dogs patiently sitting on the curb by the passenger side door.

'I don't know what's more creepy,' Connie said. 'You getting stalked by a killer or Lula walking around with a purse filled with pork chops. I'm feeling like I'm in Stephen King land.'

It was two o'clock so I called Califonte and asked if Singh was there. Califonte said no, sorry. I gave Califonte my cell number and asked him to call me if Singh showed up.

Connie and I got back into the car and put our fingers in our ears. After five minutes my shirt was soaked and sweat was running down the side of my face. This was the glorious life of a bounty hunter.

'Tell me again why we're sitting here, melting,' Connie said.

'The dog.'

'I need a better reason.'

'There's something about that dog that gives me an estrogen attack. He's small and helpless looking. And those little button eyes! The eyes are so trusting. And he's going to the *pound*. How awful is that? I can't let that happen.'

'So you have to save the dog.'

'He's counting on me.'

'Stephanie to the rescue,' Connie said.

'I could call you a cab,' I said. 'And you could go back to the hotel.'

'No way. I'd have to sit around the pool and get a tan and have half-naked waiters bring me cold drinks. Where's the fun in that when I could be sitting here listening to Lula?'

Susan Lu left the house a little after two. She walked to a bus stop on the far corner. After five minutes a bus appeared and Lu got on.

'Thank God,' Connie said. 'I'm at the end of the line with the snoring and the sweating.'

I gave Lula a shove. 'Wake up. Susan Lu left the house. We can get the dog now.'

Lula squinted at me. 'I feel like my eyes are fried. I'm not as young as I used to be. I can't do this all-night shit any more. And this place is hotter than snot. How can anyone live here?'

I cranked the car over and pulled into Lu's driveway. Lula, Connie, and I got out and walked around to the back kitchen door.

'Door's locked,' Lula said. 'Too bad you have this thing about busting in.'

'This is for a good cause,' I said. 'I suppose we could force the door if we did it really carefully.'

'Hunh,' Lula said. She swung her purse into the window beside the door and shattered the window. 'Oops,' Lula said. 'Guess I accidentally broke a window.' Then she reached in and opened the door.

'Cripes,' Connie said. 'Could you make more noise? Maybe there's someone left in the neighborhood who didn't hear that.'

I tiptoed over the glass shards, scooped up Boo, and handed him to Lula. I quickly walked through the rest of the house. I took Singh's laptop, but found nothing else of interest. I wiped Lula's prints off the doorknob and we left.

'We're like Robin Hood or something,' Lula said. 'We rescued this cute little guy. I feel like singing the Robin Hood theme song.'

We stopped and thought about that for a second.

'Damn,' Lula said. 'It's a stupid theme song.'

We got into the rental Taurus and hightailed it out of the neighborhood. Best not to delay, in case someone confused us with dognappers and called the police. The police might not understand about Robin Hood.

I stopped at a supermarket and bought a dog leash and collar, and a small bag of dog food for Boo. I bought popsicles for Connie and me and two pounds of sliced deli ham for Lula.

I didn't know if dogs were allowed at the Luxor and I didn't think it was worth the hassle to check. I wrapped the dog in my sweatshirt and smuggled him up to the room.

'Isn't this a pisser,' Lula said, going into the room. 'Look at what's here. My luggage. Came just in time to lug it back home.'

'Hopefully they won't lose it this time.'

'Damn right they won't lose it. I'm not flying. I'm done flying. I'm driving home.'

'It'll take you days.'

'I don't care. Nothing you could say would make me get back on a plane. I got the rental car and I'm driving. And I can take Boo. I don't like the idea of handing him over to those airport people.'

Boo was on the floor, snooping around.

'He's a cute little guy,' Lula said. 'I can see why Nonnie wanted him back.'

I had a problem now. There was a small chance that the flowers were a hoax and something other than death had kept Singh from showing for the job interview. I didn't want to take off only to find out down the road that Singh was alive and well in Vegas. I called Morelli and Ranger. Neither had anything to report. I called my family next.

'We're all fine,' Grandma said. 'Except for Albert, who seems to be in labor. That isn't possible, is it?'

When I was a kid my family seemed so stable. I was the flaky kid and my mom was always right, my sister was perfect, my dad was the rock. It hasn't been until recently that I've come to realize nothing is that simple. People are complicated and chock full of problems. That said, my family's problems don't seem so huge. We're a family of plodders. We put one foot in front of the other and keep going forward. And eventually we get someplace. Maybe the place isn't spectacular, but it's a place all the same. And while we're plodding sometimes the problems solve themselves, sometimes the problems get pushed low on the list of priorities and get forgotten, and sometimes the problems cause little pockets of irritation in our bowels.

Mostly we solve our problems with cake.

I was hungry and I would have liked to order room service, but I was afraid Boo would be discovered. Room service is third on my list of favorite things. Birthday cake is first. Sex is second. And then room service. Room service is better than having a mother. You order what you want and they bring it to your door, guilt free, no strings attached. Pretty amazing, huh?

'I'm going out for something to eat,' I said. 'And I'm

going to check on Susan Lu. I want to make sure she really did go to work.'

'I'm with you,' Lula said.

Connie was on her feet. 'Count me in.'

The three Mouseketeers.

We gave Boo a bowl of water and told him to be a good dog. We put the *Do Not Disturb* sign on the door, locked up, and left.

According to Connie's information, Susan Lu worked at Caesars. Caesars was exactly the wrong distance from the Luxor. Too short to feel justified taking a cab. Too long to hoof it in the heat.

We stepped outside and sucked in blast furnace-quality air and Connie made the decision for us.

'I'm not walking,' she said. 'And I'll shoot anyone who tries to make me.'

Caesars is everything a casino should be . . . noisy, smokey, gaudy, and bustling with people who can't wait to throw their money away. And if that isn't enough, it has a terrific shopping center. The waitresses servicing the game tables all wore little toga outfits. Some looked better in their togas than others. I suspected Lu would not look *wowie kazowie* in her toga. We did a casual walk around the room and didn't spot Susan Lu.

'This isn't gonna work,' Lula said. 'It's too big. There's too many of the toga women. And there are cocktail lounges on the sides, too. And restaurants.'

'I don't know how to break this to you,' Connie said, 'but I think we're being followed. You see the guy in black over by the statue of Caesar?'

Lula and I turned and looked.

'Don't look!' Connie hissed.

Lula and I stopped looking.

'You have to be sneaky,' Connie said.

Lula and I did a sneaky look.

'I don't recognize him,' I said.

Connie slid him a sideways glance. 'He was in the lobby of the Luxor when we came through.'

'Probably just a coincidence,' I said.

He was about five feet, ten inches and average build. He wore a black suit, black shirt, and black silk tie. His hair was dark and slicked back behind his ears.

'I bet he's got a purple car with a bobble-head doll on the dash,' Lula said. 'I bet he's a pimp. I guess I know a pimp when I see one. The question is, why would a pimp be following us?'

Connie and I looked at Lula.

'What?' Lula said.

Lula was wearing a skin-tight pink stretchy T-shirt with *sexy* written across her boobs in silver sequins. It had a low scoop neck showing an acre of cleavage and it was tucked into a matching Spandex miniskirt.

'Hey, I'm not the one wearing a shirt asking if you got crabs,' Lula said.

I looked down at my shirt. 'It's for the baseball team in Lakewood. Joe bought it for me.'

'Hunh,' Lula said.

I didn't think the guy in black looked like a pimp. I thought he looked like someone who bought *GQ* and took it seriously. Probably he was from LA and worked in the CAA mailroom.

'Let's go across the room and find a blackjack table,' Connie said to me. 'See if he follows you.'

'Fine, but I can't play blackjack. I'll just stand and watch.'

'That's ridiculous,' Connie said. 'Everyone can play blackjack. All you have to do is count to twenty-one.' Connie was pulling me along by my purse strap. 'I'll have Vinnie bankroll you.'

'*You* play blackjack.'

'That won't work,' Connie said. 'I want to see if he's after you. Maybe he's the carnation guy. This way, you sit down and Lula and I can sort of fade away, all the while keeping our eyes on you. Then we wait to see what he does.'

'Here he comes,' Lula said. 'He's coming along with us. He's trying not to be noticed, but I'm onto him.'

Connie tugged me toward an empty chair. 'Sit,' she said, 'there's an opening at this table.'

'This is a twenty-five-dollar table,' I said. 'Aren't there any loose change tables?'

There were two men and two women already playing at the table. They were drinking and smoking and their faces were without expression. They looked like they knew what they were doing. They'd look at the dealer and tap the table and obviously that meant something. One of the women wanted to double. She lost her chips after that, so I made a mental note not to double.

When the hand was done Connie dropped fifty dollars on the table. The dealer gave me two chips and the fifty bucks got whisked away by the dealer and stuffed into a slot on the table.

Everyone put chips out, so I put one out, too. I looked over my shoulder at Connie. Connie was gone. When I swung my attention back to the table I had two cards face up in front of me. A king and an ace.

'Twenty-one wins,' the dealer said. And he gave me a bunch of chips.

Wow. I won. I didn't even have to do anything.

Everyone else played out their hands and then we all started again with new chips on the table. I put mine out, too. The dealer gave me two cards face up. A six and a jack.

Panic. I had to add. A jack was worth what? Ten? Okay, ten seemed reasonable for a jack. So I had sixteen. I looked around. Everyone was waiting for me to say something.

The dealer asked me if I wanted a card. More panic. I didn't want to go over twenty-one. I had to subtract. I *hate* to subtract. 'Sure,' I said. 'Give me another card.'

The dealer asked me if I was *certain* I wanted another card. 'You have a six showing and *the book* says not to take another card,' the dealer said.

I didn't know what book he was talking about, but all the other players agreed with the dealer and *the book* so I decided not to take a card.

The dealer had a six and a ten on the table. He dealt himself another ten. 'Dealer busts,' he said.

And I got another chip. Hot damn. No wonder people liked to gamble. This was easy.

We started a new game and I got sixteen again with the first two cards. The dealer had a nine showing. I told him I didn't want any more cards. What the hell, it worked the first two times. Now he told me *the book* didn't like that decision. Well, God forbid I should go against *the book*. 'Okeydokey,' I said. 'I'll go with the book and take another card.'

I got dealt a king of hearts.

'Busts,' the dealer said, and he took my chips and my cards.

So much for *the book*.

I played another hand. Lost another chip. Everyone played their hands out and we started over. Connie was nowhere to be seen. The guy in black was behind me, watching me. I could feel him back there. The photo images of shattered skulls popped into my head. The memory of the heat and numbing blackness that followed the hit from the dart washed over me. I felt a panic attack trying to get a toehold.

The dealer wanted to know if I was going to play.

'What?' I asked.

'You need to put a chip in to play.'

I shoved a red chip into my circle.

'Red chips are worth ten,' the dealer said. 'This table has a twenty-five-dollar minimum.'

I pushed a different colored chip at him. The chips had numbers on them, but I was too flustered to make sense of it.

The dealer gave me a ten of spades and a two of hearts. This was easy to add. Twelve. A long way to go to twenty-one, right? I asked for another card. This started a lot of arguing. Apparently *the book* wasn't clear on this one. The dealer gave me a ten of diamonds. Damn! Busted again.

I didn't know exactly how much I had because I was having a hard time adding up all the different colored chips, but I knew I didn't have a lot. One more hand, maybe.

When the new game started I pushed a couple chips into my ring. The dealer gave me a nine of spades and a three of clubs. I bit into my lower lip, unsure what to do, and I felt a hand settle on my shoulder. I turned and looked. It was the guy in black.

'I'm going to help you,' he said.

There was a lot of noise behind me. I heard Lula let out a shriek and the guy in black gasped in surprise, jerked away from me, and went over backward. Everyone at the table stood and gawked, including me.

Lula and the guy in black were on the floor. Lula was ass up, on top of the guy in black. You could hardly see him under the pink Spandex. He was squashed spread eagle under Lula so that only his hands and feet stuck out. Connie was standing on one of his hands.

'Don't freakin' move,' Connie yelled at the poor smushed guy in black.

From what I could see there wasn't much chance of him moving. I wasn't even sure he was still breathing.

Uniformed and plainclothes security instantly appeared and wrestled Lula off the guy in black.

'He was going for a gun,' Lula said. 'He's a killer.'

The guy in black didn't move. He was still on his back,

gasping for air. 'I have identification in my inside jacket pocket,' he said. 'And I think I have a broken back.'

'Can you move your toes?' one of the security guards asked him.

'Yeah.'

'How about your fingers?'

He wiggled the fingers on one hand. Connie was still standing on the other hand.

'Ow,' the guy in black said to Connie.

Connie stepped off his hand. 'Sorry,' she said.

One of the plainclothes men lifted the identification. 'Erik Salvatora. Looks like he's a rent-a-cop.'

'I'm a licensed private investigator and a security specialist,' Salvatora said. 'I'm employed by RangeMan LLC and I was asked to protect Ms Plum while she's in town. God only knows why when she's got Big Bertha and the Bonecrusher with her.'

He was Ranger's man. RangeMan was Ranger's corporate name.

'Hey,' Lula said. 'Watch who you're calling Big Bertha. Nobody tolerates that political incorrectness any more, you little candy ass.'

'This was a terrible misunderstanding,' I told everyone. 'My friends and I didn't realize he was assigned to guard me. My usual bodyguard missed his flight.'

Now they were all wondering who the hell I was that I needed a bodyguard. And that was fine by me because I wanted this to go away. We were all carrying guns, probably illegally. I had no idea what the gun laws were in Nevada.

'I thought he was going for a gun,' Lula said.

Erik struggled to get up. 'I was going for my wallet. I was going to buy her some chips. I was supposed to keep my distance, but I couldn't stand watching her play any more. She's the worst blackjack player I've ever seen.'

'Really sorry,' I said. 'Can we take you to a hospital or something?'

'No! I'll be okay. Probably just a slipped disc and possibly a broken bone or two in my hand.'

'Don't worry about six o'clock,' I called after him. 'I might not be going to the airport.'

He looked at me blank faced. As if taking me to the airport was too terrible to contemplate right now. 'Okay,' he said. And he limped away.

'Sorry,' I said to the security people. 'I guess we'll be going now, too.'

'We'll see you out,' one of the uniforms said.

We were escorted out of Caesars, the doors closed behind us, and we stood blinking in the sun, waiting for our eyes to adjust to daylight.

'That was sort of embarrassing,' Lula said.

I whipped my phone out and I called Morelli. 'Reporting in,' I told him. 'Anything new?'

'I was just going to call you,' Morelli said. 'I know a guy on the Vegas police force. I gave him a call when I got off the phone with you and asked him to keep his eyes open for Singh. I just got a call back from him. They found Singh in his car in the airport parking lot about an hour ago. Shot twice in the back of the head, close range. We're checking the passenger lists on all Vegas flights in and out of LaGuardia, Newark, and Philadelphia.'

I had a moment's pause where I didn't know what I felt. There was an emotion struggling around inside me. Relief that there was closure on the Singh hunt. Disappointment that I hadn't been able to save him. And dread. The killer's constant presence was wearing me down.

'The Cones?' I asked.

'All present and accounted for.'

'Too bad. That would have been so easy. At least I can leave Vegas now. And I'm bringing something home with me that might be helpful . . . Singh's laptop.'

Silence at the other end. 'Susan Lu gave it to you?'

'I found it on the sidewalk. I think there might have been a break-in and the laptop got dropped and left behind somehow. And I found it.'

I wasn't sure what was going on at the other end of the

connection. Either Morelli was smiling or else he was banging his head against his desk. I was going to go with smiling.

'I'll pick you up at the airport,' Morelli said. 'Try to stay out of trouble. Do you need a police escort when you leave your hotel?'

'No. I've had enough police escorts for one day. Thanks anyway.' I disconnected and relayed the information about Singh. 'The Vegas police found Singh at the airport an hour ago. Two bullet holes in the back of his head,' I told Connie and Lula.

'I was sort of hoping it was a bluff,' Lula said. 'That the killer wasn't really here and he sent you the flowers to get you to go home. Not that I'm scared or anything.'

We all did some mental knuckle cracking and tried not to look nervous.

'We should go back to the hotel,' I said. 'If we're going to make the plane we need to pack.'

Everyone agreed, so we flagged down a cab and we all piled in. I called Ranger on the way. I told him about Singh and then I told him about Salvatora.

'I already talked to Salvatora,' Ranger said. 'His hand is okay, but he said he needs a chiropractor for his back.' Ranger paused and when he continued I could hear the laughter in his voice. 'Salvatora said a fat woman in pink Spandex and silver sequins fell on him.'

'That would be Lula. And she didn't fall on him. She tackled him.'

'She did a good job,' Ranger said. 'I'm sorry I missed it. Salvatora's partner will take you to the airport.'

'How will I know him?'

'He looks like Salvatora . . . but more.'

Five minutes later we were walking through the hotel to the elevators and we were being very vigilant. We didn't know what the killer looked like. It didn't seem likely that he would strike in a public place, but there was no guarantee.

We took the elevator to the eighteenth floor, walked halfway down the hall, and Connie unlocked our room door. She stepped in and muffled a scream. Lula and I were directly behind her and we had the same reaction.

The dog had destroyed the room. Pillows were chewed. The blanket was shredded. A corner of the mattress was missing. Toilet paper was everywhere.

Connie closed and locked the door behind us. 'Don't anybody panic. It's probably not as bad as it looks. Cheap mattress, cheap blanket, right? How much could a pillow cost?'

'Uh-oh,' Lula said. 'I think he pissed on the cable wire and shorted the television. This here's like traveling with a metal band,' Lula said.

Boo was on the bed, tail wagging.

'But look at him,' I said. 'He's so cute. And he looks sorry. Don't you think he looks sorry?'

'I think he looks happy,' Lula said. 'I think he's smiling. I'm glad we saved this little guy. That bag of monkey doody Mrs Apusenja deserves him.'

'We weren't gone that long,' Connie said. 'How could such a little dog do all this damage?'

'Guess he was feeling anxiety,' Lula said. 'Poor thing's been through a lot, what with getting dognapped and everything. And look at him, he's just a puppy. He might even be teething. At least he didn't eat the flowers. It's nice to come back to fresh flowers in the room.'

'They were sent by a serial killer! *They're death flowers*,' I said.

'Well, yeah, but they're still nice,' Lula said.

I looked at my watch. I had to pack. 'Not a lot of time to take care of this mess,' I said.

'Here's the plan,' Connie said. 'We check out and it all goes on Vinnie's bill.'

'See that,' Lula said. 'This dog's nothing but good luck. We get to stick it to Vinnie all because this dog was smart enough to eat the room. I think this here's been a positive experience. That's my new philosophy anyway. Nothing but positive experiences. That's why I'm driving home from here.'

'You've got to be kidding,' Connie said. 'It'll take you days.'

'Don't matter. I'm not getting back on a plane. I'm done with planes. They aren't any fun. All that searching and starving and standing around in lines. I don't do lines. That's another part of my new philosophy. No lines. Me and Boo can have a road trip. I'm starting to get real excited about this. I always wanted to have a dog when I was a kid, but I never had the chance. I was dog deprived.'

'Works for me,' Connie said. 'If you take Boo we don't have the hassle of crating him and getting him on the plane.'

I called valet parking and had the car brought around. I gave Lula the pepper spray and the stun gun and two hundred dollars. Connie contributed another hundred and fifty. It was all the money we had between us. We loaded Lula, Boo, and Lula's luggage into the car and waved goodbye.

'I'm not sure if she's the smart one or the dumb one,' Connie said.

There were only two of us now and we each had a loaded gun in our pockets. We stopped at the snack bar, got a bag of food, and returned to the room to finish packing.

My packing was simple. Take all the little complimentary soaps and shampoos from the bathroom and put them in my carry-on bag. Connie's packing was more complicated.

'Oh shit,' Connie said, 'look at this.'

She was holding up the wedding photo. It had a few dog tooth marks in the lower left corner.

'Do you suppose you actually got married?' I asked her.

'I don't know. I don't remember.' She closed her eyes and groaned. 'Sweet Jesus, please don't let me be married to an Elvis impersonator.'

'There must be some way you can find out,' I said. 'There have to be records. Probably you can have it annulled.'

There was a rap on the door and Connie and I went into panic mode for fear it was the maid. I looked out the security peephole and recognized Erik's partner from Ranger's description. The guy in the hall looked a lot like Erik, but bigger and weirder and scarier. He looked like a Vegas pit boss on steroids.

'It's our chauffeur,' I said.

I opened the door and invited the big scary guy in. He was dark-skinned with slicked-back black hair and dark, heavy-lidded eyes. He was wearing black cowboy boots, black leather pants, a black leather jacket, and a shiny black silk shirt that was unbuttoned half down his chest. He had a colorful crucifixion tattooed onto the back of his left hand. And he had a gun at the small of his back, under the jacket.

'I'm Miguel,' he said. 'I'm Erik's partner.'

'Jeez,' I said. 'We're all really sorry about Erik. I hope he's okay.'

Miguel gave a brief nod, which I took to mean that Erik had his back straightened out and was recovering nicely.

'I'm ready to go,' I told him, handing over the cuffs and shackles and guns. 'My partner is driving back. She has the rest of the hardware.'

Another small nod. Fine by him.

Connie was packed, but she was in the middle of the room with the photo in her hand and she was looking conflicted. 'I need to get this straightened out,' she said. 'I'm going to stay and catch a later flight.'

'I can stay with you,' I said.

She shook her head. 'Not necessary. You'll be safer in Trenton with Morelli.'

And Connie would be safer in Vegas without *me*. I gave her a hug and my room key. Miguel shouldered my bag, stepped aside, and followed me wordlessly to the elevator.

This is the thing about men who never talk. It's easier to assume that they're strong and that they have the sort of wily cunning a woman wants in a bodyguard. I try not to be judgmental, but in all honesty, I'd feel less secure if Miguel had rambled on about how difficult it was to find a decent silk shirt. So no conversation was okay by me because I needed some help being brave. I wanted to think this guy could leap tall buildings in a single bound.

I left the hotel and slipped into the air-conditioned security of a new black Mercedes. 'Your car?' I asked Miguel.

'More or less.'

He walked me to the security check, waited watchfully while I went through. No hassle this time. And then I was on my own. In theory this was a safe zone. Still, I found a seat with my back to the wall and I boarded last, looking for familiar or suspicious faces.

I was in the last row with three empty seats next to me. Lula's seat, Connie's seat, and a seat reserved for Singh. If Singh had been with me, we would have boarded first and if at all possible through a side door. Walking a guy in chains down the aisle in front of the paying customers doesn't set the tone for a stress-free flight.

I was happy to once again have my back to the wall, but I felt naked without hardware. It was a creepy thought that the killer might be on the plane. He could be the preppy-looking guy across the aisle or the hairy guy three rows up. They'd watched me take my seat. Hard to tell if they wanted to kill me or if they just didn't have anything better to do than to stare.

By the time I deplaned in Newark I was too tired to be

afraid. God bless those lucky souls who can sleep while flying. I've never been one of them.

I'd arranged to meet Morelli at baggage claim. I didn't have any baggage to claim, but it was the easiest pickup point. It was seven in the morning, Jersey time. My teeth felt furry and my eyes ached.

I searched the crowd for Morelli and felt my heart skip a beat when I found him. Morelli never blended. He was movie-star handsome and looked like a man you'd avoid in a fight. Women always looked twice at Morelli, but seldom approached. With the possible exception of Terry Gilman.

Morelli's face softened when he saw me. He reached out and drew me to him, wrapping his arms around me. He kissed my neck and held me close for a moment. 'You look beat,' he said. He stepped back, took my bag, and smiled at me. 'But pretty.'

I gave him a sideways glance. 'You want something.'

'The computer for starters.'

'Always a cop.'

'Not always. It's Sunday. How tired are you?'

I was dog tired until I saw Morelli. Now that I was next to him I was having some nonsleeping thoughts. The nonsleeping thoughts lasted about thirty seconds into the ride home.

* * *

I opened my eyes and stared up at Morelli. He was out of the truck, trying to get me awake enough to get me into the house. He had my seat belt off and my bag slung over his shoulder.

'Jeez, Steph,' he said. 'Didn't you sleep on the plane?'

'I never sleep on a plane. I have to be ready in case it crashes.' I heaved myself off the seat and shuffled up the sidewalk. Morelli opened the door and I braced myself for the Bob attack. We heard him thundering through the house, coming from the kitchen. He reached the small foyer and Morelli held up a giant dog biscuit. Bob's eyes got wide, Morelli threw the biscuit over Bob's head down the hallway, and Bob turned in midgallop and followed the biscuit.

'Pretty smart,' I said.

'I should take him to obedience training, but I never seem to get to it.'

What Morelli meant was that he should try obedience training *again*. Bob had flunked out twice before.

Morelli set the bag on the floor at the foot of the stairs and removed the computer. 'I'm not going to open this. I'm going to turn it over to the experts first thing tomorrow.'

That had been my thought, too. I hadn't fooled with the computer.

'Have you told Vinnie about Singh?' Morelli asked.

'I left that for Connie. She stayed behind to clean some things up.'

'Vinnie'll put a good spin on it. You found Singh. That's the important part. The system worked.'

'I need more sleep,' I said. 'Wake me up when it's time for dessert.'

'Bad news,' Morelli said. 'Dessert will be too late. We're expected for dinner at my mom's house. We accepted this invitation two weeks ago,' Morelli said. 'It's Mary Elizabeth's birthday.'

I'd totally forgotten. Mary Elizabeth is Joe's great-aunt. She's a chain-smoking booze hound and she's a retired nun. And no party for Mary Elizabeth would be complete without Grandma Bella because Mary Elizabeth is Bella's younger sister. I got a sharp pain in my right temple and my blood ran cold. I was having dinner with Grandma Bella.

'Are you okay?' Morelli asked. 'You look sort of white.'

'I'm having dinner with Grandma Bella. My life is passing in front of my eyes. I'm as good as dead. I should just stand outside and let the carnation killer shoot me.'

'You have to have the right attitude about Grandma Bella.'

'And that would be what?'

Joe shrugged. 'She's crazy.'

* * *

I slept until late afternoon. When I woke I was in Joe's bed, still dressed in my travel clothes, partially tangled in a lightweight summer patchwork quilt. The sheets were rumpled under me and the pillowcase was damp with sweat and humidity. Aunt Rose's gauzy curtains hung limp against the open window. The air was heavy, but the light was soft. The room felt like Joe and good sex. There were mental imprints of time spent here that didn't get smoothed away with new sheets. If I closed my eyes in this room, even if I was alone, I could feel Morelli's hands on me.

And today the room smelled like popcorn.

The popcorn aroma was drifting up from the living room where Joe and Bob were watching a ball game. I shuffled downstairs and looked in the popcorn bowl. Empty. I checked out the game. Not interesting.

Joe looked over at me. 'I could call and cancel.'

'You can't do that. It's a birthday!'

'I'd come up with something good. I'd say you broke your leg. Or you had an appendix attack. Or you insisted we stay home and have a lot of sloppy sex.'

'Thanks. I appreciate the thought, but I don't think any of those would work.'

'The sex would work.'

I smiled at him and took the empty popcorn bowl back to the kitchen. 'Nice try.'

I toasted a bagel, smeared it with too much butter, and ate it with the butter dripping down my arm. Do I know how to eat a bagel, or what? I went back upstairs, took a shower, and got dressed for dinner.

I was halfway through make-up when Morelli appeared in the bathroom doorway. He leaned a shoulder against the jamb, hands in pants pockets. 'We're late,' he said. 'How's it going?'

It wasn't going good. Dinner with Joe's family had me in a state. I'd accidentally poked myself in the eye with the mascara wand and almost gone blind. 'It's going great,' I said. 'Give me another minute.'

'You have a big black blob on your eye.'

'I know that. Go away!'

Ten minutes later I clattered down the stairs in my highheeled strappy sandals, the swirly skirt, and a stretchy top. It was the best I could do under the circumstances. I didn't have a lot of clothes at Joe's house.

'Nice,' Joe said, eyes on the skirt. 'I'm going to have fun with this outfit when we get home. You have panties on, right?'

'Right.'

'I don't suppose you'd want to take them off.'

'I don't suppose.'

'Doesn't hurt to ask,' Morelli said with a grin. 'It would make dinner more interesting.'

Everyone was at the table when we arrived. Joe's mom was at the head. Grandma Bella was next to her, then Mary Elizabeth. Joe's sister, Cathy, was next to Mary Elizabeth. Joe's Uncle Mario was at the foot of the table. Cathy's husband was seated across from her. Joe and I were seated across from Mary Elizabeth and Bella.

'Sorry we're late,' Joe said. 'Cop business.'

Mary Elizabeth was looking very happy. She had an empty highball glass in front of her and a half-empty wine glass. 'More like monkey business,' she said.

Bella shook her finger at Joe. 'All the Morelli men are sex fiends.'

'Hey,' Uncle Mario said, 'how's that to talk?'

Mario was Bella's first cousin and the only male Morelli left from Bella's generation. Morelli men weren't especially long-lived. Mario was small and wrinkled, but still had a full head of wiry black hair. It was rumored he colored it with shoe polish.

Grandma Bella fixed an eye on Mario. 'Are you telling me you're not a sex fiend?'

'There's a difference between an Italian stallion and a sex fiend. I'm an Italian stallion.'

Joe filled our wine glasses. 'Salute,' he said.

Everyone held their glasses high. 'Salute.'

'I didn't see you in church today,' Grandma Bella said to Joe.

'I had to miss today,' Joe said.

And last week. And the week before that. And come to think of it, last time Joe was in church was Christmas.

'I prayed for you,' Bella told him.

Joe took a sip of wine and looked at Bella over the rim of his glass. 'Thanks.'

'And I prayed that the bambinos would get over the death of their mother.'

Joe's mother gripped her wine glass and narrowed her eyes at Bella. I stopped breathing. Everyone else slumped in their seat with an *oh boy, here it comes* sigh.

'The bambinos?' Joe asked.

'You will have many bambinos. The mother will die. It will be very sad. I saw it in a vision.'

I bit down hard on my lower lip. My poor little bambinos!

'Don't worry,' Bella said to me. 'It's not you. The woman in the vision was blonde.'

Eleven

Joe drank more wine and draped an arm around my shoulders. 'At least you're not the dead woman in this vision.'

Mrs Morelli threw a dinner roll at him and hit him in the head. 'That's a stupid thing to say to a woman. Sometimes you're just like your father.' She crossed herself and looked penitent. 'God rest his soul.'

Everyone at the table crossed themselves except Joe. 'God rest his soul,' everyone said.

'And *you*,' Mrs Morelli said to her mother-in-law. 'No more with the visions.'

'I can't help I have visions,' Grandma Bella said. 'I'm an instrument of God.'

This brought on a lot more crossing and Uncle Mario muttered something that I think included the words *devil woman*.

Bella turned on Mario. 'You watch your step, old man. I'll

put *the eye* on you.' The table went silent. No one wanted to mess with *the eye*. *The eye* was Italian voodoo.

While all this was going on, Mary Elizabeth had put away three glasses of wine.

'I love a party,' Mary Elizabeth said, her words slightly slurred, her eyes slightly crossed. She raised her wine glass. 'Here's to me!'

We all raised our wine glasses. 'To Mary Elizabeth!'

When we were all stuffed with chicken in red sauce and meatballs and macaroni casseroles, Mrs Morelli brought out the desserts. Plates of Italian cookies from People's bakery, fresh-filled cannoli from Panorama Musicale, cheeses from Porfirio's, and the birthday cake from Little Italy.

By now it was sweltering in the Morelli dining room. All the windows were open and Mrs Morelli had brought a fan in to circulate air. Sweat was running down my breastbone, soaking my shirt. My hair was stuck to my face and my mascara was not living up to its waterproof promise. No one cared about the heat. Everyone but Joe and his mom was shit-faced, me included.

Candles were lit on the cake, raising the room temperature by another ten degrees. We all sang 'Happy Birthday,' Mary Elizabeth blew out the candles, and Mrs Morelli made the first cut in the cake.

Grandma Bella slammed her hands palms down on the

table and tossed her head back. She was having a vision.

Everyone at the table groaned.

'I see death,' Grandma Bella said. 'A woman.'

More groaning from around the table.

'I see white carnations.'

'Don't worry about it, honey,' Morelli whispered in my ear. 'There are always white carnations.'

'This woman who died,' I asked Grandma Bella. 'Is she a blonde?'

Grandma Bella opened her eyes and looked at me. 'She has curly brown hair,' Bella said. 'Shoulder length.'

My hair. Good thing I was too drunk to care.

'That's the vision,' Bella said. 'I'm tired now. I need to lay down.'

Bella always got tired after a vision.

We watched her leave the table and go upstairs.

'Good riddance,' Mary Elizabeth said. 'She's such a downer.'

And we all made the sign of the cross and had dessert.

Morelli poured me into his truck and drove me back to his house where he dragged me out of the truck and propped me against the passenger side door. 'If you're going to throw up, it'd be good if you could do it out here,' he said. 'It's supposed to rain. It'll wash away.'

I thought about that for a moment and decided I wasn't going to throw up. I took a step and went down to one knee. 'Oops,' I said. 'The curb's in my way.'

Morelli hauled me up, slung me over his shoulder, and carried me into the house and up the stairs. I flopped onto Morelli's bed and put one foot on the floor to stop the whirlies. 'Wanna have sex?' I asked.

Morelli grinned. 'I think I'll take a rain check on that one. I'm still worried you're going to be sick. Do you want me to help you get undressed?'

'No. But it'd be good if you could make the room stand still.'

I was awake but I was afraid to open my eyes. I suspected hell was lurking just beyond my eyelids. My brain didn't fit in my head and the little devil guys were poking hot sticks in my eyeballs.

I cracked an eye and squinted up at Morelli. 'Help,' I whispered.

Morelli had a coffee cup in his hand. 'You really tied one on last night.'

'Did I make an idiot of myself?'

'Honey, you were at a dinner party with my family. On your best day you couldn't even *compete* in the idiot contest.'

'Your mother isn't an idiot.'

'My mother likes you.'

'Really?' I eased myself into a sitting position, put both hands to my head, and applied pressure in an attempt to prevent my brain from exploding. 'I'm never doing this again. Never. I'm done drinking. Okay, maybe a beer once in a while, but that's it!'

'I went out and got *the cure*,' Morelli said. 'I have to leave for work, but I want to make sure you're okay first.'

I opened my other eye. I sniffed the air. '*The cure*? Really?'

'Downstairs,' Morelli said. 'I left them in the kitchen. Do you want me to bring them up?'

Not necessary. I was on my feet. I was moving. Slowly. I was at the stairs. One step at a time. I was going to make it. I put my hands over my eyes to keep my eyeballs from falling out of my head while I worked the stairs. Then I was on firm floor. I inched forward. I was in the kitchen. I squinted into the red haze and I saw it. It was sitting on the little wooden kitchen table. A large bag of McDonald's French fries and a large Coke.

I carefully eased myself onto a kitchen chair and took my first fry. 'Ahhhh,' I said.

Morelli was slouched in the chair opposite me, finishing his coffee. 'Feeling better?'

I sipped some Coke and I ate more fries. 'Much better.'

'Are you ready for ketchup?'

'Definitely.'

Morelli got the ketchup out of the fridge and dumped some on a plate for me. I mushed some fries in the ketchup and tested them out.

'I think the brain swelling is going down,' I said to Morelli. 'The pounding has stopped.'

'Always a good sign,' Morelli said. He rinsed his cup and set it in the dish drain. 'I'm out of here. I have to get the computer to the lab.' He kissed me on the top of my head. 'Be careful. Tank's outside, doing his thing. Try not to lose him.'

'I owe you,' I said.

'Yeah, I know. I already have plans.'

And he was gone.

Bob was patiently sitting beside me, waiting for his share. I fed him a couple fries, finished up the rest, and drank the Coke. I gave a big burp and felt pretty decent.

I took a shower and got dressed in a short denim skirt, white sneakers, and a white T-shirt. I pulled my hair into a ponytail, applied some lipstick and a single swipe of mascara, and I was ready for the day.

I put a call in to Lula and got her at a truck stop.

'I'm fine,' she said. 'Me and Boo are having breakfast.

We're making real good time. We're traveling straight along Route Forty all the way. This here's real interesting. I never drove through anything like this before. This is cowboys and Indians country.'

I hung up, dropped a raisin and a small chunk of cheese into Rex's cage, gave Bob a hug, and told everybody I'd be back. I locked up after myself and waved to Tank. Tank gave me a nod back.

I drove the short distance to my parents' house and parked in the driveway. My grandmother was at the door, waiting for me, responding to some mysterious instinct embedded in Burg women . . . an early warning signal that a daughter or granddaughter was approaching.

'That big guy is following you again,' Grandma said, opening the door to me.

'Tank.'

'Yeah. I wouldn't mind spending some time with him. You think he could go for an older woman?'

Young women, old women, barnyard animals. 'Hard to say with Tank.'

'Your mother's at the store and the girls are off playing somewhere,' Grandma said. 'Valerie's in the kitchen eating us out of house and home.'

'How's she doing?'

'Looks like she's going to explode.'

I went in and took a chair across from Valerie. She was picking at a bowl of macaroni and chicken salad, not showing much enthusiasm for it.

'What's up?' I asked.

'I dunno. I'm not hungry. I think I'm in a slump. My life is same old, same old.'

'You're having a baby. That's pretty exciting.'

Valerie looked down at her stomach. 'Yeah.' She gently rubbed the baby bulge. 'I'm excited about that. It's just that everything else is so unsettled. I'm living here with Mom and Dad and Gram. After the baby there'll be four of us in that one small bedroom. I feel like I'm swallowed up and there's no more Valerie. I was always perfect. I was the epitome of well-being and mental health. Remember how I was serene? Saint Valerie? And I adapted when I moved to California. I went from serene to perky. I was cute,' Valerie said. 'I was *really* cute. I made birthday cakes and pork tenderloins. I bought my jerkoff husband a grill. I had my teeth bleached.'

'Your teeth look great, Val.'

'I'm confused.'

'About Albert?'

Valerie rested her elbow on the table and her chin in her hand. 'Do you think he's boring?'

'He's too funny to be boring. He's like a puppy. Sort of floppy and goofy and wanting to be liked.' He could be a little annoying, but that's different from boring, right?

'I feel like I need a hero. I feel like I need to be rescued.'

'That's because you weigh four hundred pounds and you can't get out of a chair by yourself. After you have the baby you'll feel different.' Okay, so I was being a big fat hypocrite again. I felt the same way as Val. I wanted to be rescued, too. I was tired of being brave and semicompetent. Difference was, I refused to say it aloud. I suspected it was a basic instinct, but it felt wrong somehow. For starters, it felt like a terrible burden to dump on a man.

'Do you think Albert is at all heroic?' Valerie asked me.

'He doesn't look like a hero, but he gave you a job when you needed one and he's stood by you. I guess that's sort of heroic. And I think he'd run into a burning building to save you.' Whether he'd get her out of the building is another issue. Probably they'd both die a horrible death. 'I think you're doing the right thing by not getting married, Val. I like Albert, but you don't want to marry him just because Mom's in favor of it, or because you need a second income. You should be in love and you should be sure he's the right man for you and the girls.'

'Sometimes it's hard to tell what's love and what's only indigestion,' Valerie said.

I left Valerie with the macaroni salad and drove to the office.

Connie looked around her computer screen at me when I walked in.

'Well?' I asked. 'Are you married?'

'No. It turned out to be a joke photo. I caught the ten o'clock out of Vegas.'

'And the room damage?'

'It all went on Vinnie's credit card. Vinnie almost popped a vein when he heard. But then the reporters started showing up and Vinnie was distracted. The room bill got pushed on a back burner. You saved Vinnie's ass. You even made him look *good*. The visa bond worked. The guy fled. We found him.'

'Actually, the Vegas cops found Singh.'

'Not when Vinnie tells it. Vinnie's made some improvements on the story. So we all still have our jobs. Vinnie's not going to be selling used cars in Scottsdale. Everybody's happy.'

Everybody except me. I was being stalked by a lunatic. And it was possible that I was indirectly responsible for causing three murders.

'Now that Singh is off the books, I've got a backlog of skips,' Connie said. 'What would you like . . . first-time rapist, repeat domestic violence, assault with a deadly weapon, or possession?'

'What's the possession?'

'Kilo of heroin.'

'Whoa! That's a biggy. That's Ranger's. How about the deadly weapon?'

'Butchy Salazar and Ryan Mott got into a fight over Candace Lalor. And Butchy ran over Ryan with his Jeep Cherokee. Three times.'

'Butchy was drunk?'

'Yep.'

'Give me Butchy.' Sometimes a drunk is an easy catch if you can get him in the morning.

I took the papers from Connie. I didn't need a photo. I knew Butchy. Went to school with him. Didn't like him back then. Wasn't real crazy about him now.

'I'll give you the rapist, too. It's his first time around. Maybe he just forgot to show for court. I tried calling, but all I get is a machine.'

'Have you tried his work number?'

'He's unemployed. Got fired when he got arrested.'

I looked around. 'It feels strange not to have Lula here.'

'Quiet,' Connie said.

'Empty.'

'Glorious,' Vinnie yelled from his inner office. 'Freaking glorious.'

I hefted my bag higher on my shoulder and I headed out. Tank was standing guard on the sidewalk, in front of my car.

'I have a couple FTAs,' I said to Tank. 'One's in the Burg and one's in Hamilton Township. I have to stop at my apartment first to get some clean clothes and stuff.'

'It might be easier if we took one car for the busts,' Tank said.

I agreed. 'Do you want to drive or ride shotgun?'

Tank's eyebrows raised a fraction of an inch. Shocked that I would even consider driving. Tank only rode shotgun to Ranger.

'It's the twenty-first century,' I told Tank. 'Women drive.'

'Only in my bed,' Tank said. 'Never in my car.'

I didn't have a reply to that, but I thought it sounded like an okay philosophy. So I beeped the Escape locked, got into Tank's SUV, and we chugged off for my place.

We went through the standard routine at my apartment. Tank went in first and did a safety check. The photos were gone from the floor. Residue remained where the police had checked for prints. I gathered a few things together when Tank gave the all clear. Mostly what I wanted from my apartment was hardware. I took the cuffs and pepper spray from my bedside table and dropped them into my shoulder bag. I went to the cookie jar next and added the .38 to my bag of goodies. I knew Tank was fully armed and probably had fifty pairs of cuffs in the back of his truck, but

I wanted my own. Am I a professional, or what?

I locked up and we took the elevator. Two-hundred-year-old Mrs Bestler was in the elevator joyriding. 'Going down,' she told us, pressing the button, leaning on her walker. 'First floor, ladies' handbags, designer shoes.' She looked up at Tank. 'My goodness, you're a big one,' she said.

Tank smiled at her. Big Bad Wolf reassures Grandma he's not going to eat her for lunch. The doors opened and we got out.

'Have a nice day, Mrs Bestler,' I said.

'Don't take any wooden nickels,' Mrs Bestler sang out.

According to Butchy Salazar's bond agreement, he was renting the top half of a two-family house on Allen Street. For years now, Butchy'd worked nights tending bar at a dive on Front Street, so chances were good that he'd be at home.

Tank did a pass in front of the house. No activity. He returned and parked two houses down on the opposite side of the street. I called Butchy on my cell phone and got his machine. I didn't leave a message. Tank and I got out and approached the house. No back door to worry about, so we positioned ourselves to either side of the front door. I rang the bell for the upstairs apartment and waited. No response. I rang again.

The downstairs door opened and an older woman stuck her head out. 'Butchy isn't home and my cats hate when people ring his bell,' she said. 'The bell scares my cats. They're very sensitive.'

'Do you know where Butchy is?'

'I think he's gone out to do his grocery shopping and stuff. Not that he does a lot of cooking. Mostly he buys beer and filthy magazines. I tell you, this neighborhood's going to hell in a handbasket.'

The woman closed her door and I looked up at Tank. It was strange being on a bust with him. I was used to Lula with her crazy clothes and smart mouth.

'Okay,' I said, 'let's go for the rapist, Steven Wegan. We can come back to Butchy later. Wegan lives in Hamilton Township in one of those apartment complexes off Klockner Boulevard.'

Minutes later we were parked in the lot in front of Steven Wegan's apartment. We sat for a couple minutes, getting the feel of things. A woman left her apartment two doors down, got into her car, and drove off. Aside from that there was no activity.

'One of us should take the back door,' I said.

'Can't do that,' Tank said. 'My first job is to protect you and I can't do that if I can't see you.'

'No one followed us here. I was watching.'

Tank went stony. An unmovable object.

'Fine,' I said, 'we'll both take the front door.'

We left the truck, crossed the lot, and I rang Wegan's bell.

Wegan answered on the first ring. You've got to love first-time offenders. They don't know the drill. Next time around Wegan will be out the back door, hiding in the Dumpster.

He was a slim five feet, eight inches with close-cut brown hair and dark brown eyes. His papers listed his age as twenty-six. He was unmarried.

'Yes?' Wegan said, looking first to me, then up at Tank. The gears were turning in Wegan's head when he looked at Tank. Tank wasn't someone you wanted to unexpectedly find on your doorstep.

'Steven Wegan?' I asked.

Wegan swallowed. 'Un-hunh.'

I introduced myself and explained to Wegan that he'd missed his court date and needed to refile. Wegan bobbed his head yes, but his eyes were saying no, no, no.

I reached back and took hold of the cuffs secured under my skirt waistband. Wegan went white, turned, and bolted. And before I could make a move, Tank effortlessly grabbed Wegan by the scruff of his neck and held him two inches off the floor. Wegan kicked out and then went limp. Tank gave Wegan a shake, causing Wegan's feet to flop around. 'I'm going to put you down now,' Tank said. 'And you're not going to try anything stupid, right?'

'R-r-r-right,' Wegan said.

I cuffed Wegan, we secured his apartment, and we all marched over to Tank's SUV. We put Wegan in the back seat, cuffed and shackled.

I couldn't help thinking it would have played out differently if Tank hadn't been along. Lula and I would have chased Wegan all over his apartment, knocking over lamps and chairs in the process. We would have snagged him eventually, but the capture would have been total Abbott and Costello.

'Do all your captures go like that?' I asked Tank.

'No,' he said. 'They don't always try to run.'

It was midafternoon when we left the police station. Wegan was back behind bars. Tomorrow morning he'd go before the judge who would once again set bail, higher this time. Vinnie would get a call from a pleading Wegan, and for another bonding fee, Wegan would walk.

We stopped off at Cluck in a Bucket for a late lunch and then motored over to the Burg to try our luck with Butchy. We parked across the street and looked up at Butchy's open windows. Television sounds drifted out to us. Butchy was home. We crossed the street and took our places on the small stoop that served as a front porch.

'Do you know this guy?' Tank asked.

'Yeah.'

'Is he going to shoot at us?'

'Depends how drunk he is.'

Tank drew his gun and I rang the bell. No answer to the bell. I rang again. Still no answer.

'He's not coming down,' Tank said.

I called Butchy on my cell phone.

'Yeah?' Butchy said.

'It's Stephanie Plum,' I told him. 'I'm downstairs with my partner and we need to talk to you.'

'So go ahead and talk.'

'You missed your court date and you need to reschedule.'

'And?'

'And you need to do it now. Come downstairs and open the door.'

'Suck my dick,' Butchy said.

'Sure,' I told him. 'Just come down and open the door.'

'Fuck off,' Butchy said. 'I don't feel like going to jail today. Why don't you come back next month. Maybe I'll feel like going to jail next month.'

I told Tank to back up and stand on the sidewalk where Butchy could see him.

'Look out your window, Butchy,' I said. 'See the big guy standing on the sidewalk?'

'Yeah.'

'That's my partner. If you don't open the door, he's going

to put his foot through it. And then he's going to go upstairs and root you out like the rodent you are and put his foot up your ass.'

'I've got a gun.'

'Is it as big as Tank's?'

Tank was holding a .44 Magnum.

'I swear to God,' Butchy said, 'if you come in I'll blow your head off.' And he disconnected.

'He's not coming down,' I told Tank. 'And he says he's armed.'

Tank walked up to the door, put his boot to it just left of the handle, and the door flipped open. 'Wait here,' Tank said.

I had my gun in hand, too. 'No way. This is my bust.'

Tank turned and looked at me. 'Anything happens to you, I have to answer to Ranger. Frankly, I'd rather take a bullet from this moron.'

Okay, that made sense to me. 'I'll wait here,' I told him.

'I'm coming up the stairs,' Tank called to Butchy. 'When I get to the top I want you unarmed, face down on the floor with your hands where I can see them.'

I looked up and saw Butchy ass first, half out the window above me. He was waiting for Tank to get to the top of the stairs and then Butchy was going to go out the window, onto the small roof over the stoop, and drop to the ground.

I ducked into the doorway so Butchy wouldn't see me. I

held my breath and waited to hear him on the roof. Tank got to the top of the stairs, Butchy's feet scuffed on the roof, and I jumped out. I had my gun two-handed and I yelled for Butchy to stop and freeze.

'I've got him,' I yelled to Tank. 'He's on the porch roof.'

Tank jogged down the stairs and moved to join me on the small patch of front lawn: He cleared the porch just as Butchy catapulted himself off the roof, and the two of them crashed to the ground with Butchy on top of Tank.

I rushed in and grabbed Butchy by the arm, cuffing him behind his back while he still had the air knocked out of him. I rolled him off Tank and shoved him aside. Tank was on his back with his leg twisted at an impossible angle.

'Just shoot me,' Tank said. 'It'd be less painful.'

I called EMS and then I called Ranger. A half hour later, Tank was rolled into the EMS truck, his leg held stable by an inflated cast.

Ranger and I stood side by side and watched the truck disappear around the corner. A big, bald, jug-headed guy, neatly dressed in black jeans and T-shirt, stood by Tank's truck. He had his muscle-bound, bulging arms crossed over his massive chest and his tiny eyes fixed on Ranger and me.

'I need to go to the hospital and get Tank admitted,' Ranger said. 'I've asked Cal to follow you around.'

'Cal has a flaming skull tattooed onto his forehead. And

he has muscles in places muscles aren't supposed to grow. Cal looks like . . . Steroidasaurus.'

'Don't underestimate him,' Ranger said. 'He can spell his name. He's not overly violent as long as he remembers to take his medication. And he gives good shade.'

I did a grimace.

Ranger pulled me to him and kissed me on the forehead. 'You two are going to get along just fine.' Ranger stepped back and turned to Butchy, who was sitting cuffed and shackled on the curb. He grabbed Butchy, dragged him to his feet, and handed him over to Steroidasaurus.

It was almost six when we left the police station. Butchy was chained to a bench across from the docket lieutenant. Steven Wegan was in the lock up. I had body receipts for both of them. Not a bad day in terms of income. Not a great day in terms of Tank's leg. Definitely a weird day, having spent it in the company of Ranger's Merry Men.

Halfway through town my cell phone rang. 'Your sister's in labor,' Grandma said. 'She was working her way through a Virginia baked ham when she started getting contractions.'

'Is she going to the hospital?'

'She's trying to decide if it's time. Do you think I should call Albert?'

'Definitely call Albert. It's his baby, too. He's been going to the birthing classes with Valerie.'

'It's just that she's not in a good mood. You know how it is when she gets disturbed in the middle of a ham.'

Twelve

Valerie was sitting on the couch in the living room when I arrived. She was doing her breathing exercises and rubbing her stomach. My mother and grandmother were standing beside her, watching. The two girls were on the floor, staring bug-eyed at Valerie. My father was in his chair in front of the television, channel surfing.

'So,' I said. 'What's up?'

The front door crashed open behind me and Albert stumbled in. 'Am I too late? Did I miss anything? What's going on?'

'Mommy's having a baby,' Angie said.

Mary Alice nodded her head in agreement.

Albert looked terrible. His shirt was untucked and his eyes were glassy. His face was chalk white with red spots high on his cheeks.

'You don't look so good,' Grandma said to Albert. 'How about a ham sandwich?'

'I've never had a baby before,' Albert said. 'I'm a little flub-a-dubbed.'

'I'm having another contraction,' Valerie said. 'Is anyone timing? Aren't these coming awful close together?'

I didn't know anything about having a baby, but I knew it worked better if you delivered it in the hospital. 'Maybe we should go to St Francis,' I said. 'Do you have a suitcase ready?'

Valerie went into the breathing and rubbing mode again and my mom ran upstairs for the suitcase.

'So what do you think, Valerie?' I asked when she stopped rubbing and puffing. 'You've done this before. Are you ready to go to the hospital?'

'I was ready weeks ago,' Valerie said. 'Someone help me get up.'

Albert and I each took an arm and pulled Valerie up.

She looked down. 'I can't see my feet. Do I have shoes on?'

'Yep,' I said. 'Sneakers.'

She felt around. 'And I've got pants on, right?'

'Black stretchy shorts.' Stretched to within an inch of their lives.

My mother came down the stairs with the suitcase. 'Are you sure you don't want to get married?' she asked Valerie. 'I could call Father Gabriel. He could meet you at the hospital. People get married in the hospital all the time.'

'Contraction!' Valerie said, huffing and puffing, holding Kloughn's hand in a death grip.

Kloughn went down to one knee. 'Yow! You're breaking my hand!'

Valerie kept huffing.

'Okay,' Kloughn said. 'Okay, okay. It's not so bad now that the hand's gone numb. Besides, I got another one, right? And probably this one's not actually broken. It's just mashed. It'll be fine, right? Mashed isn't so bad. Mashed. Squished. Smushed. That's all okay. That's not like broken, right?'

The contraction passed and we propelled Valerie out the door, down the sidewalk to the driveway. While the rest of us were flub-a-dubbed, my father had slipped outside and started the car. Sometimes my father knocks me out. On the surface he's all meat and potatoes and television, but the truth is, he doesn't miss much.

We put Valerie in the front seat. Albert, my mom, and I got in the backseat. Grandma and the girls stayed behind, waving. The trip was only several blocks long. St Francis was walking distance from my parents' house, if you wanted to take a good long walk. I called Morelli from the car and told him I wouldn't be home for dinner. Morelli said that was cool since there didn't seem to be any dinner anyway.

Even with our combined abilities, Morelli and I as a

single entity didn't equal a bad housewife. Bob ate regularly because we scooped his food out of a big bag. After that it was all downhill to take-out.

Albert and I walked Valerie in through the emergency entrance and my mom and dad took off to park the car.

A nurse came forward. 'Omigod!' she said. 'Valerie Plum? I haven't seen you in years. It's Julie Singer. I'm Julie Wisneski now.'

Valerie blinked at her. 'You married Whiskey? I had a big crush on him when I was in high school.'

This caught me by surprise. I was just a couple years behind Valerie, but I had no idea she'd had a crush on Whiskey. Whiskey was drop-dead cute but not a lot upstairs. If you talked cars with Whiskey you were on solid ground. Any topic other than cars, fugeddaboudit. Last I heard he was working in a garage in Ewing. Probably happy as a clam at high tide.

'Big contraction,' Valerie said, her face turning red, her hands on her belly.

'So what do you think?' I asked Julie. 'I don't know a lot about this stuff, but she looks like she's going to have a baby, right?'

'Yeah,' Julie said. 'Either that or forty-two puppies. What have you been feeding her?'

'Everything.'

My mom and dad hustled in and went to Valerie.

'Julie Wisneski!' my mom said. 'I didn't know you were working here.'

'Two years now,' Julie said. 'I moved from Helene Fuld.'

'How are the boys? And Whiskey?' my mom wanted to know.

Big smile from Julie. 'Driving me nuts.'

My dad was looking around. He didn't care about Whiskey and the boys. He was scoping out televisions and vending machines. Good to know where the essentials are in a new environment.

Julie wedged Valerie into a wheelchair and took her away. My parents went with Valerie. Kloughn and I were left to complete the admission ritual. From the corner of my eye I caught sight of a black hulking mass, positioned against a wall. Steroidasaurus was still watching over me.

When we satisfied Admissions that the bill would be paid, I sent Albert upstairs to be with Valerie and I went over to talk to Cal.

'It's not necessary for you to stay,' I said. 'I'm going to be here for a while. When I'm done at the hospital I'm going back to Morelli's house. I don't think I'm in any danger.'

Cal didn't move. Didn't say anything.

I slipped out the emergency room door and called Ranger and filled him in. 'So I thought it didn't make sense for Cal to stay here all night while I'm with Valerie.'

'Hospitals don't screen for killers,' Ranger said. 'Keep Cal with you.'

'He's scaring people.'

'Yeah,' Ranger said. 'He's good at that.'

I disconnected, returned to the emergency room lobby, and went upstairs to look for Valerie. Cal followed close at my heels.

We found Valerie on a gurney, in a hospital gown under a sheet, her stomach a huge swollen mound on top of her. My mother and father were at her head. Albert was holding her hand. Julie was attaching an ID bracelet onto Valerie's wrist.

'Omigod,' Valerie said. '*Unh!*' And her water broke.

It was an explosion of water. A tidal wave. We're talking Hoover Dam quantity water. Water everywhere . . . but mostly on Cal. Cal had been standing at the bottom of the gurney. Cal was totally slimed from the top of his head to his knees. It dripped off the end of his nose and ran in rivulets down his bald head.

Valerie drew her legs up, the sheet fell away, and Cal gaped at the sight in front of him.

Julie stuck her head around for a look. 'Uh-oh,' Julie said, 'there's a foot sticking out. Guess this is going to be a breech baby.'

That was when Cal fainted. *CRASH*. Cal went over like he was a giant redwood cut down by Paul Bunyan. Windows rattled and the building shook.

Everyone clustered around Cal.

'Hey,' Valerie yelled. 'I'm having a baby here!'

Julie went back to Valerie.

'Is it a girl or a boy?' Valerie wanted to know.

'I don't know,' Julie said, 'but it's got big feet. And it's not a puppy.'

A doctor appeared and took charge of Valerie, wheeling her down the hall. Kloughn and my mom followed after Val and the doctor. My father wandered into a room that had a ball game going. And I watched a couple nurses pop ammonia capsules under Cal's snout.

Cal opened his eyes but it didn't look like anyone was home.

'He hit his head pretty hard when he fell,' one of the nurses said. 'We should get him checked out.'

Good thing it was his head, I thought. Not a big loss there if it's broken.

It took six people to get Cal onto a stretcher and then they rolled him away in the opposite direction they'd gone with Valerie.

One of the nurses asked if I knew him. I said his name was Cal. That was about it. That was what I knew. I wasn't allowed to use my cell phone in that part of the hospital, so I went outside to call Ranger.

'About Cal . . .' I said. 'He's sort of out of commission.'

'Used to be you destroyed my cars,' Ranger said.

'Yeah, those were the good old days.'

'How bad is it?'

'Valerie's water sort of broke on him and he fainted. Bounced his head on the floor a couple times when he went down. Lucky he was in the hospital when it happened. He was looking a little dopey, so they took him somewhere for testing.'

'St Francis?'

'Yep.'

Disconnect.

I was making a shambles of the Merry Men. I suspected Tank was somewhere in the hospital, too. I'd stop in to say hello, but I only knew him as Tank. Probably Tank wasn't the name listed on the chart.

Morelli called while I was still outside. 'So?'

'I'm at the hospital with Valerie,' I told him. 'It's been pretty uneventful except for the birth and the concussion.'

'What, no fires or explosions? No shoot-outs?'

'Like I said, it's been quiet, but it's still early.'

'I hate to ruin my tough-guy image, but to tell you the truth, I don't even like to kid about this stuff any more.'

I didn't know how to tell him . . . I wasn't kidding. 'I should get back to Valerie,' I said.

'Television sucks tonight. Maybe I'll come over to the hospital.'

'That would be nice.'

The sky was overcast and a fine mist was settling around me. Streetlights popped on in the gloom. A block away, headlights glowed golden on cars cruising Hamilton. I'd exited the emergency entrance on Bert Avenue to make the call. I'd walked toward the back of the building, going just far enough to avoid activity. I had my back pressed to the brick wall of the hospital while I talked, trying to stay dry, trying to keep my hair from frizzing. Used to be there were houses across the street, but several years ago the houses were torn down and a parking lot was created.

A kid walked out of emergency and turned toward me, moving with his head down against the light rain, hugging a small gym bag to his chest. From the brief look I'd caught of his face I'd put him somewhere in his late teens to early twenties. Not really a kid, I guess, but he dressed like a kid. Low-slung baggy homeboy pants, gym shoes, short-sleeved shirt unbuttoned over a black T-shirt, spikey green hair. Probably had multiple piercings and tattoos, but I couldn't see any from this distance.

I dropped my phone into my purse and headed back to

emergency. The green-haired kid got a couple feet from me and staggered a little, bumping against me. He picked his head up, looked me in the eye, and raised a gun level with my nose.

'Turn and walk,' he said. 'I'm really good with this gun. I'll shoot you dead if you make a single false move.'

Usually there were people hanging out around emergency, but the rain had driven everyone inside. The street was deserted. Not even car traffic. 'Is this about money?' I asked him. 'Just take my bag.'

'Hah, you wish, sweetie pie. This is The Game and I'm the winner. Just me and the Web Master left. I get to go on to the next game after I do you.'

I turned and gaped at him.

'What?' he asked. 'You didn't know it was me? You didn't think the hunter had green hair?'

'Who *are* you?'

He jumped and slashed at the air. 'I'm the Fisher Cat.'

I'd never heard of a fisher cat. I was pretty sure we didn't have any in Trenton. 'Is that a real animal or did you make it up?'

'It's a member of the weasel family. It moves along real quiet. You hardly know it's around. It's real sneaky. And it's ferocious.'

'Have you ever seen one?'

'Well, no, not exactly. You know, like, in a book.'

'If I was going to name myself after an animal I'd want to see it first.'

'That's because you have no imagination. Gamers have imagination. We create stuff.'

'What stuff?'

'The Game, stupid. And then we *transcend* the game. The game becomes the reality. Is that total whack, or what?'

'Yeah, total whack.' It had been a long day with a lot of adrenaline expended. For that matter, it had been a long week that had brought a lot of terror and death. This kid was right about one thing. I hadn't expected the bearer of that terror and death to have green hair and a tongue stud. 'So this is a game,' I said. 'With a webmaster?'

'Pretty cool, huh?'

'Did you pull wings off butterflies when you were a kid?'

'No. I was a total wimp kid. I was a wimp until I found the Web Master and got into The Game.'

'Are there rules to The Game or do you just go around randomly killing people?'

'The Web Master runs The Game. He's the one who decides who can play. Not everyone gets to play, you know. There are always five players and a prize. This time you're the prize. I know you've been getting messages from the Web Master. That's part of his job. He's the one who keeps the rabbit running while the players are in the elimination stage. This is my second game. The first game was a couple years ago. I was last man standing on that one, too. I got to hunt a cop that time.'

'What's with the flowers?'

'That's The Game designation. If you play the Web Master's game, you're a Red Roses and White Carnations player.'

I couldn't believe I was standing on the sidewalk, talking to this kid who looked more like the Green Goblin than a Fisher Cat and was holding me at gunpoint . . . and not a car drove by. No one strolled through the emergency room doors, looking for a place to sneak a smoke. No emergency vehicles barreled down the street with lights flashing.

'You look kind of young to be killing people,' I said. As if age mattered when you were insane.

'Yeah, so far as I know, I'm the youngest player. I was seventeen when I killed Lillian Paressi. I got so excited I did the deed on her after she was dead.'

'That's sick and disgusting.'

Fisher Cat giggled. 'Maybe I'll do it on you, too, after I blow your head apart. I should have done it on Singh. The Web Master sent me to Vegas to get Singh. Really nice of you to find the little jerk for us. You don't just walk out on a Game. The Game is everything.'

I thought I was sounding pretty comfortable. My voice wasn't wobbling. My breathing appeared normal. I was asking questions. Deep inside there was bone-jarring fear. This was a seriously sick person. He had a gun. And it was going to ruin his night if he didn't kill me.

'The Fisher Cat has a real good sense of smell,' he said. 'I can smell your fear.'

'I don't think that's fear you smell,' I said. 'My sister's water broke on me.'

'Don't joke about it,' he yelled. 'This is serious. This is The *Game*.'

Oh boy. Good going, Stephanie. Now he's mad.

He waved the gun at me. 'Walk toward the garage.'

I hesitated and he shoved the gun in my face. 'I swear to God, I'll kill you right here if you don't start walking,' he said, still agitated.

So maybe it was fear he smelled. I was putting out a lot of it. I walked toward the garage, thinking the garage might be helpful. It looked empty, but visiting hours were still going on and I knew there had to be people around. I'd never paid attention before, but there had to be security cameras. Whether they were working or anyone was watching was a whole other thing.

We were still on the sidewalk, almost to the back of the garage. I assumed we were going in through the rear exit and once we were inside I would make my move. My plan was to jump behind a car and then run like the wind, screaming my lungs out. Not real sophisticated, but it was all I had.

'Stop here,' he said. 'This is my truck.'

It was a dark blue pickup parked at the curb. The paint was faded and there was rust showing around the tail pipe. The bed was covered with an old white fiberglass cap. So much for escape plan A.

'Get in the back,' Fisher Cat said. 'We're going for a ride.'

No way was I getting into the truck. The gun was scary. The truck was death. I rolled out and jerked away from him. He fired off a shot and I felt the bullet bite into my arm. I turned and ran and he ran after me, snagging the back of my shirt, throwing me off balance. I went down to one knee, pulling him down with me, and the gun dropped out of his hand.

And that's when I snapped. I was suddenly really pissed off. I whacked him with my purse, a good solid *whump* on the side of his head that jarred his mouth open and had his vision unfocused. I probably should have hit him with my bag again, but I wanted to get my hands on him. I wanted to gouge his stupid eyes out. This little creep killed people for a game. And one of them was a cop. My sister was in the hospital having a baby and this jerkoff was trying to kill me. How tacky is that?

I grabbed him by his ridiculous green hair and banged his head into the truck a couple times. He was flailing out with his arms, kicking at my legs. We both went down to the ground and rolled around, locked together like a couple squirrels, scratching and clawing and hissing. We weren't bitch slapping, trying to make a statement like Lula and Mrs Apusenja. This was real life-or-death combat. Luckily, while we were rolling around, my knee connected with Fisher Cat's crotch and I shoved his gonads halfway up his throat.

Fisher Cat went dead still and, almost in slow motion, somebody's fist smashed Fisher Cat's nose. Looking back on it, I suppose it was my fist. At the time, the fist didn't seem to be connected to my brain. The nose gave with a sickening crunch and blood spurted out, killing my outrage.

'Oh crap!' I said. 'I'm *really* sorry.' I don't know why I said it because I wasn't all that sorry. It was one of those female reflex things.

His right hand blindly struck out at me, he made contact with my arm, and lights exploded behind my eyes.

When I came around I was on my back on the sidewalk. The misting rain felt good on my face. It was dark, but there were lights everywhere. Red and blue and white. The lights were haloed in the rain, giving them a surreal quality. The fog cleared from my head. I blinked and Ranger and Morelli swam into my field of vision. There were a lot of other people behind them. A lot of noise. Cops. Yellow crime-scene tape, slick with rain.

'What happened?' I asked.

'It looks like you took a few volts,' Morelli said. His lips were tight and his eyes were hard.

It took a beat for me to remember . . . Fisher Cat's arm reaching out to me. 'Stun gun,' I said. 'I didn't see it until it was too late.'

Morelli and Ranger each got a hand under an armpit and hauled me up to my feet. The first thing I saw was Fisher Cat, motionless on the grass beside his truck. A couple cops were in the process of setting lights to illuminate the body.

'Holy cow,' I said. 'He looks dead.' I had a moment of panic that I'd killed him. Now that he'd zapped me, it was sort of satisfying to know I'd broken his nose, but I wasn't crazy about the idea that I might have beat him to death. I looked closer and saw the two bullet holes in his forehead. I let out a *whoosh* of relief. I was almost certain I didn't shoot him.

'Those aren't my bullet holes, are they?' I asked Morelli.

'No. We checked your gun. It hasn't been fired.'

Ranger was grinning. 'Somebody beat the shit out of this guy before he got shot.'

'That would be me,' I said.

'Babe,' Ranger said, the grin widening.

My arm felt like it was on fire. The entire upper half was wrapped in gauze and a fine line of blood had begun to seep through the gauze. 'I'm missing a chunk of time,' I said. 'What happened after I went lights out?'

'Ranger and I pulled in minutes apart and we got worried when we couldn't find you,' Morelli said. 'We knew you went outside to make some calls, so we went looking for you.'

'And you found me laying here unconscious and the green-haired guy dead?'

'Yeah.' Again, the tight lips and flat voice.

Morelli didn't like finding me unconscious. Morelli loved me. Ranger loved me, too, but Ranger was programmed differently.

'Your turn,' Morelli said.

I told them everything I knew. I told them about the game. About Fisher Cat. About the webmaster. About the cop.

'We need to do this downtown,' Morelli said. 'We need to get this recorded.'

It was raining harder. My hair was soaked. The bandage on my arm was soaked. I was streaked with mud and blood, my legs and arms were scratched from the scuffle. 'How's

Valerie?' I asked. 'Is she okay? Did she have the baby?'

'I don't know,' Morelli said. 'We haven't checked on her.'

The ME angled his truck into the curb just in front of the blue pickup. He got out and walked toward the body. He looked over and nodded to Morelli.

'I need to talk to him,' Morelli said to me. 'And you need to go inside and get your arm looked at. It's not serious. The bullet just grazed you, but it probably needs stitches.' He looked over at Ranger. 'If anyone in her family sees her like this, they'll freak.'

'No sweat,' Ranger said. 'I'll get her cleaned up before I get her stitched up.'

Ranger loaded me into his truck and drove me to Morelli's house. He opened the front door, switched a light on, and Bob came running. Bob stopped when he saw Ranger and eyed him suspiciously.

'I can see this dog's a killer,' Ranger said.

'Ferocious,' I told him.

'I'm assuming you have clothes here,' Ranger said. 'Do you need any help?'

'I can manage.'

His eyes darkened. 'I'm good in the shower.'

My temperature went up a couple notches. 'I know. If I need help, I'll yell for you.' Our eyes held. We both knew I'd jump out the bathroom window if I heard Ranger on the stairs.

I took a boiling hot shower, scrubbing away the dirt and blood and horror, being careful not to soak my gashed arm any more than was necessary. I toweled off and gasped when I looked in the mirror and saw my hair. A huge chunk of hair was missing. The left side was four inches shorter than the right side! How the hell did that happen? It had to have been Fisher Cat. Okay, that did it. I was glad I broke his nose. To tell you the truth, I wasn't sorry he was dead, either.

I got dressed in clean jeans, T-shirt, and sneakers. I tucked my wet hair behind my ears, covered it with a ball cap I found in Morelli's closet, and went downstairs.

Ranger was slouched on the couch, watching a ball game. Bob was beside him, his big shaggy orange Bob head resting on Ranger's leg.

'Looks like male bonding going on here,' I said.

Ranger stood and clicked the television off. 'Dogs love me.' He slid an arm around my shoulders and herded me to the front door. 'I called the hospital. Valerie had a baby girl. They're both doing great.'

Happiness and relief rushed from the center of my chest clear to my fingertips, and there was a terrifying moment when I was afraid I was going to cry in front of Ranger. I ordered myself to get a grip and I steadied my voice. 'What about Cal and Tank?' I asked.

'They've both been discharged. Tank's got his leg in a cast. Cal has a concussion. Not serious enough to keep him in the hospital.'

Ranger drove me to the hospital and walked me into the emergency room. He waited while my arm was cleaned and stitched. Then he called Morelli.

'She's done,' Ranger said. 'Do you want to take over?'

Morelli arrived a couple minutes later and Ranger disappeared into the night. Some day when I had more time and emotional energy I was going to have to think about the odd dynamic that existed between Morelli and Ranger and me. Morelli and Ranger were able to work as a team when necessary, all hostility seemingly put aside. And at the same time, in an entirely different area of the brain, rivalry existed.

Morelli and I found our way to maternity and located Valerie. My parents were gone, but Kloughn was still there, sitting on the edge of a chair at her bedside.

'Sorry I missed the big event,' I said to Valerie. 'I had a mishap with my arm here.'

'She was great,' Kloughn said. 'She was amazing. I don't know how she did it. I've never seen anything like it. I don't know how she got that baby out of there. It was magic.' Kloughn's face was still flushed and his surgical gown was sweat stained. He looked dazed and a little disbelieving. 'I'm a father,' he said. 'I'm a father.' His eyes filled and his smile wobbled. He swiped at his eyes and his nose. 'I think I'm still flub-a-dubbed,' he said.

Valerie smiled at Kloughn. 'My hero,' she said.

'I was good, wasn't I? I helped you, right?'

'You were very good,' Valerie told him.

The baby was in the room with Valerie. She was wrapped in a blanket and she had a little knit cap on her head. She seemed impossibly small and at the same time too large to have exited through a vagina. When I was in school I'd taken all the usual courses in human reproduction and I knew the process . . . the uterine dilation, the flexibility of the pelvic bones, the muscle contractions. So I knew some of the biology, but it still looked to me like this was a case of threading a walrus through the eye of a needle. There were days when I wasn't sure how Morelli fit. I didn't want to contemplate trying to pass a baby.

'We've named her Lisa,' Valerie said.

'Was it hard to pick out a name?' I asked.

'No,' Valerie said. 'We both agreed on Lisa. It's the family name that's giving us problems.'

Valerie looked tired, so I gave her a hug and a kiss. And

then I gave Kloughn a hug and a kiss. And then we left. I'm not a huggy-kissy person, but this was a huggy-kissy occasion.

Morelli and I left the hospital and went straight to Pino's. We ordered take-out and ten minutes later we walked into Morelli's house carrying a six-pack of Corona and a bag full of meatball subs. Bob was real happy to see us. Bob can smell a sub a quarter mile away.

I dragged myself into the living room, flopped onto the couch, opened the sub bag, and handed them out. One for me. One for Morelli. And two for Bob. Morelli cracked open two beers. We each took a long pull and dug into the subs. Morelli channel surfed while he ate, finally settling on wrestling.

'I'm tired,' Morelli said. 'You scare the hell out of me and it makes me tired.'

I was way beyond tired. I was numb. I had a lot of questions for Morelli, but I didn't want the answers tonight. I wasn't up to thinking. I could barely chew and swallow.

Tomorrow morning I had to go to the station and tell a recording machine everything I knew about Fisher Cat and the game. Tomorrow would be a big questions-and-answers day. Hopefully when I woke up my brain would be back in thinking mode.

Good thing wrestling was on. You don't need a brain to enjoy wrestling. Lance Storm was kicking the bejeezus out of some new guy who looked like King Kong's mutant brother. Storm was wearing little bright red panties that made him easy to find in my befuddled state. I opened a second beer and silently toasted Storm's panties.

Thirteen

Morelli nudged me awake. 'Rise and shine,' he said. 'I need to get to work and you need to come with me.'

'There's something poking me in my back.'

He slid his arms around me. 'Actually we have a couple minutes to spare.'

'How many minutes?'

'Enough to get the job done.'

'Are we talking about your job or mine?'

His hand skimmed the length of my belly and settled between my legs. 'We're wasting valuable time.'

Okay, here's the real difference between men and women. I wake up thinking about coffee and doughnuts and Morelli wakes up thinking about sex. Morelli kissed the back of my neck, did some really clever things with his fingers down there, and the thoughts of coffee drifted away. Truth is, the magic fingers had my full attention and the coffee thoughts were replaced by a fear that the fingers might stop.

The fear was groundless, of course. Morelli had learned a lot since our first time behind the éclair case in the Tasty Pastry bakery.

'So,' Morelli said when we were done, 'do you want to be first in the shower?'

I was face down on the bed, my heart rate was around twelve beats per minute, and I was in a state of euphoric slobbering contentment. In fact, I think I might have been purring. 'You go first,' I said. 'Take your time.'

Morelli went downstairs and got the coffee going before taking his turn in the bathroom. After a couple minutes the coffee fumes penetrated my after-sex glow. I rolled out of bed, pulled on a pair of shorts and a T-shirt, and followed the fumes to the kitchen. I poured out a mug of coffee and padded to the front door to get the morning paper.

I opened the door and found a red rose and a white carnation wrapped in cellophane, sitting on the paper. So much for euphoria. I brought everything inside and locked the door behind me. I left the flowers on the sideboard and opened the small square white envelope that had accompanied the flowers. The envelope held a note written on card stock.

Are you pleased that I saved you for myself? Do you get

hot when you think about me and all I've done for you? I could have killed you last night just as I could have killed you when I took you down with the dart, but that would have been too easy. Your death must be worthy of a hunter. It was signed, *Lovingly yours*.

And tucked into the envelope was a lock of my hair, tied together with a slim pink satin ribbon.

I got goose bumps on my arm and a chill ripped through my stomach. The shock was short-lived and I went back into bravado mode. Okay, I told myself, so that solves the mystery of the missing hair.

I was sitting in the living room with my coffee and the note when Morelli came down the stairs. He was freshly shaved and his hair was still damp. He was dressed in jeans and boots and a black T-shirt, and if I hadn't just had the mother of all orgasms I would have attacked him and lured him back to bed.

'I saw the flowers on the sideboard,' Morelli said.

I handed him the card. 'They were left on the porch this morning. They were on top of the paper, so the webmaster stopped around when it was daylight. Maybe someone saw him.'

'He's taking chances,' Morelli said. 'He's glorying in his success and that's going to make him careless.'

'Something to look forward to.'

'I'll have the neighborhood canvassed.' Morelli read the note. 'Sick,' he said.

I took a shower and did the best I could with my hair, pushing it behind my ears, lacquering it up with hair spray. I'd get a cut as soon as possible, but I hadn't a clue what could possibly be done with it. I looked close in the mirror. Extensions, maybe? Hairweave?

Morelli was on the phone when I came downstairs. He glanced at his watch and ended his conversation when he saw me. Morelli was ready to roll. The day had started without him. That's what happens when you're a sex fiend.

'I was talking to Ed Silver,' Morelli said. 'We just got the report back from the state techs. They were able to recover some email from Singh's computer. And the email corroborates what you learned last night. There were five players and the webmaster. We know Fisher Cat was last man standing, so we're missing a dead player.'

'Do you know any more about how the game is played?'

'One of the emails spelled out the rules. The webmaster conducts the game. Players only use their game names and can communicate with each other only through the web-master. So the webmaster always knows all. The webmaster gives out clues about the players' identities and the hunt begins. All players know from the beginning that there will only be one man standing at the end of the game. All players know there's no pulling out once the game has begun. Pulling out marks a player for assassination.'

'Singh.'

'Yeah. It looks like Singh was assassinated. The game began a full month before you got involved. You might have been the prize from the very beginning. Or the webmaster might have changed the prize midway. Or maybe the webmaster didn't feel any rush to designate a prize until the game was under way.'

'And I happened along.'

Morelli shrugged. 'No way to know. You're a good prize. Bounty hunter. The webmaster had to come up with something to top the cop. The prize isn't mentioned in any of the emails to Singh. The rules were that the webmaster only gave up the prize to the last man standing.'

'And the webmaster?'

'That's the bad news. No clue to the webmaster. His emails are, so far, untraceable. And he hasn't given away anything of himself. There were some messages to Singh about his disappearance, requesting that he return to finish the game, warning of the consequences. And there were a couple earlier messages that got the game going. Player names and hunt clues.'

'Is Bart Cone still a suspect?'

'Everyone's a suspect. Cone is high up on the list.'

'What about the other victims' computers?'

'We were never able to find Rosen's or Howie's computers.'

'Fisher Cat's?'

'Fisher Cat's name is Steven Klein. Nineteen years old. Worked at Larry's video rental and lived with his parents. The state has a team going through the parents' house, but so far as I know the computer hasn't turned up yet.'

I glanced at the newspaper I'd dropped onto the coffee table. Klein's picture was on the front page. To be more precise, Klein's sneakers were on the front page because the rest of him was hidden behind a couple cops and a back shot of me, standing hands on hips, head down. My hair didn't look good.

'Crap,' I said.

Morelli looked down at the photo. He raised his eyes and looked over at me. 'Did you get a new haircut?'

'Yeah. Somewhere between getting shot and posing for this newspaper picture. I guess you didn't look in the envelope.'

Morelli took the envelope off the coffee table and looked inside. Morelli's usually pretty good at hiding emotion, but the lock of hair pushed a button that was beyond his range of control. Color rose in his cheeks and he slashed out at a table lamp, hitting it with his closed fist, sending it flying across the room to smash against the wall.

Bob was curled into a big Bob ball at the end of the couch, sound asleep. He levitated six inches off the couch when the lamp crashed and he ran for the kitchen.

'Feel better?' I asked Morelli.

'No.'

'Do you have anything else for me?'

'Klein, Rosen, Singh, Paressi were all shot at fairly close range. Howie was shot across a parking lot. Even using a laser scope, there's still a skill level required to put a twenty-two between someone's eyes at a distance. Someone in the carnations and roses group is a very good shot. I'm guessing it's the webmaster. A possible scenario is that you discovered Howie's identity and the webmaster had to take him out or risk having the game blown. And then maybe the webmaster discovered he liked killing and decided to insert himself into the game as a player.'

'Was Bart Cone in the military? Does he belong to a gun club?'

'Never in the military. No gun club that we know of.' Morelli did another watch check. 'We have to roll.'

I did a fast scan for Ranger's man when I got outside, but I couldn't spot any shiny new black cars.

Morelli beeped his truck unlocked. 'If you're looking for

your rent-a-thug, I told Ranger you'd be with me this morning.'

'Did he make you take a blood oath that you'd protect me?'

'He asked me if I had adequate health insurance.'

The rain had stopped and Jersey was steaming. Grass was growing and oil-slicked puddles were evaporating. Another hour and the sun would be bright in the sky, shimmering in the ozone haze.

It was a terrific day for sandals, but I was wearing sneakers because it's hard to run fast in sandals. And I thought there was a good possibility that I might have to run fast today. I wasn't sure if I would be running *from* the webmaster or running *after* the webmaster. No matter which, I was prepared.

Ranger wore the eye of the tiger. He was always in the zone. I felt like I was in the zone today. Of course, there was the possibility that I was just delusional after the phenomenal sex, but what the hell, whatever the reason, I felt okay. And I was hardly thinking about the lock of hair. Well, all right, maybe I was thinking about it a *little*.

The Trenton cop shop is located on Perry Street and will never be mistaken for Beverly Hills PD. No potted palms or stylish mauve carpet. Mauve carpet doesn't hold up under pepper spray-induced snot.

Morelli brought me into a small room with a table and two chairs. He plugged in a tape recorder and punched the on button. I looked around and was ready to confess to anything. Just being in the grim little room, under the flickering fluorescent lights, made me feel guilty.

I walked my way through the conversation with Steven Klein, giving as much detail as I could recall. When we got to the part where I was zapped unconscious, Morelli shut the machine off and called Ranger. 'She's all yours,' Morelli said to Ranger. Morelli disconnected and looked over at me. 'That was a figure of speech.'

Ranger was driving a black Porsche Carrera. He was wearing black cargo pants, a black T-shirt that looked like it was painted onto his biceps, black Bates boots, and a Glock in full view on his hip. Ranger was in bodyguard mode.

'Couldn't coerce any of your men into baby-sitting me?' I asked him.

He cut his eyes to me and he didn't exactly smile, but he didn't look unhappy, either. 'You're all mine today, babe.'

It sounded different when Ranger said it.

'I don't know what your plans are for the day,' I said to Ranger, 'but my plan is to go to the mall and beg for hair help. I'm finding it hard to maintain the eye of the tiger when my hair is lopsided.'

On the way to the mall, I filled Ranger in on the game. 'It has to be Bart Cone,' I said. 'Someone sent Steven Klein to Vegas to eliminate Singh. And there were only a couple people who knew Singh was in Vegas. Cone was one of them.'

'It could also be someone Cone's talking to,' Ranger said. 'There are three brothers and they all have friends and associates. I'm sure the police have cast a wide net around them, but it wouldn't hurt for you to talk to the Cones. Sometimes a man will share information with a woman that he wouldn't think to give to a cop.'

Ranger parked at a mall entrance and we walked through the mall to the salon. We passed a Victoria's Secret along the way and I couldn't resist giving Ranger the test.

'Suppose I wanted to look for a thong,' I said to Ranger. 'Would you come into the store with me?'

Ranger did the almost smile. 'Are we cutting a deal?'

'Everything's a deal with you.'

'I'm a mercenary,' Ranger said. 'What's your point?'

For a couple years now I've been getting my hair cut by Mr Alexander. The guy's name is Alexander Dubkowski, but no one calls him Al or Alex or even Alexander. It's *Mr* Alexander if you want a decent cut.

We walked into the salon and Mr Alexander looked our

way and sucked in some air. Not only did I have a hair disaster of biblical proportions, I was with the Man from SWAT. And the Man from SWAT made people nervous.

'I had a hair accident,' I said to Mr Alexander. 'Do you have time to fix it?'

Mr Alexander went pale under his tanning-salon tan. Probably afraid Ranger would shoot up the place if I didn't get an immediate appointment. 'I have a few minutes between clients,' he said, motioning me into a chair, draping a cape around me. He did some hair fluffing with his fingers, then bit his lower lip. 'I'm going to have to cut,' he said.

Panic. 'It's not going to be real short, is it? How about a weave, or something?'

'I'm good, but I'm not God,' he said. 'It's going to have to get cut.'

I blew out a sigh of resignation. 'Fine. Cut.'

'Close your eyes,' he said. 'I'll tell you when it's done.'

I opened an eye halfway through and he quickly turned the chair so I wasn't facing the mirror. 'No cheating,' he said. When he was done, he spun me around and we both stopped breathing.

It was short. Longer in the back, curling along the nape of my neck. Short enough on the sides to have my ears show. A few wispy bangs over my forehead. And the whole thing looking slightly mussed and wind tossed.

Ranger came and stood behind me, checking me out. 'Cute,' he said.

'Last time my hair was this short I was four years old.'

When we were back in the car I turned to Ranger. 'Is it really cute or were you just trying to keep me from shrieking?'

He ran a hand through my hair. 'It's sexy,' he said. And he kissed me. Tongue and everything.

'*Hey*,' I said. 'We're not supposed to be doing that.'

A smile hovered at the edges of his mouth. 'Morelli told me you were all mine today.'

'That was a figure of speech. He trusts us.'

Ranger turned the key in the ignition. 'He trusts *you*. I haven't signed on to the *trust me* program.'

'How about me? Can I trust you?'

'Are we talking about your life or your body?'

I already knew the answer so I moved on. 'Where are we going?'

'TriBro.'

Twenty minutes later, Ranger was in the industrial park where TriBro was located. He pulled into a parking lot for a moving and storage company and cut the engine.

I looked over. 'What's up?'

He reached behind me and snagged a black molded-plastic box with a snap closure. 'I'm going to wire you. I want to make sure you're safe in there.'

'You're not going in?'

'No one will talk to you if I'm along.'

I raised an eyebrow.

Ranger did the almost grin thing again. 'Sometimes people find me to be a little scary.'

'*No!* Shocking. You ever think about losing the gun? Or dressing normal?'

He opened the box and removed a matchbook-size recorder. 'I have an image to maintain.'

I was wearing a black tank top and jeans. The jeans were hot, but they covered the bruises and scratches on my legs. Not much I could do to hide the bandage on my arm. My heart did a once over, knowing where the wire was going to get taped. 'I don't think I need a wire,' I said.

Ranger pulled my shirt out of my jeans and slid his hands under the shirt. 'You're not going to ruin this for me, are you? I've been looking forward to this.' He secured the recorder against my breastbone, just below my bra, with two crisscrossed pieces of surgical tape. The wire with the pinhead microphone ran between my breasts. 'Ready to rock 'n' roll,' Ranger said. He spun the Porsche out of the moving and storage lot and into the TriBro lot.

Let's take stock here. I've got my *go fast, feet* sneakers on and I'm wired for sound. I've got pepper spray and a stun gun in my purse. And I'm cloaked in an invisible invincible protective shield. Okay, so I lied about the shield. Still, four out of five isn't too bad, right?

I crossed the lot and entered the building. I gave a big smile and hello to the receptionist and got waved through to Andrew.

Andrew gave me the hero's welcome. 'Way to go! You found him. The office called about an hour ago.'

'Yeah, but he was dead.'

'Dead or alive makes no difference to me. All right, I know that's heartless, but I didn't really know him. And you saved me a lot of money. I would have been out the bond if it wasn't for you.'

'Unfortunately, your problems aren't over. Singh was involved in a killing game. All game members are dead now with the exception of the game organizer. And I'm pretty sure the game organizer works at TriBro.'

Andrew went perfectly still and the color drained from his face. 'You're kidding, right?'

I shook my head. 'I'm serious.'

'The police have been around talking to us, but no one ever said anything about a killing game.'

I shrugged.

Andrew got up and shut his office door. 'Are you sure

about this? This isn't another witch hunt like the one Bart went through? That was a nightmare and nothing ever came of it.'

'Lillian Paressi was a player in a previous killing game.'

'What?' Color was returning to his face, the shock morphing to disbelief and anger. 'That's ridiculous. That's the most insane thing I've ever heard. Why wasn't any of this brought out by the police?'

'They didn't know at the time.'

'But they know now?'

'Yes.'

'Then why aren't *they* here?' he asked.

I did a palms-up. 'Guess I got here first.'

'When you say you suspect the *organizer* of this game works at TriBro, does that include me and my brothers in your list of suspects?'

Up to this point I hadn't considered the possibility that Andrew or Clyde might be involved, but what the hell, cast a wide net, right? I took a shallow breath and jumped in with both feet. 'Yeah.'

Even as I was saying this I was thinking to myself that I had a lot of nerve making such an accusation. There was a really good chance that the webmaster was Bart Cone. There was also a chance that the webmaster was someone entirely out of the loop. And there was pretty much *no* chance that the webmaster was Andrew or Clyde. 'So,' I said, doing some mental knuckle cracking. 'It isn't you, is it?'

He was back in his chair and he was stunned. His mouth was open, his eyes were wide and blank, and a red scald rose up his neck into his cheeks. 'Are you crazy?' he shouted. 'Do I look like a killer?'

I had a vision of Ranger listening to this in the Porsche, laughing his ass off. 'Just asking,' I said. 'No reason to get huffy.'

'Get out. *Get out now!*'

I jumped out of my chair. 'Okay, but you have my card and you'll give me a call if you want to talk, right?'

'I have your card. Here it is.' He held the card up and tore it into tiny pieces. 'That's what I think of your card.'

I left Andrew and I scurried down the hall to Bart. The door to his office was open so I peeked inside. Bart was at his desk, eating lunch.

'Can we talk?'

'Is it important?'

'Life and death.'

He had a sandwich, a bag of chips, and a can of Coke in front of him. He took a chip and watched me while he ate.

'And?' he asked.

I gave him the same suave spiel. 'I know about Lillian Paressi,' I said. 'I know she was part of a killing game.'

'Do you have proof of this?'

'Yes.' Sort of. 'I also know about the current game. And I think the game organizer works in this building.'

Bart didn't say anything. His face showed no emotion. He selected another chip and chewed thoughtfully. 'That's a serious accusation.'

'It's you, isn't it? You're the webmaster.'

'Sorry to disappoint. I have no knowledge of any of this. I'm not a webmaster. And I'm not involved in a killing game. You're going to have to leave now. And you can talk to my lawyer if you want to continue this conversation.'

'All righty then. You have my card?'

'I do.'

I backed out of Bart's office, turned, and was almost knocked off my feet by Clyde.

'Oh jeez,' he said, grabbing for me. 'I heard you were here and I came looking for you. I guess I wasn't watching where I was going. *Shit.*' He clapped a hand over his mouth. 'Sorry. I meant to say *shoot!*'

I took a step back. 'No problem. I'm fine.'

'Have you had lunch? Would you want to go to lunch with me? I'd buy. It'd be my treat.'

'Gee, thanks, but my partner's waiting for me.'

'Maybe some other time,' Clyde said, not looking the least discouraged.

'Yeah. Some other time.'

I hustled out of the building, forcing myself to walk not run across the lot to the Porsche.

'Very smooth,' Ranger said, smiling.

I ripped the wire off and threw it on the dash. 'I'm *never* wearing one of these again. You make me nervous!'

'I wanted to make sure you didn't get abducted into the broom closet and snuffed with a toilet brush,' Ranger said. 'One of these days we should talk about interrogation methods.'

'It sort of went in the wrong direction. I don't know how that happened.' I slumped in my seat. 'I need lunch. A bag of doughnuts would be good.'

'Would you settle for pizza?'

'No! Last time you took me for pizza in this neighborhood there were bloodstains on the table.'

Ranger rolled the engine over and cruised out of the lot. 'You didn't talk to Clyde.'

'I talked more than I wanted. I'm afraid I'm going to open the door for the paper some morning and find Clyde sleeping on the doormat.'

We compromised and went to Pino's for pizza. We were on our way out when my cell phone rang.

'I have a problem here,' Connie said. 'The police notified

the Apusenjas about Singh's death over the weekend and now I have them sitting in the office. They want to talk to you.'

'Why me? You were in Vegas. Why can't they talk to you?'

'Mrs Apusenja doesn't want to talk to me.'

'Tell them I'm out of town. No, better yet, tell them I'm dead. Very tragic. Car crash. No wait, that would be in the paper. Flesh-eating virus! That's always a good one.'

'How long will it take you to get here?'

'Couple minutes. We're at Pino's.'

Five minutes later, Ranger parked in front of the office. 'You're on your own with this one, babe.'

'Coward.'

'Calling me names isn't going to get me in there.'

I looked through the large plate-glass window. Mrs Apusenja and Nonnie were sitting on the couch, bodies rigid. 'What *would* get you in there?'

Ranger leaned an elbow on the steering wheel and turned in my direction. And there it was . . . the eye of the tiger, focused on me.

I blew out a sigh and shoved my door open. 'Wait here.'

Both women stood when I walked into the office.

'I'm very sorry,' I said.

'I want to know everything.' Mrs Apusenja said. 'I *demand* to know.'

Connie rolled her eyes and I heard the lock click on Vinnie's inner sanctum.

I decided it was best to give everyone the abbreviated version. 'We had a tip that Samuel was in Vegas,' I said. 'So Lula and Connie and I flew out.'

'A tip. Who would tell you about Samuel?' Mrs Apusenja wanted to know.

'He applied for a job and his previous employer was checked as a reference.'

'This makes no sense,' Mrs Apusenja said.

'Samuel was living with a woman he met on a business trip,' I said. 'I spoke to the woman, but not to Samuel.'

Nonnie and Mrs Apusenja went perfectly still.

'What do you mean, living with a woman?' Nonnie asked.

'He listed her house as his residence. And he was living there. I can't be more specific than that.'

'I never liked him,' Mrs Apusenja said, narrowing her eyes. 'I always knew he was a little pisser.'

Nonnie turned on her mother. '*You* were the one who thought he was *wonderful. You* were the one who *arranged* the engagement. I told you these things were not done in this country. I told you young women were allowed to choose their husbands here.'

'At your age you can no longer be choosy,' Mrs Apusenja said. 'You were lucky to have an arranged engagement.'

Nonnie slid me a look under lowered lashes. 'Lucky to have him disappear and die,' she murmured.

Yikes. 'Okay, then, moving along,' I said. 'We learned from the police that Samuel had been shot and killed at the airport, so we went back and got Boo.' Okay, so I rearranged it a little. It made for easier telling.

'Boo!' Nonnie shouted. 'Where is he?'

'We didn't want to put him on a plane, so he's driving back with Lula. I think they might be here tomorrow or maybe Thursday.'

'Samuel Singh should rot in hell,' Mrs Apusenja said. 'He is a dognapper and a philanderer. After all we did for him. Can you imagine such a terrible person?'

I turned and looked through the window at Ranger. He was in the car, watching with a bemused expression. Ranger found me amusing. He enjoyed watching The Stephanie Plum Show. I didn't usually mind. I'd decided his interest was a mixture of raw lust, curious disbelief, and affection. All good things. And all things that were mutual. Still, every now and then I felt his enjoyment required some payback. And this was one of those times. If I had to deal with Mrs Apusenja, so did he. Okay, so I was escalating the game, and Ranger would probably take this as a challenge issued, but I deserved to have some fun, too, right?

'Do you see that man in the black Porsche?' I asked the women.

They squinted out at Ranger.

'Yes,' they said. 'Your partner.'

'He's homeless. He's looking for a place to stay and he might be interested in renting Singh's room.'

Mrs Apusenja's eyes widened. 'We could use the income.' She looked at Nonnie and then back at Ranger. 'Is he married?'

'Nope. He's single. He's a real catch.'

Connie did something between a gasp and a snort and buried her head back behind the computer.

'Thank you for everything,' Mrs Apusenja said. 'I suppose you are not such a bad slut. I will go talk to your partner.'

'Omigod,' Connie said, when the door closed behind the Apusenjas. 'Ranger's going to kill you.'

The Apusenjas stood beside the Porsche, talking to Ranger for a few long minutes, giving him the big sales pitch. The pitch wound down, Ranger responded, and Mrs Apusenja looked disappointed. The two women crossed the road and got into the burgundy Escort and quickly drove away.

Ranger turned his head in my direction and our eyes met. His expression was still bemused, but this time it was the sort of bemused expression a kid has when he's pulling the wings off a fly.

'Uh-oh,' Connie said.

I whipped around and faced Connie. 'Quick, give me an FTA. You're backed up, right? For God's sake, give me something fast. I need a reason to stand here until he calms down!'

Connie shoved a pile of folders at me. 'Pick one. Any one! Oh shit, he's getting out of his car.'

Connie looked like she was going to bolt for the bathroom. 'You lift your ass out of that chair and I'll shoot you,' I said.

'That's a bluff,' Connie said. 'Your gun's home in Morelli's cookie jar.'

'Morelli doesn't have a cookie jar. And okay, maybe I won't shoot you, but I'll tell everyone you shave your mustache.'

Connie's fingers flew to her upper lip. 'Sometimes I wax,' she said. 'Hey, give me a break. I'm Italian. What am I supposed to do?'

I heard the front door open and my heart started tap dancing. It wasn't exactly that I was afraid of Ranger. Okay, maybe at some level I *was* afraid of Ranger, but the fear wasn't that he'd hurt me. The fear was that he'd get even. I knew from past experience that Ranger was better at getting even than I was.

I grabbed a bond agreement and tried to force myself to

read it. I wasn't making much sense of the words and it was only dumb luck that I wasn't holding the bond agreement upside down when I felt Ranger's hand on my neck. His touch was light and his hand was warm. I'd been expecting it. I'd steeled myself not to react. But I yelped and gave a startled jump anyway.

He leaned into me and his lips brushed the shell of my ear. 'Feeling playful?'

'I don't know what you're talking about.'

'Watch your back, babe. I *will* get even.'

Fourteen

Ranger reached around me and took the bond agreement I'd been holding. 'Roger Pitch,' Ranger read aloud. 'Charged with assault with a deadly weapon and attempted robbery. Tried to hold up a convenience store. Attempted to shoot the clerk. Fortunately for the clerk, Pitch's gun misfired and Pitch took out his own thumb.'

I could feel Ranger laughing behind me as he turned to the second page. Connie and I were smiling, too. We all knew Roger Pitch. He deserved to have one less thumb.

'Vinnie wrote a five-figure bond that wasn't totally secured because there seemed to be a low risk of flight,' Ranger said.

'Pitch was a local guy with only one thumb. What could go wrong?' Vinnie yelled from his inner office, his words muffled behind his closed door.

'Goddamnit,' Connie said, opening drawers, looking

under her desk. 'He's got me wired again. I *hate* when he does that.' She found the bug and dumped it into a cup of coffee.

'Pitch didn't flee,' Connie said. 'He's just refusing to show up for court. He's at home, watching television, beating on his wife when things get boring.'

'He's only a couple blocks from here,' Ranger said. 'We can pick him up and I'll call someone in to shuttle him over to the station.'

Roger Pitch was mean as a snake and twice as stupid. Not someone I wanted to tangle with. 'Yeah, but Connie has other files. Maybe there's something more fun.'

'Pitch is a fun guy,' Ranger said.

'He's a shooter.'

'Not any more,' Connie said. 'He blew his thumb clear to Connecticut. His hand's going to be bandaged.'

Connie was right about Pitch's hand being bandaged. The incident happened three weeks ago, but the hand was still wrapped in big wads of gauze.

Pitch answered the door when Ranger and I knocked and he calmly accepted that we were bond enforcement. 'I guess I forgot my date,' he said. 'It's all these pain pills they got me on. Can't remember a damn thing. Lucky I don't put my pants on my head in the morning.'

Ranger and I were both dressed for the visit in full Super Hero Utility Belts. Sidearms strapped to our legs, handcuffs tucked into the belt, pepper spray and stun gun at the ready. Plus Ranger had a two-pound Maglite, just in case we needed to see in the dark. The Maglite could also crack a head open like a walnut, but walnut cracking was a little illegal, so Ranger saved it for special occasions.

'Let me just shut the television off,' Pitch said. And then he whirled around, slammed the door shut, and threw the lock.

'Fuck,' Ranger said.

Ranger didn't often curse and he rarely raised his voice. The *fuck* had been entirely conversational. Like he was now mildly inconvenienced. He put his Bates boot to the door and the door popped open to reveal Pitch at the end of the hall with a gun in his *left* hand.

'You're just a couple amateur pussies,' Pitch yelled.

Ranger gave me a hard shove to the shoulder that knocked me off the small front stoop into a scraggly hydrangea bush. Then he stepped to the side of the door and drew his gun.

Pitch squeezed one off, but he was shooting with his left hand and clearly he wasn't ambidextrous because the round hit the hall ceiling. The second round bit into the wall.

'Goddamn,' Pitch shrieked. 'Piece of shit gun!'

Pitch had destroyed his thumb with a semiautomatic. And I guess one misfire was enough for him because he was now holding a revolver. The revolver held six rounds and Pitch fired them all off at us.

Ranger and I were counting shots. I was counting while I was trying to disengage from the hydrangea. There was silence after the sixth shot. Ranger stepped into the doorway, gun drawn, and told Pitch to drop his weapon. I climbed onto the porch and saw that Pitch was trying to get another round into the chamber. Problem was, he couldn't do it with the bandaged hand, so he had the gun rammed between his legs and he was fumbling with his left hand.

Ranger gave his head a small disbelieving shake. Like Pitch was so pathetic he was an embarrassment to felons the world over.

Pitch gave up on the gun, threw it at Ranger, and ran into the kitchen.

Ranger turned to me and smiled. 'And you said he wasn't going to be fun.'

'Maybe you should shoot him or something,' I said.

Ranger ambled into the kitchen where Pitch was rummaging in a junk drawer, presumably looking for a weapon. Pitch came up with a screwdriver and lunged at Ranger. Ranger grabbed Pitch by the front of his shirt and threw him about twelve feet across the room. Pitch hit the wall and slid to the floor like a glob of slime.

Ranger cuffed Pitch to the refrigerator and called Tank. 'Send someone over,' Ranger said. 'I have a delivery.'

We stayed to watch Pitch get taken away by yet another of the Merry Men, we secured the house, and we walked out to the car.

'You could have told me to move instead of dumping me in the bushes,' I said to Ranger.

'It was one of those instinct things. Keeping you out of harm's way.'

'Yeah, right. Maybe more like getting even with me for sending the Apusenjas out to talk to you.'

Ranger opened the passenger side door for me. 'When I get even it's going to be something much more rewarding than dumping you in the bushes.'

I buckled myself in and looked at my watch. 'My sister came home today with the baby. I should stop around and see how she's doing.'

'Tank's going to be glad he broke his leg when he finds out how I spent my afternoon.'

'You don't like babies?'

'I come from a big family. I'm used to babies.'

'Well then?'

'My grandmother is a little Cuban woman who cooks all

day and speaks Spanish. Your grandmother watches pay-per-view porn.'

'She used to watch the Weather Channel, but she said there wasn't enough action.'

'Maybe you should check the dose on her hormone replacement. Last time I saw her she was trying to imagine me naked.'

I burst out laughing. 'That's what happens when you're a hottie. Women imagine you naked. Lula imagines you naked. Connie imagines you naked. Two-hundred-year-old Mrs Bestler imagines you naked.'

'How about you?'

'I don't have to imagine. I've seen you naked. Your naked body's burned into my brain.'

Ranger turned onto my parents' street. 'I'm going to wait in the car. And if you send your grandma out to harass me, I swear . . .'

'Yeah?'

'I don't know what I swear. I can't think of anything awful enough to do to you that wouldn't leave you maimed or psychologically scarred.'

'Nice to know there are boundaries.'

Ranger parked in front of my parents' house and got out of the car.

'I thought you weren't coming in,' I said.

'I'm not. I'm going to stay out here. I can't see the entire street if I sit in the car.'

Grandma Mazur opened the front door for me. 'Is that Ranger with you? Isn't he coming in?'

'He thinks he's coming down with a cold. Doesn't want to infect everyone.'

'Isn't that thoughtful! He's such a nice young man. Lots of times men aren't nice like that when they're hot-looking. Maybe I'll bring him something from the kitchen.'

'No! He just ate. He's not hungry. And you can't take a chance on getting infected. What if you got sick and gave the cold to the baby?'

'Oh yeah. Well, you tell him I was asking about him.'

'You bet.'

Valerie was on the couch, nursing the baby. The girls were watching Valerie. My father was in his chair, concentrating on CNN.

My mother came in from the kitchen, took a look at me, and made the sign of the cross. 'Your arm is bandaged, you have grass stains on your pants, and pieces of some sort of bush are stuck in your hair. And Ranger is outside, wearing a gun.' She looked more closely. 'Is that a wig?'

'It's my real hair. I got it cut.'

With the exception of the baby, everyone stopped what they were doing and looked at me.

'Sometimes it's fun to change things,' I said. 'Right? What do you think?'

'It's . . . cute,' Valerie said.

'I wouldn't mind wearing my hair like that,' Grandma said. 'I bet it'd look real good if it was pink.'

The phone rang.

'It's Lois Kelner across the street,' Grandma said. 'She wants to know if we're being invaded. She said it looks to her like there's one of them terrorists in our driveway.'

'It's just Ranger,' I said.

'I know that,' Grandma said, 'but Lois is calling the army.'

My mother did another sign of the cross.

'Maybe you should get Ranger out of the driveway,' Valerie said. 'Paratroopers landing on the roof would upset the baby.'

Grandma's eyes lit. 'Paratroopers! Wouldn't that be something.'

'I'll try to get back later,' I told everyone. I stopped in front of the hall mirror to pick the branches out of my hair and to take a close look at the cut. I'd never before thought of myself as *cute*. Sometimes I felt sexy. And sometimes I felt downright fat and stupid. Cute was a new one.

I opened the front door and waved at Ranger. 'Visit's over.'

'That was fast.'

'The woman who lives across the street thinks you're a terrorist. She said she was calling the army.'

'You have plenty of time then,' Ranger said. 'It'll take the army a while to mobilize.'

Ranger drove me back to Morelli's house. We clipped Bob to his leash, I stuffed a couple plastic sandwich bags into my jeans pocket, and we ambled down the street after Bob. Me and the terrorist out for a stroll with the dog.

'I feel like I should be doing something to find the carnation killer,' I said.

'You have state and local police working on it now. They have a lot of resources and they have some good stuff to trace back. The photos, the emails, the flowers. And now they have interrelated murders. They can reexamine them and look for commonality. And they'll go back through case histories to see if they can find other victims of the game. Your job right now is to stay alive.'

I glanced over at Ranger. He'd gone through three of the victims' apartments. Plus Bart's townhouse. 'Have you been through Klein's house?'

'I went through it last night while the police were there.'

'The police allowed you access?'

'I have friends.'

'Morelli?'

'Juniak.'

Joe Juniak used to be police chief. He was elected mayor of Trenton and now was running for governor.

'Klein lived with his parents,' Ranger said. 'His room was a typical kid's room. Messy, posters of rock bands, small arsenal under his bed, and a personal stash of pot in his underwear drawer.'

'You think that's a typical kid's room?'

'It was in my neighborhood.'

'What about a computer?'

'Klein had a laptop. His parents said he took it everywhere with him. It wasn't in his room and it wasn't in his truck. Probably the webmaster took the computer after he shot Klein. Paressi's computer was missing. Rosen's computer was missing. By the time the police got to Howie's apartment, his computer was missing.'

'Klein slipped up somehow when he took out Singh. He didn't get Singh's computer,' I said.

'He was probably waiting for Lu to leave, but you and Connie and Lula were in place by then.'

Bob stopped, hunched in front of old Mr Galucci's house, and conversation was momentarily suspended while we watched Bob poop. How embarrassing is this? Poop is not something I feel comfortable sharing with Ranger. Actually, I'm not comfortable sharing poop with *anyone*.

I'm not even comfortable with it when I'm alone.

When Bob was done I scooped the poop up in a sandwich bag. And now the horror continued because I had a bag of poop and no place to put it.

'Babe,' Ranger said.

Hard to tell if he was horrified or impressed by my poop scooping. 'I don't suppose you have a dog in the Bat Cave?' I asked him.

'The Bat Cave is dog free.'

Bob pulled at the leash and we continued walking.

'Everyone involved had a laptop,' I said. 'Did they have anything else in common?'

'Singh, Howie, Rosen, and Klein were all computer geeks and loners. Paressi doesn't entirely fit the profile, but she became a computer junkie when she broke up with Scrugs. Probably there's a connection between her and Rosen. Maybe Paressi talked to Rosen about the game and Rosen came on board after Paressi was killed. They were all between the ages of nineteen and twenty-seven. Rosen was the oldest. None were especially successful.'

'Bart Cone doesn't fit the profile, does he?'

Ranger was looking ahead at houses and cars. 'Not entirely, but he fits better than Andrew.' Ranger turned at the sound of a car a block behind us, traveling in our direction. He had his hand resting on his gun and his eyes stayed steady on the car. The car passed without incident and Ranger dropped his hand off the gun.

'Andrew lives in a nice midrange house with his wife. It's a stable relationship. They like to cook. They vacation at the Jersey shore. They have two kids.

'Clyde lives in a rental house on State Street. He shares the house with two other guys. I'm guessing he's known them forever. I found a photo of the three of them when they were in high school. The house is pretty much a wreck inside and out. Thrift shop furniture, broken blinds, refrigerator filled with beer and take-out boxes.'

'So Andrew and Clyde aren't loner computer geeks.'

'They aren't loners. I don't know how much time they spend on the computer.'

We turned the corner and headed for home. 'You've been busy using your breaking and entering skills,' I said.

'I just enter. I don't usually break.'

'You broke down Pitch's door.'

'Lost my temper.'

Bob hunched again.

'Oh, for crissake,' I said.

Morelli was sitting on his front step when we got back with Bob. 'Lucky you,' he said. 'A two-bag day.'

'I think we should stop feeding him.'

'Yeah,' Morelli said. 'That would work.' He stood and took Bob's leash and looked over at Ranger.

'It's been quiet,' Ranger said. 'No shooting. No one tailing us. No death threats or poison darts.'

Morelli nodded.

'Your watch,' Ranger said to Morelli. And he left.

'The bodyguard thing is getting old,' I told Morelli.

'Did you tell that to Ranger?'

'Would it do any good?'

Morelli followed me into the house. 'I have some bad news and then I have some bad news,' Morelli said.

'Let's start with the bad news first.'

'I checked your email account this afternoon just before I left work. You have another carnation letter. It's on the sideboard. I printed it out for you.'

I looked at the email.

It will happen soon. Nothing can stop it. Are you excited?

'This guy's turning out to be a real pain in the ass,' I said. 'Now what's the bad news?'

'Grandma Bella's on her way over.'

'*What?*'

'She called just as you were coming down the street with Bob. She said she had another vision and she had to tell you.'

'You're kidding!'

'I'm not kidding.'

'Why didn't you tell her not to come? Why didn't you tell her I wasn't home?' All right, maybe I sounded a little whiney, but this was Grandma Bella we were expecting. And whiney was better than flat-out hysteria, right?

'She's coming with a dish of my mother's manicotti. Have you ever tasted my mother's manicotti?'

'You sold me out for manicotti!'

Morelli grinned and kissed me on the forehead. 'You can have some, too. And by the way, your hair is cute.'

I narrowed my eyes at him. I wasn't feeling cute. In fact, I'd decided I didn't like cute. *Cute* wasn't a word anyone would use to describe Morelli or Ranger. Cute implied a degree of helplessness. Kittens were cute.

A car stopped in front of the house and I took a deep breath. Calm down, I thought. Don't want to be rude. Don't want to let them sense fear. There was a knock at the door and Joe reached for the handle.

'Touch that handle and you die,' I said. 'She's coming here to see me. *I'll* let her in.'

The grin returned. 'Woman in charge,' Morelli said.

I opened the door and smiled at the two women. 'How nice to see you again,' I said. 'Come in.'

'We can't stay,' Joe's mother said. 'We're on our way to church. We just wanted to drop this manicotti off.'

I took the casserole and Grandma Bella fixed her scary eye on me.

'I had a vision,' Bella said.

I looked down at her and screwed my face into an expression that I hoped conveyed mild interest. 'Really?'

'It was you. You were dead. Just like the last time. You went into the ground.'

'Uh-hunh.'

'I saw you in the box.'

'Mahogany? The model with the scroll work?'

'Top of the line,' Bella said.

I turned to Joe. 'Nice to know.'

'A comfort,' Joe said.

'So was there anything different about the vision this time?' I asked Bella.

'It was the same vision. But last time I forgot to tell you . . . you were old.'

'How old?'

'*Real* old.'

'We have to go now,' Joe's mother said. 'It wouldn't hurt you to come to church once in a while, Joseph.'

Joe smiled and gave her and Bella a kiss on the cheek. 'Be careful.' He closed the door after them and took the manicotti from me. 'Way to go. That was impressive.'

'I'm fearless.'

'Cupcake, you are *not* fearless. But you can bluff with the best of them.'

'What gave me away?'

'You had a death grip on the manicotti. Your knuckles were turning white.'

Bob and I followed Morelli into the kitchen.

'I was old in Bella's vision,' I said to Morelli. 'I guess I can stop worrying about the carnation killer now. And I definitely don't need a bodyguard.'

'I can hardly wait for you to explain this to Ranger,' Morelli said.

I woke up to sun streaming in through Morelli's bedroom window. Morelli was long gone and Bob was asleep in his place, head on the pillow, one eye open and watching me.

I got up, went to the window, and looked out. There was a shiny black Ford Explorer parked two houses away on the opposite side of the street. Not Ranger. Ranger never drove the Explorer. Not Tank. Tank was sitting somewhere in the Bat Cave with his leg elevated. Probably Cal. Hard to tell at this distance.

I took a shower, dressed in a tank top, jeans, and sneakers and wrinkled my nose at my hair. I had a tube of hair gunk that was a combination of wallpaper paste and mustache wax. I pulled a big glob of it through my hair with my fingers and my curls stood up at attention. I was a couple inches taller with the gunk in my hair and I wasn't a real good judge, but I suspected I was no longer cute.

A half hour later, I rolled into the office.

'Whoa,' Connie said at my hair. 'What happened to you?'

'I got a haircut.'

'I hope you didn't give him a tip.'

'Am I cute?'

'That's not the first word that comes to mind.'

Vinnie stuck his head out and grimaced at me. 'Holy shit. What'd you do, tag yourself with the stun gun? I wouldn't show that hairdo to your mother if I was you.' And he went back into his office.

'I didn't think it was *that* bad,' I said to Connie.

'You look like you soaked your head in liquid starch and then stood in a wind tunnel.'

Vinnie jumped out of his office. 'I got it! I know who it is that you look like . . . Don King!' And Vinnie jumped back inside and slammed and locked his door.

I felt my hair. It was pretty stiff. Maybe I overdid the hair gunk.

'Omigod,' Connie said, looking out the big front window. 'It's Lula!'

Sure enough, the red Firebird was parked at the curb and Lula was at the door with Boo under her arm.

'What did I miss?' Lula wanted to know, coming over to the desk. 'What's going on? Did I miss anything?'

I didn't know where to begin. There'd been death, birth, sex, and hair loss.

Lula shifted Boo on her hip. 'Are you still looking for that carnation guy?'

'Yep,' I said. 'Haven't found him yet. I tried calling you, but your phone wasn't working.'

'I stopped to take a break, got out of the car, the phone fell on the ground, and the dog peed on it.'

'You made good time,' Connie said.

'That is one motherfucker long trip,' Lula said. 'I was in the car for eight hours and my ass was asleep when I hit Little Rock and I said, "Stick a fork in me, 'cause I'm done." So I handed the rental car in and I hooked up with a couple truckers who drove day and night. And here I am. They dropped me off late last night.'

Connie took a closer look at Lula. 'Did you lose weight?'

'I lost ten pounds. Can you believe it? All you gotta do is eat meat all day. I've eaten so much meat in the last five days I can't remember ever eating anything else. I got meat oozing out my ears. And to tell you the truth, I'm starting to feel funny about all this meat. You don't think I could turn into like a *meat vampire* or something, do you?'

'I never heard of a meat vampire,' I said.

'For the last couple days my teeth have been feeling funny. You know, like they're growing. Just these two ones in front. What do they call them . . . canines. And then I was looking at myself in the mirror this morning when I was brushing my teeth and I was thinking they looked bigger. Like vampire teeth. Like I'm eating so much meat I'm turning into a carnivore. And I'm getting dog teeth.'

Connie and I were speechless.

'What happened to your hair?' Lula asked me. 'You look like Don King.'

'Yes, but I'm not cute,' I said.

'Fuckin' A,' Lula said.

Lula and I packed off in my car and headed for the Apusenjas. Boo was on Lula's lap, ears up, eyes bright.

'Look at him,' Lula said. 'He knows he's going home. Isn't it something the way dogs know these things? I tell you, I'm going to miss this little guy.' Lula cut her eyes to the rear-view mirror. 'Looks like you still got a bodyguard.'

I turned and squinted back at the Explorer. Cal was behind the wheel. And he had someone riding shotgun. Great. Now I had two baby-sitters.

I whipped out my cell phone and called Ranger.

'Lula's back,' I told him. 'So, thanks anyway, but I don't need Cal.'

'He's staying,' Ranger said.

'I can take care of myself. I want you to tell Cal to stop following me.'

'The carnation killer isn't going to move on you when you're so obviously guarded. He doesn't want to shoot you in the head from a distance. He wants to play with you.'

'Yeah, but this is really annoying and it could go on forever.'

'Not forever,' Ranger said. 'Just long enough for the police to do their thing. They have some leads. Having Cal in place buys them some time.'

'Grandma Bella said I wasn't going to die until I was real old.'

'That makes me feel so much better,' Ranger said. And he disconnected.

I parked in front of the Apusenjas' house. Lula leaned forward and adjusted the rear-view mirror and checked out her teeth.

'You're starting to creep me out with this teeth stuff,' I said.

'How do you think *I* feel? I'm the one turning into a . . . creature. I feel like Michael J. Fox in that werewolf movie. Remember when he started growing hair all over? It was like he was turning into Connie.'

Lula gave up on the teeth and looked over at the house. 'I'm bringing this dog back because that's the right thing to do, but the bride of Frankenstein better not start on me.'

'The bride of Frankenstein likes us now. She said she guessed I wasn't such a bad slut.'

'Bet you got all excited over that.' Lula levered herself out of the Escape, holding tight to Boo. She set him down on the ground. Boo ran to the Apusenjas' front door and started yapping to be let in.

Mrs Apusenja opened the door and let out a shriek. She scooped up Boo and held him close and got a lot of sloppy Boo kisses.

'Isn't that nice,' Lula said. 'A family reunited. It almost makes me want to get a dog. Except for the peeing and pooping part.'

Tell me about it.

Fifteen

I was on my way back to the office when Grandma Mazur called.

'We got a situation here,' she said. 'I don't suppose you're in the neighborhood?'

'What kind of a situation?'

'Valerie decided she's going to marry Albert.'

'That's great.'

'Yeah, except Albert's been living with his mom and his mom isn't happy that Albert's not marrying in his faith. Albert's mom wants him to marry a Jewish girl and so she's kicked him out of the house. That means everyone's going to be living here. Albert just showed up with a couple boxes of his stuff and he's moving it into that little room upstairs with Valerie and the girls.'

'Oh boy.'

'Exactly. We need to put rubber walls on this house. We don't all fit in it anymore. Your father says he's moving in with Harry Farnsworth. He's upstairs packing and your mother's all upset.'

'My dad's moving out?'

'I can sort of see his point on this. He had to drive to the gas station on Hamilton to use the bathroom this morning. So I don't exactly blame him, but what's your mother going to do if your father moves out permanent? Where's she going to find another man? It's not like she's a live wire.'

I did a large mental sigh. 'I'll be right there.'

'Don't tell nobody I called you,' Grandma said.

I made a U-turn on Hamilton and smiled, knowing Cal was scrambling to follow me in the big Explorer.

Lula leaned over the seat, watching him. 'Good to keep a man on his toes,' Lula said. 'I bet he's all worried back there, cursing you out. He can't find a place to wheel that SUV around. Uh-oh, he just jumped the curb and knocked over a garbage can. Ranger won't be happy to see a scratch on that shiny new car.'

I pulled into the driveway, blocking my father's car so he couldn't make a getaway. Then I ran back to Cal, who was parking in front of the house. His face was red and a trickle of sweat traced a path down his temple.

'It's okay if you park here,' I said to Cal and Junior, 'but don't get out of the car. Both of you stay here and try to look normal.' Even as I said it, I knew it was an impossible request. 'And don't worry about that big gash in the right front fender. It's really not all that bad,' I said.

The red in Cal's face kicked up a notch.

Lula was waiting for me on my parents' front porch. 'You are *so evil*,' she said. 'There's no gash in the right front fender.'

Grandma Mazur opened the door to me. 'What a surprise,' she said, real loud. 'Look everyone. Stephanie's here.'

Mary Alice was back to being a horse, galloping around the house, making horse sounds. The baby was screaming surprisingly loud for a newborn and Valerie was furiously rocking it in the rocking chair. Angie was drawing on a pad in the dining room. She had cotton wads stuck in her ears and she was singing, trying to drown out the noise. Albert Kloughn was pacing in front of Valerie.

'Maybe there's something wrong with her,' Kloughn said to Valerie. 'Maybe we should take her back to the hospital. Maybe she's hungry. Maybe she's wet.'

'Maybe she's got gas,' Grandma Mazur said. 'I know I do. This family's getting on my nerves. I can't stand all this noise and commotion. It gives me indigestion. I gotta get some Maalox.'

'I'm outta here,' Lula said. 'Nice seeing you all, but I'm going to wait in the car. I'm not good with crying babies. I've been locked in a truck cab with a dog and two horny truck drivers for the last couple days and on top of that I'm worried I'm turning into a carnivore.'

'I wouldn't mind hearing about the two horny truck drivers,' Grandma said.

I went into the kitchen where my mother was ironing. She always irons when she's upset. Ordinarily no one would approach my mother when she's got an iron in her hand, but I thought I should say something. 'This house is bedlam,' I said to her.

'I got a nice almond ring from the bakery,' my mother said. 'Help yourself. And there's fresh coffee.'

Even when my mother was in a state, she was still a mother.

'What do you think of my hair?' I asked her.

She looked at me and made the sign of the cross. 'Holy Mary, mother of God,' she said. Then she smiled. 'I can always count on you to top anything we have going on here.'

'I hear Val's getting married.'

'Thank goodness.'

'And I hear they're all going to live here.'

'What can I do?' my mother said. 'They have to live someplace. Am I going to turn my daughter out on the street? They're going to buy a house as soon as Albert gets a little more established.'

There were heavy footsteps on the stairs.

'Your father,' my mother said. 'He's moving out. We've been married for over thirty years and now he's moving out.'

Only if he pushed my car out of the driveway.

I went back to Val in the living room and shouted over the baby. 'I'm living with Morelli these days,' I said. 'Why don't you and the kids and Albert move into my apartment?' This was right up there with poking myself in the eye with a hot stick. I didn't really want to turn my apartment over to Valerie, but it was the only way I could immediately get her out of my parents' house.

'It would just be temporary,' Kloughn said. 'Just until we find a place of our own. Boy, that's really nice of you. Valerie, isn't that nice of Stephanie?'

'It is,' Valerie said, shifting the baby so it could nurse.

Lisa stopped crying and Valerie looked like she was morphing back to the serene Saint Valerie. I was thinking that there was probably a lot of my mother in Valerie.

'There's nothing like a baby,' Grandma said.

Mary Alice galloped by and stopped to look. 'I'd rather have a horse,' she said.

'When she gets older you'll be able to help feed her,' Valerie said. 'And she'll be as much fun as a horse.'

'Horses have nice silky tails,' Mary Alice said.

'Maybe we'll let Lisa grow her hair long into a ponytail,'

Valerie said. 'Would you like to take the little cap off her head so you can see her hair?'

Mary Alice took the cap off Lisa's head and we were all transfixed by the wispy dark hair that swirled from Lisa's crown and framed her face. Lisa's tiny hands were balled into fists, her eyes were open, and fixed on Valerie.

And just like that, as of that instant, I wanted a baby. I didn't care if it had to come out of my vagina.

'I'll tell your father about the apartment,' Kloughn said. 'I don't think he really wanted to move in with Harry Farnsworth.'

'I'll go over and box my stuff so you have room in the closet. You can move in anytime. Only thing, if there are any flower deliveries you should be sure to call me right away.'

'Thanks,' Valerie said. 'You're a good sister. I'll make it up to you. And we'll start looking for a place of our own right away.'

I yelled goodbye to my mom and I went out to Lula.

Lula was in the car, looking antsy. 'I don't know what's wrong with me,' Lula said. 'I just feel all jumpy. I'm just not myself.'

'You're not still worried about your teeth, are you?'

'I know they're growing. I can feel it. It's unnatural. And I got these cravings. I want to bite down on something. I want to feel it crunch in my mouth.'

'Jeez. You mean like a bone?'

'Like an apple. Or a Cheez Doodle. Nothing crunches on this diet. Meat doesn't crunch. I'm crunch deprived.'

I was a baton twirler when I was in high school. And that's how I felt now . . . like I was leading a parade. I pulled away from the curb and Cal pulled away from the curb. I drove to my apartment building. Cal followed me to my apartment building. We all parked in the lot. We all got out of our cars. We all took the elevator to the second floor. Then everyone followed me down the hall to my apartment. First Lula, then Cal, and then Junior. Junior was a clone of Cal, except for the tattoo. Junior was tattoo free. At least what I could see of him was tattoo free, and that was more than enough for me.

Cal opened the door to my apartment and took a look inside. Nothing out of the ordinary popped up, so we all trooped in. I filled a laundry basket with clothes and personal stuff and moved some things around to free up space for Valerie. While I was freeing space I could hear Lula trying to make conversation with Cal.

'Hey,' Lula said, 'what's going on?'

'What do you mean?' Cal asked.

'I don't mean anything,' Lula said. 'That's one of those things you say when you're trying to be friendly. That's an opening line.'

'Oh.'

'I heard you hit your head when you fainted in the hospital,' Lula said.

'Yeah.'

'Are you okay now?'

'Yeah.'

'I could be wrong here,' Lula said, 'but I think you're dumb as a box of rocks.'

'Sticks and stones,' Cal said.

There was a moment of silence where I figured Lula was regrouping.

'So,' Lula finally said to Cal. 'Are you married?'

The whole packing process took less than ten minutes. I'd been moving clothes piece by piece to Morelli's house over the last couple days and there wasn't a lot left. I handed the laundry basket over to Junior and everyone marched out to the hall and waited while I locked up. I took a last look at the closed door and had to choke back a panic attack. I was turning my apartment over to my sister. I was homeless. What if I had a fight with Morelli? What then?

Junior put the laundry basket in the back of the Escape and we all got into our cars.

'Where are we going?' Lula wanted to know.

'We're going to TriBro. I'm not sure what I'm going to do once I get there. I guess I'll figure it out then.'

I cut across town and picked up Route 1. It was the middle of the day and traffic was light. Cal had no problem following me. I took the off-ramp that led to the industrial park and wound through the park to TriBro. I parked toward the back of the lot and I sat there, watching.

'The killer's in that building,' I said to Lula.

'You think it's Bart?'

'I don't know. I just know it has to be someone at TriBro.'

After a half hour Lula was restless. 'I gotta get something to eat,' she said. 'I gotta stretch my legs. I'm all cramped up in this car.'

I was hungry, too. I didn't know what I was doing in the lot anyway. Waiting for divine intervention, I supposed. A message from God. A sign. A clue!

I put the car in gear and left the lot with the Steroidapods following close behind. I drove down Route I for a couple miles, took the turnoff to the mall, and parked at the Macy's entrance. This is always a good place to park because you hit the shoe department first thing while you still have lots of energy.

Lula pushed through the double glass doors and stood in the middle of the aisle. 'They're having a sale!' she said. 'Look at all those racks of shoes on sale.'

I looked at the racks and for the first time in Plum history, I didn't want to shop. My mind wouldn't move off the carnation killer. I was thinking of Lillian Paressi and Fisher Cat and Singh and Howie. And probably there were a lot of others. I knew of two games, but there might have been more. I was thinking of my sister's baby and the fact that I didn't have one. And maybe never would.

'Look at those sandals with the four-inch heels and rhinestones,' Lula said. 'You can't go wrong with rhinestones. And heels always make your legs look real shapely. I read that in a magazine.'

Lula had her shoes off, looking for a pair of the sandals in her size. She was wearing a poison green Spandex tube top and yellow stretch pants that matched my car and came to midcalf. She found the sandals, slipped them on and paraded in front of the mirror.

Cal and Junior were at the edge of the aisle, looking uncomfortable. They probably had expected to follow me around and catch some scofflaws when they got their marching orders from Ranger. And here they were in the Macy's shoe department, gaping at Lula, who was all boobs and booty in the rhinestone shoes.

'What do you think?' Lula wanted to know. 'Should I get these shoes?'

'Sure,' I said. 'They'll go with the pink outfit you got in Vegas.'

What if Ranger's wrong, I thought. What if the carnation

killer is tired of the game and doesn't want to play with me? What if he just wants to kill me? He could be watching me now. Lining me up in his sights.

Lula paid for the shoes and we hit the food court next. Lula got a chicken. I got a cheeseburger. Cal and Junior got nothing. Guess they didn't eat while working. Didn't want to have a burger in their hand if they had to go for their guns. That was fine by me. I was scanning the mall and my eyes were rolling around in my head so fast I was getting a headache.

I watched Lula tear into her food and I had a creepy thought that she might be right about her teeth. She could really rip apart a chicken.

'What are you staring at?' Lula wanted to know. 'Are you staring at my teeth?'

'No! Swear to God. I was just . . . daydreaming.'

After we ate we went back to the cars. I drove about a half mile down Route 1 and Lula and I turned our attention to the motel coming up on the right. It was the Morelli and Gilman motel.

'Probably I didn't see what I thought I saw that day,' Lula said. 'Probably I was just imagining . . .'

Lula stopped talking because Morelli's truck was parked in front of one of the units.

'Uh-oh,' Lula said.

I'd been doing eighty and I was a quarter mile past the motel by the time I screeched to a stop. Cal and Junior went flying past me, utter surprise and horror on their faces. I put the Escape into reverse, backed up on the shoulder at a modest fifty miles per hour, and turned into the motel parking lot. No sign of Cal and Junior.

'Suppose it's police business?' Lula wanted to know. 'Like maybe it's a sting.'

'He's not working vice any more. And this isn't even in Trenton.'

'You aren't going to do something stupid like beat down the door, are you?'

I parked at the far end of the lot, behind a tan van. 'Do you have a better idea?'

'We could sneak around back and listen in. Then if we hear them doing the deed we can beat down the door.'

I'd rather knock and have Morelli answer the door halfdressed than catch Morelli and Gilman in the act. I couldn't think of too many things that would be more depressing than hearing or seeing Morelli playing hide the salami with someone other than me. On the other hand, I didn't want to make a false accusation. 'Okay,' I said, 'we'll go around back.'

We walked around the side of the motel and began counting off units. Each unit had two windows on the back side. I was guessing one window was in the bathroom and one in the bedroom. There were twelve units in the first building. All were at ground level. A strip of grass hugged the back of the building. Beyond the grass was a chunk of overgrown woods filled with refuse. A plastic milk crate. Soda cans. A torn mattress. I had no idea what was on the other side of the wooded area.

Curtains were drawn on all the units. We listened briefly at each window, hearing nothing. We got to the seventh unit and heard voices. Lula and I pressed closer to the window. The voices were muted, difficult to hear. The back window was closed. The air-conditioner was running in the front window. There was a slight break in the curtain halfway up the back window. Lula tippytoed to the woods and got the milk crate. She put the milk crate under the window and motioned that I should get on the crate and look in the window.

No way was I going to look in the window. I didn't want to see what was going on inside. I whispered to Lula that she should look.

Lula got up on the milk crate, pressed her nose to the window . . . and her phone rang. Lula grabbed at the phone hooked onto her stretch pants and stopped the ringing, but it was too late. *Everyone* heard the phone.

Shouting erupted from inside the motel room. A gunshot

rang out. And a large man in a tan suit crashed through the window and knocked Lula off the milk crate.

'What the hell?' Lula said, sprawled on the ground in a tangle of curtain, sprinkled with window glass.

I wasn't sure what any of this was about, but I'd heard the shot and the guy who came through the window wasn't Joe, so I roundhoused him with my purse and sent him to his knees. I had him at gunpoint when Morelli stuck his head out the broken window.

'Oh Christ,' Morelli said when he saw me. And he ducked back inside.

Guys came running from either side of the building. Obviously cops, but I didn't know any of them. Two were in FBI T-shirts. Morelli joined them. I didn't see anything of Terry Gilman.

Morelli grabbed me by the arm and pulled me aside. 'What the hell are you doing here?'

'I saw your truck.'

'And?'

'I thought I'd stop by to say hello.'

'I'm working!'

I was getting annoyed. He was just a notch below yelling at me. 'How was I to know? This isn't Trenton. You're not driving your crappy cop car. And a couple weeks ago Lula saw you coming out of this motel with Terry Gilman.'

Morelli's eyes narrowed. 'You went around back to spy on me and Gilman?'

'Actually, Lula was going to do the spying. I didn't want to look.'

The guy in the suit was getting dragged away in bracelets.

'Isn't that Tommy Galucci?' I asked Morelli.

Tommy Galucci was famous in the Burg. Everyone knew he was a Mob boss, but the police had never been able to get anything to stick on him. Maybe because in the past the police never really cared all that much. Being a Mob boss in Trenton didn't get you on *America's Most Wanted*. Trenton was just a midsize pothole in the organized crime highway. And Galucci was a good citizen. He gave to the church. He kept his yard nice. He went out of town to cheat on his wife. But lately it was rumored Galucci was having a midlife crisis, wanting to make more of a name for himself, pushing his associates around.

'Yes, it's Tommy Galucci. Some of his *business partners* aren't happy with him and want to see him removed some way other than a one-way ticket to the landfill. They decided it would be a good thing for everyone if Tommy got to spend a couple years relaxing on a farm.'

'Like a federal-run farm surrounded by razor wire?'

'Yeah, something like that. The *business partners* decided they wanted me to run the operation. Probably that was

Uncle Spud's suggestion. And Gilman was acting as the go-between. People see me and Gilman together and the first thought isn't *sting.*'

'It wasn't my first thought. Why this motel?'

'It's owned by Galucci's brother-in-law. Galucci did a lot of business here. Felt safe to him.'

'Guess I screwed things up.'

'I don't know what it is with you. You fall into a hole filled with shit and you come up smelling like a rose. Galucci wasn't cooperating. I wasn't getting anywhere with him. When he heard the phone he freaked, thinking he was set up. He shot the fed who was in the room with me and then he tried to escape by going out the window. The fed in the room with me just got a superficial flesh wound, but now we have Galucci on assault with a deadly weapon.'

I looked beyond Morelli and saw two suits grilling Lula.

'You better rescue Lula,' I said. 'Probably it's not a good idea to let those guys look in her purse.'

Morelli did some negotiating with the feds involved in the bust and it was suggested that Lula and I should leave the scene immediately and never return. Lula and I were happy to comply with the suggestion.

Cal and Junior had backtracked and found me and were parked two cars down in the motel lot. Their faces were red and they had deodorant failure. Ranger wouldn't have been happy if they'd lost me.

'See that?' Lula said when we were all heading south on Route 1. 'I told you Morelli was there on account of work. You should be more trusting of Morelli.'

'If you'd been in my shoes, would you have trusted him?'

'Hell no,' Lula said.

Truth is, I did trust Morelli. But there's a limit to trust. Even the most trusting woman who saw her boyfriend's truck at a motel in the middle of the day, *twice*, would have doubts. There's a difference between being trusting and being stupid.

Traffic was heavy and slow going in and out of Trenton. It was coming up on rush hour. Drivers looked sweaty and impatient. Men drummed their fingers. Women chewed on their cheeks.

I was still feeling the pull from TriBro. I turned off Route 1 and found my place in the TriBro lot.

'I don't get it,' Lula said. 'What's with this parking thing? What are you waiting for?'

I didn't know. Instinct kept dragging me here today. I half expected to see ominous dark clouds boiling over the building. Ghostbuster clouds. Portents of danger.

We sat there for a while and employees started to leave. The lot was almost empty and my phone rang.

It was Clyde. 'Hey, Stephanie Plum,' he said. 'Is that you out in the lot? I see a yellow car and it looks like you inside. I'm watching you with binoculars. Wave to me.'

I waved to Clyde.

'What are you doing in the lot?' he wanted to know.

'Just sitting,' I said. 'Watching.'

'Is that your partner with you?'

'Yeah. That's Lula.'

'It's quitting time,' he said. 'Do you and Lula want to go to dinner? We could all get a burger someplace.'

'I don't think so.'

'Okay,' Clyde said. 'Call me if you change your mind.'

'Pretty soon we're gonna be in this lot all by ourselves,' Lula said. 'You and me and the two big dummies over there. You aren't planning on breaking in, are you? Maybe see if Bart Cone left his computer on?'

'Bart's smarter than that. He's not going to leave anything incriminating on his computer. Even if he did, I'm not that good at computers to be able to find it. And I'm sure the building has an alarm system.'

The idea was tempting, though. Just not practical. And it was out of my league. It was a Ranger escapade.

'Okay, then how about the guy who just called you? The goofy Cone brother that doesn't do anything and wants to be a junior G-man. He's always wanting to take you out, right?

I bet you could get him to let you in. I bet he doesn't even like his brother.'

'*No*. I'll never get rid of him. It would be like feeding a stray cat. Once you give it a bowl of food you're stuck with the cat for life. I don't even *talk* to Clyde Cone.'

'Too bad,' Lula said, 'because I bet he'd let you in and you could go snooping through ol' Bart's files and drawers and everything. You couldn't get into his email, but you could take a look at the desktop on his computer.'

Truth was, I didn't want to go into the building. Not even with Cal and Junior doing backup. There was something bad in the building. The monster was there. He was waiting for me.

I got a call from Morelli wondering where I was. I didn't know what to say. I was sitting in an empty parking lot. Waiting for the mystery to be resolved. 'I'll be home soon,' I told him. 'Don't worry.'

The *don't worry* message was insincere. I was worried. I was really, really worried.

'Steph,' Lula finally said. 'Maybe we should go home.'

She was right, of course. So I cranked my yellow Escape over and drove out of the lot. I dropped Lula off at her car at the office and then I went home to Morelli.

I made peanut butter and olive sandwiches for supper and we ate in silence in front of the television. Probably we should have talked about the motel thing, but neither of us knew how to begin. Maybe it wasn't important anyway. We seemed to still like each other.

At nine o'clock Morelli was glued to the television and I was still fighting the fear or dread or whatever the hell it was that had its grip on me. I went to the kitchen and got a beer and took it out to the back porch. The air was soft and smelled nice, like fresh dirt and new grass. Joe didn't do much with his backyard, but his next-door neighbor, Mrs Lukach, had flower beds and a dogwood tree. Joe and I had gardening skills that were almost as good as our house-keeping and cooking skills.

I finished my beer and stood. I turned toward the house and I felt a familiar piercing pain in my back. In my mind I called for Morelli, but either he didn't hear over the drone of the television or else it was only a mental plea for help, because the blackness came and there was no Morelli.

Even before I opened my eyes I knew I was in trouble. Fear filled every part of me. The fear was a hard knot in my chest. The fear clogged my throat. The fear slid in a greasy wave through my stomach. I forced my eyes open and I looked around. I was on the floor, in the dark. I didn't seem to be hurt. I wasn't restrained. I moved my leg and realized I had a chain padlocked around my ankle.

There were jingle bells attached to the chain. The potential significance of the ankle chain took my breath away.

I had a dull throbbing ache behind my eyes. It was from the drug, I thought. Like last time, when I was shot with a dart in the parking lot.

The only source of light was a single candle burning on a desk to my right. The light was dim, but I knew where I was. I was at TriBro. I was in Clyde's office. I could make out the action figures in the bookcase to my left.

I pushed myself up so I was sitting and realized someone was slouched in a chair, lost in shadow, watching me from across the room. The shadowed figure leaned forward into the candlelight and I saw that it was Clyde.

'You're awake,' he said. 'And you look scared. Sometimes when I get scared I get sexually excited. Do you get excited when you get scared? Are you hot?'

The words sent a new rush of cold fear into my chest. I looked into Clyde's eyes and I saw the monster emerging.

'Get up,' Clyde said. 'Go around the desk and open the drawer. I have a surprise for you.'

I steadied myself on the desk and got to my feet, swallowing back nausea from the drug. I inched around the desk, carefully opened the drawer, and looked down at another lock of my hair, tied with the slim pink ribbon.

I looked up and my eyes met Clyde's. 'Now you know,' Clyde said. 'You're surprised, right? I bet you never thought it was me.'

Everything fell into place. Web Master wasn't a computer term as we'd all assumed. It was a Spider-Man reference. Days ago, I asked Clyde what he wanted to do, and he said he wanted to be Spider-Man. Spider-Man was known as the webslinger and Clyde's game name was the Web Master.

'Spider-Man didn't kill innocent people,' I said. 'Spider-Man was a good guy.'

'I'm not the web*slinger*,' Clyde said. 'I'm the Web *Master*. There's a difference. And I don't kill innocent people. I run a game so people can kill each other. How cool is that?'

'What about the prey? Aren't they innocent?'

'I pick the prey out real careful. And they're never innocent. The cop killed a guy in the line of duty. And so have you. As soon as I saw you at the plant that day I knew you had to be the next prize. Bart tried to warn you away, but you wouldn't listen. It wouldn't have mattered. I had my mind made up right away.'

'Bart knows about The Game?'

Clyde was smiling, rocking back on his heels, enjoying his moment. 'Bart's confused. I got careless with The Game two years ago and Bart got to read an email. Paressi and Fisher

Cat were left in The Game and I was giving them the kill clue. Bart didn't know it was a game. He thought I was involved with Paressi and he went to the kill spot to stop me from a crime of passion. Problem was, he got there too late. Paressi was dead and Fisher Cat was gone.'

'And Bart was accused of the crime.'

'Yeah. And he was being a hero, protecting me. What a moron. Then when the DNA came back he was totally confused. It wasn't his DNA, of course. And Bart knows enough science to know that the DNA couldn't have been mine, either. It had the wrong structure. It was Fisher Cat's DNA.'

'Didn't Bart ask you about the email?'

'Yeah. I gave him some bullshit story about unrequited love. And he wanted to believe it. He wasn't warning you off because of The Game. He was worried I'd go gonzo for you and write another nutcase letter.'

'What about Andrew? Did Andrew know about The Game?'

'Andrew? You gotta be kidding. Andrew's got his perfect office, and his perfect family, and his freaking perfect house. Andrew doesn't see bad things. Doesn't allow them into his life. Doesn't ask questions that might have troubling answers. Andrew lives in Denial Land.

'Everyone always thinks Andrew's so perfect and

everyone always underestimates me. Silly, lazy Clyde. Poor, dumb Clyde.'

'And?'

'I'm not dumb. I'm smarter than everybody. Ask any of the people who play my game.'

'They're all dead,' I said.

'Oh yeah,' Clyde said on a giggle. 'I forgot.'

'Why did Singh take off?'

'He was scared. He went after Bag Man, who you know as Howie. Somehow, Singh managed to screw up the kill and then his cover was blown. He turned chicken and ran.'

'Now what?'

'Now we play. I've got a new game I thought up just for you. It's sort of a treasure hunt. And the grand prize is death. It's going to be a real good death, too. Scary and sexy and bloody.'

This guy was so crazy. He'd been letting the insanity leak out little by little over the years and no one had noticed. Or maybe his family had noticed and chose not to recognize it for what it was.

'Okay, here we go,' Clyde said. 'I'm going to tell you about The Game.'

Morelli would have discovered I was gone by now. He'd call Ranger and they'd be out looking for me. If I dragged this on long enough, they might find me in time.

'I can't think,' I said. 'I have a headache and nausea from the drug.'

'That should be passing. I gave you a small dose. Just enough to have you unconscious for the capture. Probably what you're experiencing is a blood pressure rise from the fear. You're scared, right?'

I looked at Clyde. I didn't say anything.

'Yeah,' Clyde said. 'You're scared big time. I can feel it. I'm very sensitive to these things.'

I raised an eyebrow.

'I *am*,' Clyde said. 'I have heightened senses . . . like a superhero or a werewolf.'

'I understand pigs have a superior sense of smell. Maybe you're part pig.' I was relieved not to have stuttered. I was so scared my mouth felt detached from my face.

'Here's the game plan,' Clyde said. 'All the doors are locked. You can't get out. Your only hope is to find a weapon and eliminate me before I get tired of playing with you. I have a loaded gun, a stun gun, and a big sharp knife hidden somewhere in the plant. Plus, there are things you'd naturally find here . . . like acid and hammers and shit like that.

'I've got two of your buddies hanging out here, waiting for you to find them. If you die, they die, too. In fact, if you don't find them soon enough, they'll die. You have a half hour to find the first one.'

'Who are they?'

'That's for you to discover. Oh yeah, and I forgot to tell you . . . you'll be doing this in the dark. You can take the candle if you want. Romantic, right?'

He was smiling again. I guessed this was his idea of a date.

'I've disconnected the alarm system,' he said. 'If you trip the smoke detectors the signal won't get sent out anywhere. The sprinklers will go off and we'll all get wet, but nobody'll come to save you. That might be fun . . . seeing you in a wet T-shirt.'

Clyde stood so I could see he was armed. 'I have a twenty-two for the kill,' he said. 'And I have a paintball gun and a pellet gun for the rabbit in the shooting gallery. That's you. You're the rabbit. Oh yeah, and I have a taser. It's new. I always wanted to use a taser.' He pointed the taser at me. 'This is the start of playtime. I'm going to give you a chance to run. I'm gonna count to twenty and then I'm going to shoot you with the taser. *Go!*'

He started counting and I took off, forgetting the candle. Halfway down the hall I had to stop running. It was pitch black and I had no idea what was in front of me. I put my hand to the wall, feeling my way, jingling with every step. The hall led to the front foyer and I was prepared to crash through the glass door if necessary. I needed to get out of the building. Crazy Clyde was going to kill me and he wasn't going to spare his hostages. It didn't matter who I found. We were all going to die unless I could escape and get help. Clyde wasn't going to leave witnesses.

I saw the ambient light from the foyer and broke into a run. I turned the corner, heard gunshot, and felt the sting of impact. I felt blood run down my side, down my leg. I cried out and put my hand to my side. Paint. I was hit with a paintball.

'I'm right behind you,' Clyde said. 'If you go toward the door I'll shoot you with the taser. I'm dying to use the taser. Sometimes they use these things for torture. The electric lead stays hooked into you with a barb and you can keep getting shocked. How cool is that?'

I was in the middle of the floor and I was breathing heavy. 'What do you want me to do?'

'I want you to run, rabbit. Run *away* from the door.'

I took a step and stumbled down to one knee. I was too scared to run. Too scared to think. Not good, I told myself. I had to try to stay calm. I managed to get myself to my feet and I ran in blind panic down the other side of the hall, toward Andrew's and Bart's offices.

There was a faint bar of light under a doorjamb in front of me. I pushed the door and it swung open. It was Bart's office. The office was lit by a single candle on the desk.

Albert Kloughn was duct-taped to the desk chair behind the desk. He had duct tape across his mouth and wrapped around his ankles. His eyes were huge and tears rolled down his cheeks.

I ripped the tape off his mouth and was about to go for the tape around his torso when I saw the bomb.

'Don't touch me,' he said. 'I'm b-b-b-booby-trapped.'

I snatched at the desk phone. No dial tone. I locked the door from the inside and pawed through the junk on Bart's desk, looking for something helpful. My hands were shaking and my heart was thundering in my chest. 'I *hate* this,' I said. 'I *hate* this game. And I *hate* the pathetic excuse for a human being who's out there stalking me.'

'You have to get help,' Kloughn said. 'This guy is crazy. He's going to kill us.'

'There are just nuts and bolts on this desk,' I said. 'I need something I can use as a weapon.'

'I know where there's a weapon,' Kloughn said. 'I can swivel myself in this chair and I was looking out the window into the warehouse when the crazy guy was hiding things. There's a room off to the side with glass windows all along.'

'The quality control area.'

'I don't know, but there's a workstation just by the door to that room. And he hid a gun there. It's right on top of the table part of the machine.'

There was a knock on the door. 'You're not allowed to lock yourself in Bart's office,' Clyde said. 'It doesn't matter anyway, I've got a key. But now you're gonna have to get punished before we can go on with the playtime.'

I heard the key scrape in the lock and I grabbed a wooden crate half-filled with gears and threw it at the window that led to the warehouse. The glass shattered and I dove through the window. If I got cut it wasn't going to be any worse than what was going to happen to me at Clyde's hands.

I hit the ground and rolled. I'd seen the roll done in the movies and it seemed like a good idea. Problem was, in the movies they weren't usually landing on two thousand metal gears. Still, I wasn't decapitated from the glass shards when I pitched myself through the broken window, so that was a point in my favor. I scrambled to my feet, sliding on the debris, and ran for the first workstation. Beyond the first workstation the room blacked out and I was going to have to feel my way to the side room where the quality control people worked.

I was almost to the workstation when I was hit by another paintball. Thank God, I must have been beyond the reach of the taser. The paintball hit square in my upper back. If I lived to see another day, I'd be bruised. I dropped to the floor and put the workstation between me and Clyde. I heard Kloughn give an unearthly blood-curdling shriek, the candlelight went out, and then everything was quiet.

I was guessing that Clyde didn't want to chance going through the broken window. He was going to have to go back to the hall and enter the warehouse through the door at the end of the adjoining corridor. That gave me some time.

I crossed the room as fast as I could, creeping along low to the ground, my hands outstretched to keep from smashing into a workstation. I found the wall with the windows and knew I was in the right place. I followed the wall to the door and then paced off to the workstation. Sure enough, there was the gun just like Kloughn said. I couldn't see the gun even when I held it inches from my face, but I could feel that it was a six-shot revolver and it was loaded.

I backed myself into the test room and closed the door. I took up a position behind a desk, kneeling with my forearms resting on the desk, two-handing the gun to keep it from shaking. I was doing deep controlled breaths, telling myself to focus, to be a professional.

I heard the door open and I shouted for Clyde to stop. There was a gunshot and I felt the hit to my shoulder. And in that instant, I unloaded everything I had. I squeezed off all six rounds, shooting blind. The last shot was followed by silence. It was solid black in the office. I couldn't see my hand in front of my face. Either Clyde was dead or else he'd retreated. I wasn't willing to leave the desk to find out. It was Dolly Freedman's desk. I reached into her top drawer and got her pepper spray. Then I ducked under the desk and waited.

I heard something scuff in the direction of the door and my heart stuttered. He wasn't dead! The monster wasn't dead. A sob caught in my throat and I blinked back tears. There was the rustle of clothing directly in front of me and I covered my face with my arm and hit the trigger on the pepper spray.

'Oh shit. *Fuck!*' A man's voice. Not Clyde.

The spray was knocked out of my grasp, a hand grabbed me by the front of my shirt, hauled me out from under the desk and dragged me to my feet, moving me out of the area, away from the spray.

I was told to hold still. I knew this voice. I was held tight to Ranger. He slid goggles over my head and I was able to see in the dark. Ranger had two men with him. Cal and Junior. And Junior was bent at the waist, gagging. That was the one I got with the spray.

'Sorry,' I said.

He made a dismissive gesture with his hand.

I looked to the door and saw feet. Clyde's. The feet weren't moving. Clyde hadn't jumped away fast enough.

Turned out Clyde wasn't as smart as he thought.

'Dead?' I asked.

'Looks that way. From what I can see, he took three in the upper body.'

'I was shooting blind in the dark,' I said. 'I didn't know if I hit him.'

'Anyone else in the building?'

'He has Albert Kloughn tied up with a bomb strapped to his chest in one of the offices. He said he had another hostage. I don't know who that is. I didn't find the other hostage.' My knees gave out and I sort of sunk into Ranger and dissolved into tears. He had his arms tight around me, holding me to him. He sent Junior in search of the mechanical room to get the lights back on. He sent Cal to search for the second hostage. Then he called Morelli.

'I've got Stephanie,' Ranger said. 'She's safe, but there's a hostage unfound and a hostage potentially carrying a bomb. I haven't seen the bomb. I'm going to check it out now.'

'Where's Joe?' I asked, wiping my nose with the back of my hand, trying to regain some control.

'We split up. I got the factory and he went to Clyde's house.'

'How did you know it was Clyde?'

'Cal saw the truck tear past him. He didn't know what the truck driver was up to, but he thought it was suspicious enough to check with Morelli. Cal got part of the plate and Morelli ran it through the system, checking it against the principals.'

The lights flickered and we took our goggles off. Every light flashed on at full power and we got a better look at Clyde. He was lying face up. The monster was gone and Clyde looked very ordinary in death. In fact, he looked oddly peaceful. Maybe it had been a relief to give up The Game.

'Help,' Albert Kloughn said. His voice was barely a whisper.

We all turned and stared at him, strapped to his chair on the other side of the warehouse. His face was red and mottled and he looked like he wasn't going to live long enough for the bomb to explode.

Ranger jogged across the room. 'Try not to move,' Ranger said to Kloughn. 'I'm coming around to take a closer look.'

We all followed after Ranger, watching from the hall while Ranger went into the office.

'I think it's a dummy,' Ranger said, 'but I'm not an expert.' He took out a pocketknife and cut the duct tape away from Kloughn's ankles. He sliced into the tape binding Kloughn to the chair. 'I'm not going to touch the device you've got strapped to your chest,' Ranger said. 'Stay here in the chair until the police get here with a demolition team.'

Ranger's walkie-talkie chirped.

It was Cal. 'You have to see this,' he said. 'I think I found the second hostage. I'm in the lunchroom.'

We left Junior with Kloughn and we followed the hall to the lunchroom. Cal was standing hands on hips, smiling up at Lula. She was swinging like a giant piñata from a rope attached to a ceiling fan. She was still wearing the poison green top and the yellow stretch pants and her feet were treading air about fifteen feet off the ground. Her arms were duct-taped to her sides and she had duct tape across her mouth. A thick rope was wrapped around and threaded through the duct tape on her body and then looped around the fan. She had the beady little charging bull eyes, she was making angry *mmmmrf mmrff* sounds under the duct tape, and she was kicking her feet. Plaster dust was sifting down on her head from the ceiling fixture.

Ranger's face creased into a smile. 'I love my job,' he said.

'He must have gotten her up there with a forklift,' Cal said. 'There's one parked down the hall. Do you want me to drive it down here?'

'Don't need it,' Ranger said, shoving a table under Lula, climbing onto the table.

Her feet were still swinging in the air and she was still kicking.

'You kick me and I'm leaving you here,' Ranger said.

'*Hmmph,*' Lula said under the duct tape.

Ranger worked at the rope with his knife, the rope gave, and Lula dropped onto the table. Cal reached out to support her and the two of them went to the floor.

I ripped the tape off Lula's mouth and Ranger cut the tape that was binding her arms.

'I was drugged!' Lula said. 'Do you believe it? I was taking the garbage out and he shot me in the ass with a dart. That little shit, Clyde. Next thing I know I'm swinging around from the ceiling. I'm beside myself. I'm in a state. I didn't know what to think. I saw some kinky shit when I was a 'ho, but I never did anything like this.' She looked around, wild-eyed. 'I need something to eat. This here's an eating situation.' She spied the vending machine and stormed across the room. 'I need money. I need quarters or dollars, or something. Omigod, they got Twinkies in here. I need a Twinkie real bad.'

'What about the supermodel diet?' I asked Lula.

'Fuck that. I hate those bony-ass supermodels anyway. I don't know what I was thinking.' Lula was shaking the vending machine. 'Who's got a hammer?' she asked. 'Somebody help me out here.'

Ranger slid a dollar into the machine and Lula punched the button.

'Hello, Twinkie,' she said. 'I'm coming home. Lula's back in town.'

* * *

It was way after midnight when Morelli and I got back to his house. Morelli dragged me up the stairs, stripped my clothes off, and shoved me into the shower. I had paint everywhere. Yellow, red, blue.

'You're a disaster,' Morelli said, standing to one side, watching me.

'Is it coming out of my hair?'

'It's out of your hair, but I think you might have a permanent blue stain down the back of your neck. You're not going to believe this,' Morelli said, 'but I'm too tired for sex. I'm beat. I'm not even forty and you've turned me into a burnout. I'm standing here, looking at you naked in the shower, and nothing's happening.'

The soap slid from my fingers, I bent to retrieve it and Morelli changed his mind on the burnout.

'Move over,' Morelli said, peeling his clothes off. 'I can see you need help here.'

I woke up feeling great. I opened my eyes and I knew it was over. No more red roses and white carnations. The sun was shining. Birds were chirping. Albert Kloughn didn't explode with the bomb. Morelli was beside me, still sleeping. Life was good. Okay, so I was slightly homeless and I had a blue stain down the back of my neck. Ranger was still at large, waiting to get even for the Apusenja event, but that was in the future. It could be worse. Eventually I'd get my apartment back. And in the meantime I was with Morelli. Who knows, maybe I'll just stay here. Then again . . .

The doorbell rang. I propped myself up on an elbow and looked at the bedside clock. Eight-thirty.

Joe put his hands to his face and groaned. 'Was that the doorbell?'

I got out of bed and went to the window. Joe's mother and Grandmother Bella were on the front porch. They looked up at me and smiled.

Shit.

'It's your mom and Bella,' I said. 'You'd better go see what they want.'

'I can't go,' Joe said. 'My mother would fall off the porch if she saw me like this.'

I looked under the sheet. He was right. His mother would fall off the porch. 'Fine!' I said, rolling my eyes. 'I'll go. But you'd better throw some cold water on yourself and come down and rescue me.'

I wrapped a robe around myself and ran a hand through my hair on the way down the stairs. I opened the door and tried my best to smile, but my mouth only partly cooperated.

'Coffee cake,' Joe's mother said, handing me the bakery bag. 'Fresh-made today. And Bella has something to tell you.' Joe's mother elbowed Bella.

'It's about the vision,' Bella said. 'I was wrong about the dead blonde wife and the babies. It wasn't Joseph in the vision. It was Bobby Bartalucci.'

'That's a relief,' I said. 'But poor Mrs Bartalucci.'

'I could have been wrong about the dead part, too,' Bella said. 'Maybe she was just sleeping.'

I heard Morelli on the stairs behind me. Felt his hand rest on my shoulder. 'Morning,' he said to his mother and grandmother.

'And one more thing,' Bella said to me. 'It's about your car. It's going to be blown up. *Kaboom*. There's going to be nothing left of it, but don't worry, you won't be in it. I had a vision.'

Bella and Joe's mom drove away and Joe and I stood in the open doorway, staring at my car.

'Something to look forward to,' Joe said. And then he kissed me and took the bakery bag into the kitchen.

JANET EVANOVICH

Seven Up

'Pithy, witty and fast-paced' *The Sunday Times*

In her most explosive adventure yet, bombshell bounty hunter Stephanie Plum is dropped into a smorgasbord of murder, kidnapping and extortion – a magnificent buffet of mud wrestling, motorcycles, fast cars, fast food and fast men.

Stephanie Plum thinks she's going after an easy FTA: a senior citizen charged with smuggling contraband cigarettes. But when she and Lula show up at his house, they get more than they bargained for – a corpse in the woodshed and an old man who's learned a lot of tricks during his years in the mob, and isn't afraid to use his gun. Then there's his involvement with Walter 'MoonMan' Dunphy and Dougie 'The Dealer' Kruper (Stephanie's former high-school classmates). They've been sucked into an operation which is much more than simple smuggling, one that holds risks far greater than anyone could have imagined. And when they disappear, Stephanie goes into high-octane search mode.

But Stephanie's mind is on other matters as well, because she has two proposals to consider: vice cop Joe Morelli is proposing marriage, and fellow bounty hunter Ranger is proposing a single perfect night . . .

All in all, a typical dilemma in the world of Plum.

'Hilarious reading, with a gorgeous fistful of believable and only occasionally murderous eccentrics' *Mail on Sunday*

'Hooray for Janet Evanovich, who continues to enliven the literary crime scene' *Sunday Telegraph*

'The funniest, sassiest crime writer going' *Good Book Guide*

0 7472 6761 8 (A format)

0 7553 2906 6 (B format)

review

JANET EVANOVICH

Hard Eight

'Hooray for Janet, who continues to enliven the literary crime scene' *Sunday Telegraph*

'That girl has some class' *New York Times*

The stakes get higher, the chases get faster, and the men get hotter.

Bounty hunter Stephanie Plum has a big problem. Seven-year-old Annie Soder and her mother Evelyn have disappeared – and estranged husband, Steven, shady owner of a seedy bar, is not at all happy. Finding a missing child is an unusual assignment, but as a favour to her parents' neighbour, Evelyn's grandmother, Stephanie agrees to follow the trail – and finds a lot more than she bargained for.

The case is somehow linked to the very scary Eddie Abruzzi. Both cop Joe Morelli, Stephanie's on-again, off-again fiancé, and Ranger, her mentor and tormentor, have warned her about Abruzzi – but it's Abruzzi's soulless eyes and mannerisms that frighten her most. Stephanie needs Ranger's expertise, and she's willing to accept his help to find Annie even though it might mean getting *too* involved with him. Also with her are Lula (who's not going to miss the action) and Albert, Evelyn's almost-qualified lawyer (and Laundromat manager). The search turns out to be a race between Stephanie's posse, the True Blue Bonds' agent – a Rangerette known as Jeanne Ellen Burrows – and the Abruzzi crew. Not to mention the killer rabbit on the loose!

Get ready for the ride of your life with Stephanie's funniest, most riotous misadventure yet. The world of Plum has never been wilder.

Praise for Janet Evanovich:

'Pithy, witty and fast-paced' *The Sunday Times*

'Razor-sharp' *Sunday Express*

'A screwball comedy that is also a genuinely taut thriller' *Daily Mail*

'As smart and sassy as high-gloss wet paint' *Time Out*

0 7472 6762 6 (A format)
0 7553 2907 4 (B format)

review

If you have enjoyed **To The Nines**, you may enjoy the following **Janet Evanovich** titles also available from your bookshop or *direct from the publisher*.

FREE P&P AND UK DELIVERY
(Overseas and Ireland £3.50 per book)

S..n Up	Janet Evanovich	£7.99
Ha.. Eight	Janet Evanovich	£7.99
Ten.. g Ones	Janet Evanovich	£7.99
Full H..se	Janet Evanovich & Charlotte Hughes	£6.99
Full Tilt	Janet Evanovich & Charlotte Hughes	£6.99
Full Speed	Janet Evanovich & Charlotte Hughes	£6.99
Full Blast	Janet Evanovich & Charlotte Hughes	£6.99

TO ORDER SIMPLY CALL THIS NUMBER

01235 400 414

or visit our website: www.madaboutbooks.com

Prices and availability subject to change without notice.